PAPA DEAREST

A Novel

I0672200

Table of Contents

BETTY KUFFEL

PAPA DEAREST

Papa Dearest is fictional. The content is based on victim interviews and extensive incest research. Characters, events, and settings are a work of imagination. Any resemblance to places or persons, living or dead, is coincidental.

Trigger/Content Warning

Readers may find portions of the story of sexual and psychological abuse of children disturbing. Content includes support and empowerment of incest victims to escape and begin recovery.

DEDICATION

To Great Aunt Anna and her beautiful daughter Sophia born of incest.

Note from the Author
Betty J. Kuffel, M.D. F.A.C.P.

The World Health Organization considers incest a silent health emergency. Any sexual activity between close blood relatives, family members including mothers, fathers, brothers, cousins, uncles and grandfathers, or step relatives defines incest and is illegal.

I wrote *Papa Dearest* for all incest victims to help them escape abuse and charge their abusers. Child incest victims are some of the most vulnerable of the abused. Victims are usually threatened with harm, death, and abandonment if they tell. A child may report the abuse and not be believed, placing them at increased risk, trapped and unable to escape. Paralyzed to do otherwise, the children are forced to live with the continued trauma.

Incest is as common around the world today as it has been through the ages. Statistical information on incest is sparse due to lack of reporting. The U.S. Department of Justice estimated incest occurs in more than 10% of American families but 80% of incidences go unreported.

Reporting to law enforcement is low due to fear of retribution, especially when the abuser is a prominent community or religious figure providing financial support to the family. Men who use children for sexual satisfaction are from all levels of society but are commonly pillars of the community, shielded by families who hide the shame. By exposure, the perpetrator's future is uncertain and standing in a community is destroyed.

Abused children sustain severe physical and emotional damage. Victims are more likely to act out, bully, use drugs, fail in school and function poorly as adults. PTSD is common and may be lifelong. Victims experience depression, alcoholism, prostitution, and self-harm. Studies also show sexual abuse victims have a higher risk of autoimmune disorders and chronic health problems.

Even after years, sometimes decades of hiding abuse, incest victims feel they cannot expose the perpetrator. Many die without revealing the anguish they felt at the hands of controlling men, often their fathers.

Stories of pain and survival in this novel stem from interviews with incest victims. Their willingness to speak to me about their angst stemmed from hope of helping others and to stop abuse. None of them told authorities. They are my friends and relatives, both men and women, left physically and emotionally scarred by those deemed protectors. Some complicit mothers allowed abuse to continue. Family members were often aware and didn't stop or report the behavior.

I also wrote this for my great aunt Anna who long ago as a young teen bore a little girl she named Sophia. Anna was impregnated by her father following the death of her mother. In photos, Sophia and Anna bear a strong resemblance. Relatives knew and hid the truth.

My great grandfather's obituary described him as a man of indomitable spirit, a kind neighbor, a man of the church, a willing worker, and his death, an unbearable loss to his surviving children. Sophia was not listed as a surviving relative though she was raised in the family from birth as Cousin Sophie.

I wonder if Sophie felt rejected her whole life. Non-existent. No one in the family would speak of her. My mother acknowledged her but had little information about Sophie's adult life, only saying Sophia was treated as a daughter and loved.

Anna, Sophia's mother, married and bore a son, remaining an active part of the family.

No one spoke of Sophia.

Even at age ninety-five, my last surviving aunt who knew Sophia refused to speak to me about the family secret. She took the information to her grave.

Old family photographs reveal Sophia grew to be a beautiful young woman. My only knowledge of her adult life told by my aged mother is that Sophie became an accomplished photographer. Information about her life ends there.

Lost to the family, a family who today would accept her completely with love.

Acknowledgements

Skilled guidance from my critique partners and beta readers brought *Papa Dearest* to completion. I thank all of them for their time, comments, and willingness to explore how best to portray this difficult topic.

Storyline development stretched over decades of researching haunting secrets in my own family and interviewing many people. Strangers and close friends trusted me with their previously undisclosed personal stories of abuse. They shared painful details to help others escape frightening victimization, find professional counseling, and recovery. I thank all of them for trusting me.

Work in emergency medicine brought me close to assault victims. The proximity motivated me to first write a true crime book about pedophiles. *Eyes of a Pedophile* provides information to help recognize common identifiable traits of child predators that may help keep children safer. Most child sexual abuse occurs at the hands of family members and others the child trusts.

Sexual abuse of children is so common few families are spared from knowing an abuser or a child harmed by one. Often vulnerable children without adult protectors become victims. I encourage readers to help protect children, report abusers to the police and child protective services, and to seek counseling to help recover from personal unreported abuse.

Chapter 1 – The Dying

Mama rests near a narrow dirt road winding beneath an ornate iron arch at the entrance to the garden of the dead. A few days after she died, I walked about a mile to the cemetery to talk to her. I cried all the way and sheltered behind her tombstone where Papa couldn't see me. Harsh Montana prairie winds rustled my hair, curly like hers before chemo took Mama's away. The winds erased words no one could hear, sweeping them away with her flowers.

Dust devils swirled across nearby fields leaving a path of destruction just like the cancer that swirled through Mama's body. After the cancer came, I prayed, but I didn't pray enough or say the right words because she got sicker and sicker. I ran home from sixth grade each day to be with her, to wash her face and feed her soup. Mama would say, "Anna, come read to me." We cuddled in bed while I read library books to her. Often, we just talked as she taught me life lessons while she lay dying.

During the year she slid toward her grave, Papa rode the rails, driving trains, drinking himself to sleep in faraway towns and I took care of Mama with her blond hair falling like my grades.

Papa worked extra after she got weak. When he rolled back into town, he'd stomp into her bedroom yelling, "Tess ... Tess! Get up and make my dinner." He complained about how thin she looked and stupid things like dust or a dead fly lying on a windowsill. He didn't scream as much if I had the house spiffy and dishes washed so I tried hard to keep him calm for Mama's sake.

Sometimes he brought us presents like matching pink satin pillowcases or sweet-smelling hand cream. Maybe it was his way of showing love because he never hugged me, never.

No matter what your age, when your mother dies, I suppose things will never be the same. For me, I think it is worse because she died on my birthday. That was seven years ago, and I have missed her every day since. We shared birthdays. She said I was her best gift. Mine was the gold ring with two rubies she gave me on her deathbed. The ring is a reminder she would always be with me. She was right. Mama lives in my heart and our birthstones sparkle on my finger.

From the time I was four, we lived in a simple house at the edge of a small town near the railyards. I don't remember much before that time. After we moved to the northern prairieland, I recalled the sharp wind making little goosebumps rise on my skin and blowing our hair when we went for walks.

We dodged tumble weeds that bounced and rolled down the road till they stuck along a fence line. We made a game running to catch them, but they usually got away, especially on days when dust devils swirled. I'm eighteen, now, but I still go to the cemetery to talk to my mother where the wind carries her spirit, where Tess rests in the ground near her mother.

Mama loved the prairie stretching all the way to the horizon as much as she loved books. She taught me about faraway places. We often spent time in the library where her childhood friend Opal worked. We could talk to Opal away from Papa's stink eyes.

For years before Mama took sick, we waited till Papa was gone on one of his long railroad trips, then rode our bicycles to the library where we'd spend hours in the aisles. I sat on the floor flipping pages in picture books between towering skyscraper shelves of books filled with adventure.

We always checked out books to read, little kid books for me, big ones for Mama. Sometimes I had to help her carry them home.

We kept her books under my bed where Papa wouldn't look. He ruled the roost as she said, wouldn't even let us go to the grocery store where Mama might talk to someone. We had little money because she said Papa held the purse strings too tight. I thought that was funny because he didn't carry a purse. He gave us an allowance for emergencies when he went out on the rails, but the library was free if you signed up for a borrowing card. I was proud to have one of my own.

There was little we could do without money but go bicycling, take walks, read or visit with George the scarecrow while we pulled weeds. One day she took me to a matinee movie for kids. We had enough allowance for that.

She told me Papa had moved us here to Riverside back to where he and Mama grew up. It's a small prairie town northeast of a much bigger place named Falls City. That was after her parents were in the ground and he knew they couldn't interfere. I never met my mother's parents, but I feel like I know them because Mama and I would sneak to their graves with flowers from our garden when Papa was gone, and she would talk to them. I never felt creepy out there talking to the dead because Mama said they kept her company.

Her mother liked little blue flowers called Forget-me-nots. We'd put them near the headstone with *Sally Anna Inman* chiseled in it. Then sit nearby in the shade of a big oak tree to talk and read stories to her. Mama named me for her.

At the cemetery, sometimes a nice man in work clothes named Jimmy stopped by to visit us. It was Opal's husband. He'd say things like, "Out here talking to Sally again, Tess?"

Her blue eyes twinkled when Jimmy spoke and in a cheerful voice, she'd pass the time with him. Once when I was still in elementary school, she asked him to sit and have a cookie with us. When they talked, her words and laugh were musical, like a meadowlark. She never laughed when Papa was home.

One day Jimmy removed his baseball hat, sat close to Mama on a gravestone and looked around at me. "My wife says you're doing some heavy reading, Anna."

I nodded. "Mama and I like math and biology."

"Those are big subjects for a little girl. I hope you listen to your smart mother."

I smiled as Mama opened her Tupperware container and offered it to Jimmy. "Chocolate chip. Take a couple."

"My favorite." He took a bite. "Delicious." Jimmy nodded toward a fresh grave. "Suppose you heard. Rex Davidson got killed in a rollover. Buried him this morning."

Mama gasped. "Horrible. They have a daughter Anna's age. It'll be tough for them. Charlene doesn't make much money working at the beer joint." She closed the cookie box. "I'm surprised Dave didn't tell me about Rex. Sometimes he stops by Mack's Shack on his way home from the railyard so he must have known."

Jimmy stood to leave. "I've seen his car there. I'd better get back to work or the residents will complain about me loafing on the job."

The corners of Mama's eyes wrinkled with her smile. It was real, not fake like the smiles I usually saw.

Jimmy touched her shoulder. "Take care, you hear?" His little pickup with tools in the back rattled down the narrow road to a pile of fresh dirt where he got out.

I watched him shovel the dark soil and rake it smooth around the new grave.

Mama placed the cookie box in the basket on her bike. "I like it out here where it's safe and quiet. Don't tell Papa I talked to Jimmy, or he'll get jealous and mean."

Her words reminded me of a time when the two of us accepted a ride home from a movie with a man from church. One of Papa's friends told him he saw us in the car. Papa accused Mama of being sweet on the fat old man. We both laughed and it made Papa furious. He left the house and slammed the door so hard on his way out the windows shook. I heard them arguing that night.

Over years of working side-by-side, Mama helped me learn to cook and showed me where she kept favorite recipes. Some were Grandma Sally's. One day when I made chicken and dumplings, Papa ate two bowls and said it was as tasty as Mama's. He was short on nice words, so it made me feel good.

I loved school but when my math teacher in sixth grade asked me about the only question I'd missed on a test, I felt horrible. I figured out the right answer later but felt bad about getting it wrong. All the other kids had left for home when she talked to me. I felt a failure and put the next assignment into my book bag, getting ready to walk home. "I'm sorry I didn't get them all right. I can't concentrate. I have to get home. My mother needs me; she is dying." I slung the bag strap over my shoulder.

The teacher hugged me. "My dear child, I'm so sorry. I didn't know." She pulled me to a table near her desk. "Come sit over here. Let's share a soda and chocolate bar."

Her hug helped a lot that day when I was feeling so bad. "Thank you. My dad won't let me have treats like these. Says they'll rot my teeth."

She smiled. "It's our secret. You are particularly good at math, but I'll give you extra help anytime."

That day, Mrs. Hensley became my friend, someone I could talk to. At Christmas break, she sent cookies home with me. I shared them with Mama, but we didn't tell Papa because he'd get mad and complain about nosey people.

After Mama got cancer, Papa stayed away more than before. Mama said, "It's not catchy, Anna, but he acts like he's afraid of me." When he did come home, sometimes he smelled like beer and fried onions from eating burgers at Mack's Shack.

I was so happy when school ended the summer Mama died. Then I could be with her all day. I sang songs to her and played the piano. Papa made me continue taking piano lessons even though I begged to stay home. Music made Mama happy, so I tried hard and learned one of her favorite songs, "I'll Walk in the Garden with You." He made me play it at her funeral. I played it from memory because I couldn't see through my tears. I felt her hand on my shoulder, so I think she liked it.

One hot summer evening just before she died, church-ladies knocked on the door carrying a gift. I guess someone told them Mama was sick because we hadn't been to church in months. After accepting their casserole and good wishes, Papa sent them on their way. That night, he ate with us before packing his grip. Papa left saying he'd be back in a few days, then walked out.

Mama's frown disappeared after the door closed behind him. She relaxed back on her pillow. Like me, she felt less stress with him gone.

That was the last meal Mama ate, two bites of tuna fish hotdish. She took sips of water and a little apple sauce over the next few days, but after her eyes and skin turned yellow, she quit eating.

Weeks earlier, mother had told me about growing up and having menstrual periods. She gave me a book I didn't want to read. Sex sounded nasty.

Mama squeezed my hand. "Please, Anna, be smart about being a girl." Her eyes teared. "My mother told me nothing. Being dumb about sex can ruin your life."

That day she explained no more. Later, before she got too sick to talk much she said, "At eleven, you're too young to be troubled with some of what I have to tell you, but these are things you must remember when I'm not here." Her bony fingers found both of my hands and squeezed. "Remember when I talked to you about sex and how humans make babies?"

I nodded, wanting to block my ears.

"That should be an act between adults who love each other more than anyone else in the whole world." She spit out the next words. "I don't love Papa. Never have."

I tried to grasp what she was saying, comparing his behavior to a friend's father. "I know he's not a hugger like Janey's dad."

Tess's voice turned loud, harsh like I'd never heard her speak before. "He's twenty years older than I am. He forced sex on me when I was a child your age." Her eyes squeezed tight, teeth clenched, hands shaking. Her eyes looked like she'd just seen the devil. "Dave was driving past and waved to me. Then stopped and offered me a ride home from school."

Mama stared faraway, remembering. "Instead, he took me into the woods and hurt me bad, then dropped me at home. I ran into the house crying. Mother took one look at me all messed up and screamed for my father. Daddy made me tell and I showed them my bloody underwear."

I squeezed her hands. "Oh, Mama. That's terrible."

Mama said her father flew into a rage and wanted to kill Dave, but her mother held him back saying, "Sam, control yourself. You'll lose your job if we call the police and, if you hurt him, you'll be the one in jail. Besides no one would believe her." Mama said she tried to run away, feeling like it was her fault, but her mother hugged her tight and wouldn't let go.

Tears streamed down Mama's face as she spoke in a soft voice. "My father sat, head in his hands. It was the only time I ever saw him cry. He said he'd never forgive himself for not protecting me." Mama sat up, balancing herself on the soft mattress on her bony elbows. "At that time, my dad was forty-five years old, a hard worker. My brother, Steve, worked with him at the same box factory where Dave's father was boss. We would have starved without their pay checks."

Mama collapsed on her back. "Four months later when they realized I was pregnant because I was throwing up and my belly stuck out my parents made Dave marry me." She closed her eyes tight, but tears escaped. "I am so glad I have you, but I was too young to understand any of it. I didn't know what sex was until Dave raped me." She was silent a few moments. "After the courthouse wedding, he took me far away to another county and cut me off from friends and family. That's the way I've lived my life."

Mama pointed. "See that little doll high on the bookshelf? I brought her with me when I walked out of the house with my suitcase." She laughed a mournful sound. "My treasure from a lost childhood."

I squinted. "A little girl in lace. I knew she wasn't a toy because you put her on display like a special vase. Now I know her story and yours. I guess it's mine, too. The story of three little girls."

"Dolly kept me company. Too young to talk for myself and trapped by a man I feared. Deserted by my parents. When Dave left the house to go to work, I talked to Dolly."

Thinking of her story stabbed me with guilt. "I'm so sorry, Mama. I should never have been born. You'd have had a better life without me."

"No, Anna. I love you more than you'll ever know. I could talk to you and didn't need Dolly, so I put her in a safe place."

I sat down, looking at my hands, feeling responsible for her pain.

"You have to hear the rest." She returned to her story. "Later, when my belly grew bigger people looked at Dave and me funny. Probably because I was so young and small. He closed the drapes on our little shack to keep snoopy eyes out. After you were born and he got a job on the railroad we moved to a nicer home, but other than church people, I knew no one."

Mama's fingers clenched. "Anna, I'm telling you this because I don't want it to happen to you. I don't think I was the only young girl Papa went after. He likes young girls. I worry about your safety when I'm no longer here to protect you. If he ever calls you *honey*, watch out. Go to the police if he wants you to undress for him or if he touches you."

"I would run away."

Tess shook her head. "I tried that, Anna. He found me and brought me back. I had no money except a few dollars he left me when he was on the rails. I had no friends, no family, no transportation and I never learned to drive."

"Why didn't your mother come and get you? You would never let a man take me away."

"Sally was a proper church lady who couldn't bear the shame of a pregnant young daughter and being such a failure as a mother." Mama looked over at the stack of her library books. "He wouldn't let me go to school, so I've learned from books."

I squeezed her hand in fear. "Will he make me stop going to school, just like you?"

Mama's eyes closed partway to block the bright sun streaming into her room. "Papa promised me he'd pay for your college. But I don't believe him. You'll have to do it yourself. Be strong."

I laid my head on her chest and cried. She wiped my tears and ran trembling fingers through my curls. "I bought you something by saving my emergency money. It will remind you I am always with you. Open the lowest drawer in the dresser. There's a little box way in the back. Bring it to me, please."

My fingers found it and I handed it to her.

She shook her head. "You open it."

Tears blinded my eyes as I pulled out a gold band with two red stones.

"Ruby is our birthstone. July. Wear it. Touch it when you're sad and pretend I'm hugging you." She smiled.

That day, I placed it on a finger and walked near the window in the setting sun to admire the ring in sunlight. The stones sparkled. "It's beautiful. Thank you."

"I am so sorry, Anna. I wish I were stronger, but I think I'll be gone soon." She whispered, "Please take Dolly from the shelf. She will give you company like she helped me. Take good care of her."

My heart broke. I cried so hard I couldn't breathe. Like a fish out of water, struggling. My mouth opened and closed but no words could come out.

She pulled me to her. The springs creaked as I crawled into her bed and pulled the blanket over us. I folded my hands feeling the beautiful ring. Mama hugged me and Dolly. I lay still watching shadows on the walls fade. Darkness fell around me, a smothering feeling. Mama's breathing slowed. Her hugging arms relaxed. I finally slept after the midnight train rattled through town.

I awakened in dawn light. Her body, still. My breath locked. One of her stiffening arms draped my chest. I couldn't move for a long time. I had to tell someone, but I didn't want to leave her last hug. Finally, I sat up.

Sun beamed in on her thin relaxed face. A pleasant expression. Not pained. Maybe, just maybe, a little smile on her lips. I didn't know what to do sitting on the edge of the creaking bed with my dead mother beside me. I recalled her words, "Anna, be strong. You must be strong."

I kissed my mama and our ring, then hid Dolly in my room and returned to Mama. I placed her stiffening hands at her sides and pulled the soft blue blanket up to cover her chest, but not her face.

Mama didn't even like turtlenecks. They made her short of breath.

She wouldn't like the coffin.

I combed her thin hair, wondering what dress she'd like to wear to her funeral.

Chapter 2 - Deathday

My mother died on her 24th birthday. I didn't know how to call Papa when he was on the rails. If I walked to the church, the pastor would say prayers for the dead, but how about for the living?

I cried for two hours lying on my bed with Dolly. I dressed, then rested on the rocking chair on the back porch hugging a neighborhood cat and Dolly, rocking and wondering what life would be like without my mother, not knowing who to tell she had died.

The cat alerted to a robin perched on a branch of a nearby lilac with most of its lavender flowers browning in the July heat. A few moments after it flew off, I set the cat down, picked a lilac bloom and brought it to Mama. It looked pretty in her hands against her yellow skin.

Dressed in pedal pusher jeans and my favorite purple T-shirt, I bicycled to the library. Opal would know what to do. The moment I saw her, my tears streamed out like our leaky garden hose. She ran to me, arms open, and pulled me into the office. "Is she gone?"

Sobs shook my body and choked my words. I nodded. We both cried.

I finally spoke. "Today is our birthday and her *deathday*." Our wailing echoed off the library walls.

"Where is your father?"

I shrugged. "Somewhere on the rails. He might be back tomorrow."

Opal picked up the phone to call her husband. She talked to Jimmy and hung up. "He'll call the funeral home and meet them at your house."

I headed to the door. "I have to go home to be with her. I need to be there. I'll let them in."

"Wait." Opal dialed. "I'm calling Blanche to cover for me. I'll go home with you."

I shook my head. "Mama said to be strong. I'm okay."

She followed me to the door. "I don't want you to be alone."

I smiled through tears. "I won't be alone. I'll be with Mama."

Pastor Bob was on the doorstep when I bicycled up and propped the bike against a tree. I walked to the door. His fat arms encircled me. "Jimmy called. I'm so sorry, Anna. My wife will send the kids over with a casserole for you."

I moved out of his bearhug. "I don't need food. I need God to bring back Mama."

"I want the same thing, Anna, but we don't always have our prayers answered." The pastor hung his head. "This is a sad day for everyone. I'd like to say a prayer for your mother."

Pastor Bob was too fat from eating all those casseroles. Walking up four steps to the screen porch made him huff and puff to catch his breath. At Mama's bedside, in the room where Papa put her after the last hospital trip, Pastor stood, hands folded, mumbling prayers I didn't want to hear. I was saved by a knock on the bedroom door.

Opal's husband Jimmy came in, followed by a tall skinny man wearing a black shirt and pants. Jimmy squatted down and looked into my eyes. "I'm so sad for you. I will miss Tess, so will Opal." He held my hand. "You can always call us or stay with us if your dad can't be home."

I felt better with Jimmy because I knew how much Mama liked and trusted him.

I kissed Mama for the last time, then Jimmy waited with me in the kitchen with his arm around my shoulders while the undertaker took her away.

Through the screen door I watched the man close the door of the hearse, ending my life with Mama. As the hearse drove away, Opal arrived with cookies and a loaf of home-made bread. She and Jimmy stayed a while making sure I was safe and were assured I wanted to be alone.

After they left, in the silence, the house creaked and moaned. Late in the afternoon on that sad day, sitting on the back porch with Dolly and the cat on my lap, thunder rumbled in the distance and rain fell like my tears.

Mama in a casket.

Papa riding the rails.

Toward evening, the Pastor's wife knocked on the front door and left a macaroni hotdish for my dinner. She said Papa's train was in the yard, so he'd be with me soon.

About an hour later, Papa came home smelling of beer. "The funeral is day after tomorrow. Go find a dress for your mother. I have to take it to the funeral home tonight."

I opened her closet door. She had few dresses. The only place we dressed up for was church and we only went when Papa was in town. I settled on a pale blue silky long-sleeved dress trimmed with lace. She'd worn it to Easter Sunday church services. I hugged it and smelled her smell. I didn't want to part with it.

After the funeral, after they put her in the ground, after graveside prayers, after the condolences, after the food and "I'm sorry" messages from church people, Papa dropped me off at home and left.

The house was dark like my thoughts. I wandered from room to room and played, "I'll Walk in the Garden with You." I tried to sing but only got through the first verse because my voice choked with sobs. I sat outside on the back porch hoping kitty would come for a visit, but she didn't show up.

After the summer sky darkened and the stars appeared, I went to bed feeling lost and listened to the creaking house until I slept.

Later, I don't know how long, my bedroom door opened. I awakened smelling beer breath and lay still with my eyes closed pretending to be asleep, wanting him to go to bed without speaking because drinking always made him mean.

Papa never hugged me so when he crawled into my bed and put his arm around me, it felt good. I thought it was strange, but I somehow felt comforted and not so alone.

He said nothing.

I closed my eyes.

My twin bed sagged with his weight. Gravity rolled me toward him. I was uncomfortable being so close to him and hated the stinking beer smell. I held very still barely breathing until he snored.

Gripping the mattress, I edged away from him, planning to sneak out of the room but his slow regular breathing quickened. He coughed, then settled into regular breathing and I thought he was asleep.

Again, I moved away. I had one foot on the floor when his hand gripped my arm and his voice rasped, "Where do you think you're going. I need a little *honey*."

Mama's words screamed a warning in my brain. She'd said to go to the police if he touched me.

I gasped and pulled away. "Let go. Get away from me...." His calloused hand smothered my mouth and nose, until I thought I would die, stopping my screams. Then his rough hands pulled up my nightgown and the crush of his weight stopped my breath. I wasn't sure what happened. I sensed cold floorboards against my back. He lay on his stomach on my bed. His arm hung over the side with his fingers gripping my nightgown.

I screamed.

Only he heard me.

I tried to get away.

Papa pushed me against the floor.

No one could help me.

I waited till his breathing was even and his grip relaxed, then inched away.

My naked skin came alive on the cold floor, fog cleared from my thoughts and spun to stark terror of the devil wind spinning in my house. Mama was in the ground. She couldn't protect me. She had tried. She warned. *Protect yourself. Don't let him take you for his honey.*

I failed.

In the darkness, I found clothes to wear and crept out of my bedroom to the bathroom and locked myself inside.

I looked at the child in the long mirror on the door, someone I didn't know.

Defiled, terrified, bleeding.

I didn't run water in the tub because it might awaken him. Scrubbing myself with a soapy washcloth was a pain I would never forget or forgive. I dressed, checked the lock, then curled up on the bathroom floor wishing I had Dolly for comfort. Trembling and whimpering, I wrapped in a bath towel to hide my shame and shield eyes from the rising sun. I hurt bad physically, but the worst pain was failing Mama.

Chapter 3 - Honey

Papa said nothing about what he did to me. Not sorry, nothing. He went back to work. Opal and Jimmy had wanted me to stay with them when he left town, but I couldn't. I had to be home, or I'd unravel. I would fall apart.

My brain didn't work.

I couldn't think, couldn't sleep.

I felt dirty even after long baths and couldn't stop thinking about Mama in the ground. I cried till I had no tears. That was when I knew I had to go to the graveyard and talk to her.

With all the shades down so it would look like no one was home in the day, I wouldn't answer the door. In the evenings after dark, with all the house lights out, I walked around the backyard and stood close to George in the garden watching the stars and zooming nighthawks.

After nights of wandering in the yard out of view, one evening before dark I bicycled to the cemetery. I had to talk to Mama.

I stood by her new grave, dark dirt with rake marks, next to Sally's. Close together. Maybe they had finally made peace after Sally had deserted her child.

I couldn't find the words to tell Mama I had failed her.

Instead, I sat on the grass near Grandma Sally and spoke to her and the wind. "You could have been a good grand-mother to me, but you deserted my mother, your little girl. You could have stopped Dave and saved her, but you didn't. I'm sorry you lived out your life without her. Tess was a won-derful smart mother who protected me." Tears flooded my view of her headstone. "Mama stayed with me as long as she could. I learned many lessons from her and even learned to bake some of your good recipes, but now, my brain won't let me stop crying.

"I can't forgive you for making your little girl get mar-ried. Mind you, I'm glad to be here because Tess loved me, but my brain feels like tangled yarn when I try to understand why you and Sam forced her to marry a bad man who is now doing it to me."

I had no friends and was sort of a book worm but didn't read much right after Mama died. Distraction and confusion paralyzed my thoughts. Papa came home from his trips with presents. He brought me dresses, a new bicycle, things to cheer me. Perfume, lipstick, and pretty nightgowns he made me model for him at night.

Church ladies brought food, but I lost weight. They wor-ried.

I gave them a fake smile and lied, saying I was doing okay.

Isolated in pain and fear of a man who pretended he was a god-loving churchgoer, I couldn't tell the church ladies I was trapped by a madman. They wouldn't believe me any-way.

On a day in the past I will never forget, Mama and I sat on a bluff above the Missouri River eating peanut butter cookies in a strong wind whipping bushes and stirring dust. I was five years old and confused because Mama was so serious. Her words that didn't make sense. That was the first time she told me to tell her right away if Papa ever tried to hurt me. I promised.

He didn't try.

She had been there to protect me.

He waited till Mama was dead.

No one would believe a churchman and reliable railroader could ever rape his child.

At church, people whispered *sorry* messages to me.

Grandmothers said *it* would get better with time.

The other deacons with Papa, murmured *it* was grief.

It would take time.

I knew *it* wouldn't stop till Papa was in the ground.

Papa never spoke of his abuse.

Never said, "Sorry."

No explanations for his behavior.

I screamed when he entered my bedroom again, but it didn't matter. His hands covered my mouth. No one heard and I couldn't tell. He said he'd throw me out with the trash, dead.

I hated his face. His smell. His beer breath. And being isolated.

I wanted him gone. Working. Not touching. I worried. Would let me go to school in the fall or lock me in the house like he imprisoned Mama.

In public, he dressed up nice in clothes I ironed. Wore after-shave, combed his brown hair, and walked with his hand on my shoulder. He looked like a real father, but he was a fake.

Papa said being a railroader was like being a long-haul trucker. He was exhausted by trying to keep the train on time. At the end of his line, when another crew took over, he would eat and drop into bed hundreds of miles from home. His layovers were rest-overs, so the trainmen didn't get too tired and have accidents. Just like when Mama was alive, he left me alone at home for days each week and never let me know when he'd return.

I loved being alone and feared his return.

Dolly and my ring were connections to Mama that helped me survive the sadness. I could take care of myself. As weeks passed, when he was away, I was calmer. I locked the doors at night and played the piano and talked to Dolly. The stray gray cat hung around sometimes. For the first month, Dolly and the cat were my only friends. Later, I got back to reading about faraway places. I reread books Mama had read to me. Sometimes I read out loud and tried to make my voice sound like hers. The books kept me company. But every time the train whistle blew at the edge of town, far away, it was like a warning. *Get ready, Anna. He's coming.*

My heart sped up like I was pedaling my bike uphill. My hands would go cold and shake. I'd heard the engine, the rattle of the cars on the tracks getting louder and closer. I raced from room to room checking to be sure everything was in order.

I never knew if it was his train coming home but every time I heard a whistle, my heart pounded. When the train rumbled on through town without stopping and I heard the whistle fading into the distance, my heart and breathing slowed.

He had yelled at me if there was a dirty dish in the sink, so even when he was gone, I made sure the house was always clean. I was happier with Papa gone but I was never alone. Cop cars inched past the house many times a day, his friends were watching me.

Mama's deathbed words looped through my thoughts, spinning in my brain wondering what I could do to escape. I plotted various ways and wondered if her older brother, my uncle Steve, would help me. I decided I'd look through Mama's papers to see if she had known where he was living and kept his address. I had never met him. Papa wouldn't allow her to have any contact.

Weeks after Mama died, I wanted to stay home, away from people, away from snoopy eyes, but on Labor Day weekend Papa took me to the carnival. He'd never taken me to one before. I was afraid to refuse. I wondered why he was doing this. I couldn't be for me.

At the fairgrounds, we waited in long lines under hot sun. Cotton Candy. A hotdog. Carnival rides. I have to say, I smiled a few times. I loved the treats and watched other parents and children wondering if they had fathers like him and only looked good in public. I was afraid to look people in the eye. Maybe they would see my inside dirt. They wouldn't like me if they knew what he did to me.

After a spinning riding on the Tilt-a-Whirl, Papa pulled me out of the rocking cage on unsteady legs up to the platform. I felt dizzy, weak, and nauseous.

"Guess that dawg didn't sit too well on your stomach. You're acting like my old drinking buddy instead of a young girl. I'd better get you home to bed."

After he said that, my thoughts spun to him getting in bed with me. My hearing and vision dimmed. His rough hands caught me as I slumped and barfed all over my new dress and shoes.

The hand I hated squeezed mine as he dragged me along the dusty fairgrounds, stumbling, falling. I wanted to go anywhere but home. Suddenly, he jerked me upright and whispered loud in my ear. "Shape up, girl. Here comes Pastor Bob and his family. Greet the kids. Be friendly."

He waved and chuckled as he apologized for my appearance. "I'm afraid, Anna had one too many rides."

I felt ugly, smelly, and sick but gave the pastor a fake smile. His wife's eyes examined my stained dress, then locked on my stone face. I wonder if she knew. Did she suspect his abuse?

I closed my eyes. I didn't want to go home, but years of ducking his anger, avoiding stares and nasty words taught me to hide my thoughts. When I had to be polite for other people, like at the fair, I had a ready fake smile that seemed to fool everyone. My plastic smile. Not real.

Papa took my elbow and led me to his dusty Ford, a junker-car he called it. I got in and swallowed hard, feeling acid rise and burn in my throat, afraid I might throw up again. He slammed the car door and lowered his window. "You smell like puke." His eyes rolled over me. "Sure am glad I didn't drive the Chevy. Wouldn't want you stinking up my baby with your damn vomit."

Papa took the corners too fast on our way home.

I clung to the armrest to keep from scooting sideways on the slick seat. I nearly threw up again from the rocking and weaving. I tightened my seatbelt.

At home, I lay in the tub with warm water melting my muscles. Globs of green Prell shampoo cleaned my blond curls. I scrubbed my skin with Ivory soap that bobbed on the surface. When I was little, Mama had washed me with the pure white soap. It floated along carrying me on its raft to South Sea islands in my dreams like stories she'd read at my bedtime. That was long ago when Ivory made me feel clean. Now, I knew it carried dirt away but could never wash away the filth my father left in me.

I got out of the tub and reached for the Lava soap on the sink, the harsh soap Papa used to wash his railroad hands. I climbed back in the water and used the gritty gray bar, scrubbing my skin red, trying to get rid of the dirt only I could feel and wash it down the drain.

I rinsed and then toweled off in front of the long mirror on the back of the closed bathroom door, hating my developing breasts.

Chapter 4 – The Confession

On a cold December afternoon during Christmas break six months after Mama died, I walked to the cemetery to talk to her as soon as Papa's train left town. My hood blunted the icy wind as hot tears streamed down my cold cheeks. I fell on the slippery rut in the narrow road where tire tracks made parallel snowy paths. I got up and struggled to Mama's grave where I huddled out of the wind behind a large stone monument. I wasn't sure how to tell her, but I couldn't leave town without her knowing.

I spoke to her out loud because no one in their right mind and not dead would be out on the cemetery grounds in the nasty weather. A freezing wind whistled through barren branches of the oak tree over Grandma Sally's grave where a gnarled twig pointed at me like the finger of a scolding old woman. I turned away from the finger of shame. This is what I said to my mother:

"I hope you're listening. You tried to warn me, but I didn't understand what you meant when you said Papa likes young girls. I thought it was wonderful he liked young girls, but it made me sad he never hugged me. I thought he didn't like me. On your funeral night when I was so sad and lonely, wishing I could die to be with you, he came to my room, and I was glad."

I looked around at the desolate cemetery with snow drifting against sad gray granite markers. I bit my gloved finger, having trouble getting the words out but continued talking to her.

"Then, I learned what you meant by being his honey. I remembered your warnings when I was eating that peanut butter cookie on the bluff so long ago, and again when you were dying. You said, 'Go to the police if he hurts you.' I couldn't tell you until now because I couldn't bear to tell you I failed."

The oak tree shook its finger at me again. "Mama, I'm so upset. - The night of your funeral Papa took me for his honey."

Was that a gasp I heard? Maybe it was the wind. I looked around the graveyard where snow drifted to the tops of granite markers. Snow covered the names. No one heard.

"Mama, I thought you'd gasp if you knew. Anyway, that's why I'm here today. I was going to tell you sooner and came out here one evening crying, but Papa found me right where I'm sitting now and forbade me to ever come out here again."

I recalled how frightened I was. "I am very afraid of him. Sometimes I'm paralyzed. That day, he yelled all the way home, pounding the steering wheel, speeding around corners, calling me a slut. I had to use your dictionary to look up that word. He's crazy."

I pulled the hood down around my face. "Papa said he didn't want me out at night messing with boys. He lied. He wanted me for his honey and that night, he did it again, and day after day. I wanted to die. I wanted to tell but couldn't. Papa laughed when I said I'd call the police. They're his drinking buddies. He said they wouldn't believe me."

When my hood blew down exposing my ears, the traffic on the highway near the cemetery grew louder, but no one turned onto Cemetery Road. I continued, "He brought lotion, perfume, pink satin sheets. Candlelight. I closed my eyes each time he came in my room. My heart and I went somewhere else, to a happy place down on the river bluff, listening to the rushing water while his rough hands hurt me. He beats me in places that don't show, warning me to tell no one our secret. You are the only one I can tell."

I felt like she was listening. The wind stopped. "I'm sick and scared like always but worse today because something more horrible has happened. Three nights ago, he suddenly jumped out of my bed and turned on the lights. I thought he was going to beat me again. I squeezed my eyes shut. When I opened them, he stood over me pulling up his underwear, glaring and breathing fast. He bent over and pushed on my belly and said, 'Shit girl, you're pregnant.'"

I stood up and turned away from her grave. "I screamed at him. Papa, I'm twelve. I can't have a baby."

"His eyes stabbed me. 'No, you can't. Why didn't you tell me you started your monthly's?' I didn't, Mama. I didn't. I'm so confused."

My hand went to my belly bulging beneath my heavy coat. "That night, Papa jerked me to my feet saying, 'Get some clothes on. We have to get rid of your problem.' He stomped out of my room and returned a few minutes later, yelling to hurry it up that we were going for a ride.'

"I'd noticed a grapefruit sized lump in my lower belly and was throwing up every morning, even missing some school. I wondered if a baby was growing inside me but who could I tell? I hoped the lump would go away. Maybe it was ovarian cancer like yours and I would just die like I wanted to."

I told her about the trip to Falls City, to an old house with a dim light in the window, about arriving after midnight, about the old man with bloodshot eyes and smelling of pipe smoke who opened the door. Papa said, "Hello Doc. This is the girl you need to get out of a fix."

The ugly doctor had led us through his living room filled with boxes of junk to a back room with a padded table and a glaring overhead light that nearly blinded me when I climbed on the table and Papa pushed me down on my back. The old man bent over me without a word and pulled up my shirt exposing my chest. Then, he pulled down my pants.

I looked up into his fat face with hair sticking out of his nostrils. His beady eyes looked at my breasts and grimy hands pushed on my belly. He shook his head. "Can't help you, Dave. She's too far along." His lips parted in a smile showing snaggle brown teeth. "You're going to be a father."

The wind howled and it was getting dark, but I had to tell her the rest. "After that, Papa sped down the highway like a maniac on our way home. My heart skipped beats. I was so scared, I thought I might die. Kids can't have babies, but then, I guess I'm like you Mama. You had me when you were about my age.

"On the way, I didn't talk or cry so he wouldn't hit me. At home, I tucked in the blankets all the way around and slid down under the sheets and covers from the top by my pillow. I was thinking maybe the tucked in bedding would stop him from trying to make me his honey again. Block him out. I felt safer with the blankets tucked in. That sounds dumb when I say it out loud, magical, but I finally fell asleep."

I finished my confession hiding behind a big tombstone after the streetlights came on. A few dim ones lit the cemetery road and I didn't want anyone to see me. "The next morning my bedroom door flew open and hit the wall. Papa announced, 'You're going to a home for sluts when I get back. I'll be on the rails for two days. Pack a suitcase. You'll be sorry you ever messed around with that ugly neighbor boy and got yourself pregnant.'

"Mama, I sat up straight and yelled at him. 'That's stupid. You did this. You did it!' He walked over, jerked me out of bed and shook me, hard, leaving bruises on my arms that hurt tonight. He jabbed a finger in my chest and told me, 'That's what happened to you. You, hear? You screwed a neighbor kid, right?'

"I shook my head. He squeezed my arms so hard it hurt bad. I said I did - but I didn't. He made me lie. Mama, my suitcase is ready. I'll be on the passenger train to Minneapolis tomorrow. I'll talk to you when I get back. I love you, Mama. I'm so sorry I failed you. I'm so scared. Bye."

I stumbled away crying hard, following the ruts out of the cemetery, across the highway and into neighborhood streets, walking in icy wind till I reached home and my warm bed.

I cried myself to sleep.

Chapter 5 – Cousin Julie's Birthday

In the morning, an approaching train whistle told me Papa would be home soon. Wind shook the house. Snow drifted across the driveway. I sat on the couch, wearing my special ring, ready to leave. My suitcase sat by the door with Dolly packed inside. I knew she'd keep me company. I wouldn't be able to talk to Mama for a long time.

Papa stomped in. "Fry me a couple eggs. The passenger train leaves in two hours. Pack sandwiches and a bottle of milk for the ride. It'll take about twenty-four-hours to get there."

In the afternoon, we boarded a passenger train sleeper compartment. I threw up rocking and rolling all the way across North Dakota while he made me his honey over and over again.

In Minneapolis, he dragged me into a taxi that stopped at a huge brick building he called a home for sluts.

I felt dirty and scared as we were introduced to Mother Superior, who handed us off to an old nun who was half deaf. I huddled in a creaking chair in a cold room and listened to him yell lies to the old woman. "Sister, this is my daughter Anna, my only child. My wife died of cancer." He faked a sniffle. "It's hard raising a girl by myself."

I guess the deaf woman heard some of what he said because she glared at me.

"I don't know what got into her. She's been hard to control ever since she turned fifteen. Going out at night alone, you know."

I stared at him, clenching my teeth, wanting to scream that I was twelve and he was lying.

"She won't say who did this to her, but boys are harder to raise than girls. If she has a girl, I'll raise her as my own. If it's a boy, adopt him out."

At those words, my heart broke. He would throw a baby boy away, but he would keep a girl so he could abuse her, too.

I wore the stone face I learned from Mama. No expression but I was so afraid, I didn't know what to do. I felt like the statue of Mary by the front door of the building.

No words. No heart. No life.

Afraid of him.

Afraid of nuns.

Afraid of having a baby but suddenly feeling protective of the little creature growing inside of me. The nun's voice stopped my scared thoughts. "Mr. Stanton, you'll have to sign the papers for Anna because she is underage."

Papa signed and stood to leave. He took my elbow and led me into an area away from other nuns and two pregnant girls. "I'll never come back if you tell the secret. You'll have no money, no home and a baby to take care of. Make your choice." His evil eyes stabbed my heart. "If you keep the secret, I'll pay for your college like I told your dead mother I would do. Make your choice." He walked out.

The nuns were strict, but tutors came to the home to teach all the girls, so I kept up with classes. Nuns and helpers taught us kitchen skills. One taught us how to change diapers, hold babies, and feed them from bottles. I'd never been around a baby, so I concentrated on what she said about baby care. The house library with big lounge chairs and a fireplace was a refuge where I read every minute that I wasn't doing assigned chores.

I talked with some of the eight pregnant girls I lived with during those months of prison. There was a lot of crying and praying going on around me. Some came and left, mostly leaving without their babies. The saddest part was Christmas eve when they were all wailing about being away from their families. For me it was just another day. We had never celebrated Christmas or had a tree. We prayed in church, that's all. I felt sorry for the other girls, but in my room, I spent Christmas with Dolly and Mama.

During quiet thinking times, I wondered if Papa was hurting other young girls while I was gone. It made me sad. I felt terrible I couldn't help them. I had to put those thoughts in a box and close the lid to focus on my future with the little baby that was moving inside of me. I had to do well in high school and go to college so I could earn a living and escape Papa's control.

As the baby inside me grew, I talked to the other girls. Some of them told me stories of nuns stealing newborn babies. I became more fearful, staring at the nuns and wondering which one of the pious praying women was a kidnapper. Would she come in the night when I was sleeping? I had nightmares about waking up and finding my stomach flat and the baby gone.

I vowed I would tell everyone what happened to me if I had a little boy and Papa tried to give him away. I couldn't bear the thought of giving him to the nuns, never knowing what might happen to him. I would have fought for his life and to keep him.

My body changed, stretched to the point of looking like it might burst and like a balloon, I'd fly around backwards. One girl calmed my fears. "Everything stretches like rubber and then snaps back. You'll be okay and will never know you were ever pregnant."

My breasts grew and belly stuck out so much I used it as a rest for books I read in bed. Nuns gave me elastic pants and long comfortable sweatshirts. As the weather warmed, I traded them in for light weight knit shirts and pants.

Some of the girls delivered in the home, but for me they "expected trouble." I didn't know what they were talking about. But one night fluid gushed out of me, and a nun drove me to a hospital across town where they put me in a private room in an area designated *Maternity*.

A doctor about Papa's age took care of me, two nurses helped, one stayed with me most of the time. After hours of pain and fright, wondering if the baby might be dying, the doctor came in and examined me. His dark eyes watched my face. "Anna, because the baby is making no progress to come out, I will have to do surgery to take the baby." A nurse with a worried expression held my hand.

"What do you mean 'take the baby?' I want to keep the baby." But another pain came, and I cried out. When the pain was over, I looked into their faces. "Mama's friend had a C-section. Is that what I need?"

The doctor nodded. "You do. You're small for a sixteen-year-old and it's getting dangerous for you and the baby to let labor continue."

I almost screamed, "Sixteen? Papa's lied." But another pain stopped the words.

The doctor explained what would happen as they wheeled me into a bright, cold operating room where I went to sleep. I woke up with a sore belly and a beautiful baby girl.

Julie was born on May 18, 1975, about two months before my thirteenth birthday.

Two weeks later, Papa showed up and took us home on the train. The peaceful rocking helped Julie sleep. The nuns sent lots of baby formula and bottles with us, so we didn't run out.

Papa brought sandwiches for us to eat during the ride home. Julie and I slept well while he rolled along the rails sitting in the club car drinking.

I wanted to stay on the train forever. Protected, rocking and safe with Julie's tiny fingers curled around mine. Bright blue eyes looked around. I held her up so she could see the prairieland and all the cattle as we rattled along the rails headed West, back home to Montana. I told her someday she might be a cowgirl or maybe a photographer taking beautiful pictures.

I compared our hands and noticed we both had crooked little fingers like Papa's. He didn't even look at Julie or ask how she was doing. He just stumbled into the sleeper and sat with us mumbling about losing his job and what people would think. He decided our story would be that his cousin died in childbirth, and we offered to raise the baby we'd call a cousin. I picked her name. We called my daughter Cousin Julie.

His rule was, "Never tell." No one can ever know the truth, or he'd lose his job, be rejected by the townsfolk, and kicked out of church. If I *never* told, he would pay for my college but only if I got good grades and took good care of the baby.

If anyone found out, he'd kick me out, no money, no home, no school, and – he would keep Julie.

That would never happen. I'd kill him, first.

Chapter 6 – The Family

Rocking Julie in rhythm with the gently swaying sleeper car, my thoughts drifted to our future with Papa. As the train slowed nearing Riverside, my heartbeat turned erratic. I trembled. How could I keep this secret in a town with many snoopy eyes?

Looking at Julie's adorable face steadied my heart and reinforced my vow to protect her. I left the weak, frightened, powerless girl named Anna in Minnesota. Still a five-foot tall twelve-year-old with curly blond hair, but holding my baby steeled me with determination I had never felt before. The new girl, *Ann*, feeling taller and older vowed to one day reveal Papa's abuse.

I sat straight up and draped the strap of a small duffel bag holding diapers and formula over my shoulder and waited for the train to stop. Papa stood rocking with the train movement, holding onto the door frame with his rough calloused hand and his crooked pinky finger. Seeing the hand that had hurt me so many times strengthened my reserve to stop the abuse, but I'd have to bide my time.

The train stopped at the station not far from our home. Papa carried our suitcases into the waiting area and dropped them by a bench. "I'll be back as soon as I can with the car." He bent toward me, partially covering his mouth and whispered. "Keep your mouth shut."

My legs wobbled and my arms felt like lead, but I held Julie close to my chest and sat down. A few people milled around the ticket counter paying me no attention. Papa strode past the windows cutting across the tracks, taking the quickest route to our house.

A few minutes later, he entered and picked up our bags, motioning for me to follow him. The green Ford junker idled close by. He opened the front passenger door and I sat down holding Julie.

At home, I placed the baby on my bed with pillows around her. She was too little to turn over, but the nuns had cautioned us about preventing babies from falling off beds. Papa walked in behind me and peered over my shoulder. "Sure glad she looks like you and not that neighbor kid."

Hate filled my body. I tensed and said nothing. I would have to choose important times to confront him.

He headed for the living room. "Let's go get a crib and some baby clothes."

My legs would barely hold me. "I have to rest and feed Julie first." I ate a sandwich and warmed a bottle, then lay on the bed with her beside me. Lying on my own bed brought a calm I hadn't felt since getting on the train heading to MN. My life had changed dramatically since that day, since telling Mama the night before that I was leaving, now with a precious bundle beside me. It felt surreal.

Papa drove us to a second-hand store that afternoon where we found a nice crib. The white paint looked like new, and I loved the little pink and blue spinning balls that decorated the head and foot frames. At J.C. Penney, we bought flannel sheets, little gowns, shirts, lots of diapers, flannel blankets and a knitted shawl. Just before we got to the counter, I spied a pink sweater and hat set with matching booties. I examined the package. Papa nodded. "Let's get it. The outfit will look good when we take her to church for baptism."

We drove home without a word. I watched him assembled the crib while lying on the bed feeding Julie. He lowered the railings making sure everything worked and then sat on bed beside us. "I leave tonight on a run. If you have questions about the baby, call Opal. Before I picked you up at the train station, I stopped at the library and talked to her about our situation and Cousin Julie."

I scowled, fearing our secret would be out.

"She knows an old woman named Edith who lives three blocks from here who babysits. Says she'll see if Edith will help you. I'll pay her."

With it being May, I would have the summer off school, three months to adjust, and get a routine. Hearing about Edith eased my fear of him making me quit school to take care of her.

Papa loomed in the doorway as I placed sleeping Julie on a soft flannel blanket in her new crib. I blocked his view of the baby, not wanting his evil eyes on her. He said, "I'm going back on the rails today. I have to work extra after taking the time off to bring you home. Don't know when I'll be back." He walked out.

I listened for the car to leave, then took a long hot shower. Seeing the gross red surgical scar across my belly made me cringe but it didn't hurt much. I was relieved to dress in my favorite pedal pushers. I got the zipper up but couldn't quite button the waist. A short-sleeved pink T-shirt with an edging of lace at the neck covered my hips and belly. It felt good to wear real clothes and not the baggy pants I'd worn for months in Minnesota.

After I heard a freight train rattle out of town, my spirits improved, I turned on the radio, covered the baby with a light blanket and lay on my bed. With her safely in the crib an arm's length away, I fell into a dead sleep.

Later, her cry shot me out of bed. I grabbed her, calmed her and was relieved to find she was just hungry. I didn't know how to take care of a baby. I had never babysat or been around kids.

Papa being gone was good. I hoped Julie and I would have developed a routine before he returned so he wouldn't yell and get us both upset.

I loved Julie from the moment I saw her and now that we were home, in our own house, my tension decreased. I slept well between her feedings and found great comfort having someone to talk to. I unpacked my suitcase and placed Dolly in a corner of her crib. Now, I had a baby of my own to love, just like Mama. As soon as Julie was old enough for a doll,

I would be sure she played with Dolly. Maybe it was a small way to begin breaking the cycle I'd found myself in. One day she'd be free, playing with dolls and other kids.

My baby would not become another incest victim.

Opal knocked on the door the next morning with Edith at her side. I invited them in but felt uneasy bringing someone into our home. That never happened before Mama died except for church ladies with casseroles who were let into the living room. Since Jimmy, Opal and the undertaker left, no one had been inside but me and Papa.

Edith, a grey-haired lady who looked like she was a good cook had a sweet smile. "Your father asked Opal and me to check on you. I think you have your hands full and could use a little help. I'm great with babies."

Opal reiterated Papa's sad story about the tragic loss of his cousin, how I had stayed with her when she was ill with a complicated pregnancy.

I brought them into the bedroom and picked Cousin Julie up from her bed. They exclaimed about her beauty and Edith held out her arms to hold the baby. Their visit was short, but they returned about an hour later with a couple bags of groceries and made dinner for me. We ate together and it was the most wonderful feeling. It was as if I had a family. They couldn't know the secret, but I trusted Opal because of Mama and if Edith was her friend, that was good enough for me.

Chapter 7 - School Days

Throughout the summer, Edith came over for about an hour almost every day to help with cleaning, cooking and caring for Julie. Sometimes we'd take walks and bring a few groceries home for recipes she wanted to fix. Papa started leaving money on the kitchen table for what he called "essentials" to use when he was on the rails.

Before school started, Edith and I had a plan. She arrived early, giving me time to walk to school, and stayed till I got home. She usually had dinner in the oven.

I called the loving overweight woman Grandma Edith. She taught me things about baby care like Mama would have. Between the two of us, Julie grew smiley and seldom cried.

+

Challenging seventh grade classes and caring for a newborn required the calming support of Grandma Edith. She sent me out the door with a full stomach and Julie in her arms. In winter months, walking the few blocks to school in windy fresh air cleared my thoughts of the darkness I often felt in our house. I feared the times Papa would drag me to his room after Julie was asleep forcing me to endure the physical and mental pain he left behind.

My body was my enemy.

It didn't really belong to me. I wondered who "me" was.

One body washed clothes like Mama taught me, ironed Papa's shirts and vacuumed. Like being in a play, it kept busy with studies and taking care of Julie, playing with her like a little doll.

The other a damaged body with the C-section scar as a constant reminder of what Papa had done and kept on doing lived an invisible nightmare, harboring hate, and searching for an escape. Threatened with abandonment and poverty if it didn't comply with his demands, or worse, death. Getting rid of it and keeping Julie if I didn't do everything he said.

Julie and I lived in a rut like the dirt road in the graveyard. Papa coming and going, seldom speaking except to complain about all the money he had to pay Edith. Leaving on a train trip. The whistle blowing a warning when he was coming back. Stomping into the house complaining, hurting me, shunning Julie, and leaving, only to return again bringing chaos like the dust devils Mama and I watched tear up the fields and disappear. Both of my bodies wanted him to disappear, too.

One day I heard his train approaching, first the whistle at the edge of town, then the engine louder, and louder, a rattle on the rails.

Then the junker car engine's characteristic sound.

I was feeding Julie when he stomped in and yelled, "You're quitting school to stay home with Julie. This is costing me too much money."

Julie stiffened in my arms and wailed at his yelling. I jumped up, "No!" I screamed loud enough for anyone passing by to hear, "No! You promised me and Mama. You promised me! You promised at the Catholic home you'd pay for my college." Julie squalled, adding to my voice. "You promised. Do it or I'll tell!"

His hand flung out connecting with the side of my head snapping it, hurting my neck.

I refused to cry out. Through clenched teeth, I stood straight and glared, then turned away from him and left the room to calm Julie.

I'm not sure where he went. We didn't see him for a couple days and that suited me fine. When Julie and I walked to the library, I saw his car at Mack's Shack and wondered if he was sweet on Charlene, Rex's poor widow, trying to support her daughter.

I feared more he might be sweet on her teenage daughter Penny, about a year younger than me.

I turned thirteen two months after Julie's birth. Mama had been in the ground for a year. Throughout that time, I found comfort in the library. Sometimes Opal would hold Julie for me as I scoured the shelves for child development books. The library expanded my knowledge and interests, with a focus on subjects that could change my life. I read about emergencies like floods and fires, how people packed important belongings they'd need if they had to flee.

I had to flee.

Be ready.

Not knowing when but believing the time would come when Papa would try to take Julie for his honey. I never forgot what he said when he spoke to the deaf nun at the girls' home. "If it's a boy, adopt him out. If it's a girl, I'll keep her for my own."

At that time, I was too frightened to realize what he meant.

Well, now I know.

I'm skinny again, but my breasts have grown, and the surgical scar is fading but looking at it reminds me I'm still in prison. I escape to school each day, leaving Julie in Edith's loving care. My brain absorbs information when my troubled thoughts allow it.

Mama never drove a car, never had a checkbook, never had money of her own. I am glad her allowance bought our ring because the sparkling stones hold memories of her love and the words, *be strong*. I felt her presence. She taught me to think and plan. She'd say, "Attend college, then leave home as soon as possible."

I kept the cardboard box we used to place her books in beneath my bed as part of my escape plan. I really had nothing to put in it yet. The only things I owned were a few clothes, Dolly, our ring, and Julie.

After Julie started walking and Edith potty trained her, when I wasn't in school, I would take her hand and we'd explore the neighborhoods, often walking in empty fields where alfalfa with purple flowers grew. She giggled watching bees in the blooms. The prairie winds blew her curls. When she was bigger, we went to a small park with swings and a slide. She babbled a lot and words came easy. Opal helped me find the right library books to read to her. Like Mama did for me, I tried to teach Julie something every day.

Opal and Edith were Mama's replacements. I shouldn't say it like that because no one could replace Tess. What I mean is, they would share a recipe with me or a new book, talk to me like a daughter, give me hugs that provided comfort and strength. Just like the ladies at church, they asked no questions and seemed to accept fully what Papa said about "Cousin Julie."

Papa seldom took us anywhere. When he was in town, we walked to church on Sunday morning. We'd get up early and dress up, instead of slacks or peddle-pushers in summer, Julie and I each had a few dresses he'd brought home to us. He had a good eye for clothing. I felt good in my bright dresses and made sure Julie looked perfect. She particularly like black patent leather shoes and would skip down the sidewalk to church after we ate our eggs and toast.

Papa followed his routine of work and was away for days on end.

Fewer honey sessions.

Time alone with Julie.

I loved having him gone.

When she was old enough, I decided I would tell her the truth. It would have to be a time when she could keep the secret so we would be safe until we escaped together. I would have to wait. I was too young to drive, had no money, and no family to help. Everyone was dead except my mother's brother Steve, and I didn't know how to find him.

I thought Papa must be sweet on another girl. He hadn't bothered me as much.

Maybe he sensed my intense anger and worried I might tell someone what he was doing to me. I was frightened all the time because I believed if I told anyone or they suspected and went to authorities, he would kill me. It would look like an accident. I'd be gone and he'd have Julie all to himself.

I don't know where he got them, but he made me take birth control pills every day. He watched me swallow them at first but then he left town with threats of death if I became pregnant again. I could have refused but didn't want to become pregnant. If it wasn't for Julie, I know I would just kill myself to stop the abuse.

Sometimes I wondered if he was bringing gifts to his other girl instead of to us.

Am I jealous?

No, I only wish we lived a different life, where the daddy was a real daddy not a horrible lying faker pretending to be a churchman respected by community leaders and even the cops.

Most important to me, Julie was safe. Happy. Unknowingly, she lived inside the invisible cloud of my anguish and fear. I kept the abuse a secret, feeling powerless for years. But growing older, learning more, made me stronger and led me to believe I'd be able to act if I saw his eyes on my beautiful daughter. I'd be ready to do something other than hide in a shameful situation that was all my fault.

Mama had warned me. "Be strong."

I'm learning and planning. Papa's bruising grip on my shoulder at church each Sunday reminds me I must hold my tongue.

I've held my tongue but am old enough to make secret plans. I decided to take driver education and fake his signature allowing me to take the class. I don't like lying because I live a lie every day, but driving might provide an escape and I know he wouldn't sign for me.

Papa is strict and orderly. He demands everything in its place. No messes. He says, "Cleanliness is next to godliness." Thinking about his words and knowing what he did to my mother and me, I sneer. At least he showers after a long trip and smells good after cleaning up, but based on his behavior, he isn't godly and won't be going to heaven.

I think he was trying to be a better man. He became some sort of church board member and is called a deacon. He attends meetings at the parsonage when he's in town. He attends church services more often and is taking on parish responsibilities. I hope it isn't with young girls.

He's an actor, wanting to look good, acting the part of a good man, pretending in public, and working as a nasty prison guard in his home.

We all look good on the outside, wear nice clothes, but we're dirty.

No one would talk to us if they knew.

No one asks about Cousin Julie.

The church people just exclaim how generous we are to take in a family orphan. They exclaim about the family resemblance. Papa smiles.

The pastor and his wife invited us to a church social at their home, a potluck. Papa demanded I make Julie behave. "Show them we're a good Christian family."

I know the ugly truth. Nothing could change that, but Julie is perfect, a wonderful little girl. We aren't angels, but we mind our manners.

Mama had taught me how to wash clothes and hang them out to dry. I'm better at cooking after practicing some of her mother's recipes but I'm still not so good at baking. The potluck church women raved about my tasty green Jell-O salad with pineapple chunks and marshmallows. One of the women even invited me to Bible study. I kindly thanked her but said I had to devote time to schoolwork. I would never leave Julie alone with Papa. Besides, she's too young to sit around coloring pictures of Jesus. Instead, like my Mama did for me, I read her stories about faraway places I dream about us visiting.

Papa made sure we went to church as a family when he was in town but wanted us at home if he wasn't around to control our moves. On a summer Sunday after Julie turned four, we sat in *our* pew on the left side of the small Lutheran church beneath a stained-glass window picturing Jesus holding a little lamb. The morning sun shining through Jesus's dark red robe cast a reddish light over me turning my arms and sundress rose-colored. I was twiddling my fingers and not listening to the preacher. Julie looked at me. I smiled and she started laughing and choking, trying to muffle her giggling.

I elbowed her. She laughed harder. The preacher stopped talking and stared at us. Heads of stern old women in funny hats turned and frowned.

Papa's eyes stabbed us so viciously I thought they might draw blood and add to the polka dots on my dress.

I glared at Julie and shook my head. She finally settled down, but I could see the laugh spasms in her belly continue.

After church when we were walking home, I asked why she was laughing. She said my face and teeth had turned pink because of the light shining through the colored glass. I laughed, too, and told her about a time at a church picnic with my friend who laughed so hard she snorted corn kernels out her nose and I couldn't stop laughing. Julie's laugh spasms started again.

We had walked almost three blocks toward home by the time Papa caught up with us. He'd stayed back to talk to some of the men. "Cousin Julie, you're an embarrassment to me. Everyone saw your behavior during the reading of the Gospel."

"I'm sorry Papa, I got a tickle bug and couldn't stop. Anna's teeth were pink in the sunlight, and it made me laugh."

"Don't let it happen again or I'll send you back where you came from."

Julie sunk to the ground with tears in her eyes.

Tears stung my eyes seeing his treatment of my beautiful child. "She is not a throw-away! Papa, she's a child. Don't be so harsh."

His voice boomed so loud I wondered if the people milling around outside the church could hear him. "Who the hell are you to tell me what to do?"

I took Julie's hand and walked ahead of him, furious. At home, I pulled her inside and closed the door. We were in the living room just inside the front door, when Papa snatched it open and grabbed my arm turning me into a slap that smacked my cheek. "I don't allow sassing. Shut up if you know what's good for you."

I jerked loose from his grip and spun to face him. "Don't touch me."

Julie screeched and ducked past him, running toward the door.

Papa blocked the doorway. "Where in hell do you think you're going?"

I took Julie's hand and reached for the doorknob. "To show the police my face."

Papa laughed out loud. "I'll just call and tell them you're lying and to throw you in jail." He sneered. "I'm your father. You're sixteen now. You can leave home and be on your own. Go live under the Missouri River bridge with the bums, but Julie is staying with me."

Fear struck my heart. Julie squeezed my fingers tight, fright in her eyes, increasing my rage against him. My eyes stabbed. "Never."

He entered his bedroom and slammed the door. Julie and I were in our room removing our church clothes and dressing in play clothes when he appeared in the doorway, glared at us and then stormed out the back door. I waited for the sound of a car motor, thankful when he drove away.

It was on that day I knew I must make a plan. I could never let him touch Julie and I sensed he was looking at her with honey eyes when he brought her a short, skimpy sundress, not adoring eyes of a loving father, but those of an evil man.

Chapter 8 - High School

Gramma Edith came every day, but I worried her health was failing when I saw she had trouble bending and picking up things she dropped. She moved slower and had to rest after walking across the room. The twinkle in her eyes had turned to worry. When I asked about her health, she said her doctor had changed her heart medication recently and she was feeling better.

A few days later, when I returned from school, I found Edith sound asleep on the couch. However, Julie was happily sitting near Edith's feet reading to a stuffed kitty. I let Edith sleep and went to work on school assignments. Her sleeping worried me. It meant Julie, at age 5, was unattended.

When Edith awakened, she seemed confused as if she didn't know where she was. I gave her a glass of milk and we talked for a while. Edith assured us she'd had a bad night, not sleeping well, but felt fine after the nap.

I took her arm to help, but the elderly woman walked fine, just a little slow. The thought of not having the stability of Edith in our lives would be disastrous. What would I do with Julie when I was in school?

Julie and I walked Edith home. I called Opal from Edith's phone to tell her Edith was feeling tired. Then, the two friends talked. After staying with Edith for about an hour, I asked about getting more help so she would not have childcare responsibility for Julie every day. She said if anything happened, Opal could watch Julie because she had the flexibility to close the library for short periods in an emergency.

Edith said Opal suggested pre-school. I had thought about that, too. When we left Edith, she seemed fine. We had fixed her dinner and she was resting.

The next day I stopped by a preschool daycare I walked past every day on my way to and from school. I inquired about the cost and hours.

Things went along in the Stanton family rut. My grades were great and at sixteen I qualified for driver education. I brought the parental approval form home and practiced copying Papa's signature from one I found on a carbon in his checkbook. I admired my work and finally wrote his signature on the form.

It looked authentic when I carried it to school and submitted it, no questions asked.

I memorized road rules and passed the written test without missing any questions. When I began driving, I worried one of Papa's friends would see me behind the wheel. During the lessons, I pulled my hair up into a ponytail, sort of a disguise because I never wore my hair that way. Luckily, the instructor usually took us on back roads. We even drove through the cemetery where he said, smiling, that the residents wouldn't complain.

I laughed. If my mother's spirit blowing in the wind was aware, Mama would be smiling.

Billy Brothers, a tall athlete my age, was the only boy I talked with much in my class. We took driver education together. I liked him and hoped he would not grow up to be like Papa. He seemed comfortable in any situation based on his behavior in the classes we shared. We were both good drivers, but he said he'd gotten a head start driving tractors on their farm as soon as his feet could reach the pedals.

He teased me that I was too short to see over the steering wheel without sitting on a pillow. I chose one just the right height from a stack of cushions the instructor carried in the trunk for his students to get them situated before handing over the keys.

Earning my permit was greater achievement than getting straight As. It was a goal I had looked forward to for years. Although I had no one to drive with me to practice, I took the driving test in the school training car and passed.

That day I ran with the wind, hurrying home with the temporary one in my hand.

I had to be sure to retrieve my permanent license from the mail before Papa saw it. He couldn't know.

When the license arrived, I put it deep in the pages of a book in my bedroom on the bottom shelf. I thought it would be safe because the only book I ever saw Papa open was a hymnal. I didn't trust my escape ticket to be visible in the emergency box sitting empty beneath my bed.

Chapter 9 - Secret Blood Ties

On a sunny morning in July, as soon as we heard the freight train rattle out of town, Julie and I left for the graveyard with bouquets of flowers. It was about a mile walk. We crossed the highway, but most of the distance took us through neighborhoods of boxy houses with screened front porches much like ours, then along a dirt road. We entered beneath a metal arch designating Evergreen Cemetery.

Papa left the house about half an hour earlier in a hurry, carrying his grip. His parting words were: "I won't be back for a week. Behave yourselves. Here's a five-spot in case you need some groceries." He handed me the money and left.

He often just left a couple dollars on the kitchen table but was usually gone only a few days. I wondered why this trip was longer than most but didn't ask. I'd learned not to question anything to avoid an explosion of emotion from him.

Luckily, Julie and I had each other for company. Without her, it would have been very lonely. I know how to entertain myself, but being very alone right after Mama died, my confused brain sometimes wished Papa would return from the rails. Being with someone bad was better than no one at all, besides, sometimes he brought me nice presents.

At the end of my school year when Julie was five, Papa announced. "Girls should play the piano. It's time Julie started, and I expect you to help her."

We didn't disagree because I'd been teaching her some simple songs and she had a special talent. After starting lessons with a woman living a couple blocks from our house, a church lady Papa paid, Julie and I borrowed some music books from her to play duets. It was a great way to spend time and we fit practice periods into most days. One day when we were playing, Julie stopped and held up a hand. "Look, we both have funny pinkie fingers!"

Our crooked fingers matched. They matched Papa's but I didn't say that. Seeing my hands looked like his, made me hate him just like the C-section scar I carried on my belly. I felt like the inherited bad fingers were sirens of shame. People would know if they saw mine and Julie's, so I tended to hide my hands in public.

Julie held my hands and compared our fingers. Her hands were a mirror image of mine.

My thoughts swept me back to the wavy mirror at the carnival where Papa took me the day I puked all over myself. The trick mirror distorted my face and body. It made me look pregnant. It was as if it had looked inside and saw Julie before I even knew what was happening to my body.

I probably threw up that day because I was pregnant. The morning sickness got worse and worse on the rocking train all the way to the girls' home.

Sitting at the piano with Julie holding my hands, I closed my eyes and willed my brain to just stop thinking. STOP!

I kissed her little fingers. "They're a little strange but they work just fine." I straightened my fingers and then made fists a couple times. "We're related, cousins. It must run in the family."

Being so closely related, closer than cousins, I knew we were lucky. One day when I was scanning library books, I had run across one on inheritance. My eyes locked on *inter-family marriage. Blood relatives* they called it, producing babies often born with genetic abnormalities.

I had held my breath as I read on. Having Papa father a child with me could have produced a child with large defects and mental disabilities.

For a while, I worried something might show up as Julie grew. I saw photos of kids with crooked faces and twisted legs, unable to walk or speak. I watched Julie carefully as she developed into a bright talented child. In my eyes, Julie was perfect, but we had no professional opinion because Papa hated doctors. We only went when someone was very sick or for an immunization. The doctor had never said Julie had anything wrong with her body or brain.

We decided to talk with Tess about the coming school year. It would help me to discuss changes in her presence, out loud, because there were big changes ahead with Julie entering preschool and me beginning my senior year in the fall. A few days after Julie and I stopped at a daycare to speak with the director and solidify a plan, we walked out to the Stanton family plot.

Julie would be in daycare during my hours in class. It cost more than Papa paid for Edith, but when I inquired about working there a few hours each day to help pay the fee, the director loved the idea. Her afternoons were always busier and said she'd welcome my help each day after school.

Papa was gone on the rails as usual so we could tell him when he returned from his long run. There was no hurry in making decisions, but knowing we had this opportunity provided me relief. Grandma Edith's knees were giving out and she had trouble walking the three blocks to our house and up the three steps to the front door.

We placed flowers on the family graves, including Sam's, Tess's father. She had no photos of her parents, so I had to recall her descriptions. I pictured Sam with a kind face and blue eyes like hers. Tess said she resembled her mother, but her brother Steve had auburn hair like Sam's. I thought about her words when I placed painted daisies on his grave. The flowers had brown centers with a glint of red similar to his hair color. Mama and her mother Sally both got bouquets of white daisies mixed with Forget-me-nots from Julie.

After placing the flowers, we sat atop the large Stanton Family granite stone to talk. I had to boost Julie up first before I climbed up to the perch where we could easily look across the graveyard. Julie pointed to a couple of new graves. "I wonder who died."

There were mounds of dark dirt not far away. Of course, we were so isolated, I knew few people except for some I'd met at church, no one I would call friends and knew few family names. Our eyes followed Jimmy's little pickup driving up to the site and stopping. We watched him smoothing the ground. He stood up and leaned on his long-handled shovel, stretching his back. He turned and surveyed the cemetery, seeing us, he waved and walked our way for a visit.

When he drew close, I called, "Hi, Jimmy. People have to quit dying. You're working too hard."

He nodded and checked out the name on a headstone. "I don't think old Ben would care if I took a break sitting with him, talking to you." Jimmy sat down and removed his baseball cap. "Don't you look cute high up on the family marker. Wish I had a camera."

Julie smiled. "Sorry we don't have cookies to share. We just brought flowers."

"I ate breakfast." He patted his belly. "Opal packed me a lunch today, so I could finish up smoothing and seeding those graves to get some grass growing before it gets too hot." He invited us to stop by for a visit anytime, then went back to work.

Julie and I talked for a time, discussing preschool and how to behave around other children. "Manners are important. I learned mine from Mama." I looked at her headstone, "Didn't I, Tess?"

Julie and I looked at each other as if listening for a response.

A gust of wind whipped around us shaking the little blue flowers on Tess's grave. I raised my eyebrows questioning. "Hmm. Maybe she heard me."

"She would be very proud of you, Anna. You and Edith have both taken good care of me, being that I'm Cousin Julie and not really a beginning member of this family. You saved me."

"Tess would love you very much just as I do."

Julie hopped to the ground. "I would like to know what my mother was like. Would you tell me about her? I'm so sorry she died." Julie's words broke. "I heard someone say she died in childbirth. I guess that means I killed her." She choked on the word *killed*, and tears ran down her cheeks.

I hugged her, turning away, hoping she wouldn't see the tears welling in my eyes. "Sweetie, I will tell you about her soon."

I had been thinking about telling Julie the truth but keeping the secret was a matter of life and death for both of us. My actual death and her living in bondage. I couldn't let that happen.

Chapter 10 - The Recipe Box

Julie and I planted a nice garden. We dressed George in a new bright red plaid shirt we'd bought at the thrift store and put him back in place to scare crows away from our little strawberry patch. He was one of our few friends, so Julie and I told him stories. It was nice looking out the window, knowing he'd be there. He'd wave to us. Julie commented that he was not a very scary scarecrow because the crows perched on his shoulders. We laughed.

At times, we dug through a box of recipes to find different things to cook. Most of them were Grandma Sally's, some marked with Mama's notes in writing similar to her mother's. She'd penciled in slight changes or comments on how tasty some turned out. Julie and I treasured the recipes just as Mama had. It was a comforting touch of the past from a person we never knew. I recalled the day we hurried home with the box from the library.

Opal brought it out saying she had forgotten she'd placed it on a shelf in her basement years earlier after Sally took sick and Mama lived faraway. When things didn't look too good for Sally, she'd asked Opal to give her little box to Tess if she ever saw her again. It was something Sally could share with the daughter she'd lost. At the time, Opal said she didn't know if she'd ever see her friend Tess again.

Opal told Tess about Sally's sadness when her only son had gone into the military after Sam died. Through her illness, Sally lived in pain and grief without any of her family by her side.

Mama said the first time she walked into the library after they moved back and found Opal there working, they both burst into tears of joy. Opal dug out the box of recipes and surprised Tess with it. My mother treasured the recipes, now the box was mine and Julie's.

One day, Papa came home and found us reading recipes. He glared at the mess we'd made on the kitchen table sorting them into piles, such as cookies, cakes and hotdishes. He picked up one and read it out loud. "Beef Stroganoff. Tess was good at making this. Why don't you two make yourselves useful? Fix this for me today for dinner."

I scanned the ingredients. "Could you get some sour cream for us? We'll need it and we don't have any. We have everything else."

He nodded and after taking a nap, left for hours, returning drunk, but carrying a container of sour cream that he placed in the refrigerator.

We cleared our mess, stashing the recipes to sort another day and Julie made little meatballs while I set the table and put water on the stove for the noodles. The kitchen smelled wonderful. I thought Papa might comment on it when he returned, instead, he flopped on his bed and snored so loud, we closed the door to blunt the sound.

I turned on the radio and we listened to music like Mama and I used to do as we cooked.

Papa got up mean and demanded dinner.

Luckily, we were ready to add the cream and drop noodles into the boiling water. While we readied the salad and
noodles, he washed up and combed his hair. Within minutes, he appeared looking presentable and sat at the small
kitchen table opposite Julie.

I placed the food in the center of the table easily within
reach for all of us. Papa bowed his head. We all folded our
hands. He said grace, then served himself first as usual. He
ate a few bites in silence and reached for more. "Girls, this is
the best food I've had in weeks. Keep up the good work." He
ate the second helping and left.

Julie took a second helping. "I think we should make this
one again. It's really good and that is the first nice thing he's
said in a long time."

I agreed. After we finished eating, washed the dishes and
put them back in their places, we played the piano. We went
for a walk before sunset and stopped to swing in the city
park. Dog-walkers and lovers holding hands strolled past.
Before going to bed, we agreed it was a nice afternoon and
evening, unusually peaceful.

I fell asleep wondering what had changed to make Papa
a nicer happier man.

The next morning at breakfast, we decided it was a good
time to talk to him about Edith's health issues and our possible plan of Julie attending a daycare preschool until she was
old enough to begin kindergarten. Summer would be over
soon and my last year of high school would begin in the fall.

As soon as I brought up the topic, Papa's body stiffened. He clenched his fists. One held his butter knife like a weapon. Raspberry jelly dripped from the tip like blood. He stared first at me then at Julie. "So, the two of you have been cooking up mischief that will cost me more money."

I faced him. "No. I inquired about working at her school to help pay the cost."

He stood up. "No! I don't like my women working."

"Papa, it's not a real job. I would just be helping so it won't cost as much. I can't leave Julie at home at her age when I'm in school."

He spread his toast with the jam and slammed the knife down. "Like I said before, the easiest solution is to quit school."

Julie shook her curls. "No, Papa. Anna is very smart, and she wants to go to college like I do."

"Dammit, so now the two of you are teamed up against me after everything I do for you." He left his toast on the plate and walked out.

We sat looking at each other. "What now?" Julie leaned back in her chair. Tears gleamed inside her lower lids.

"We'll have to see. I never know what to expect. He just likes to order us around without discussing anything. Thanks for supporting me."

Julie was asleep, breathing regularly, when I heard the back door open and Papa's footsteps crossing the squeaky kitchen floor. They went across the living room and when I heard his bedroom door open and close, I felt relief. I willed him to go to bed and go to sleep. Just like past prayers that went unanswered, willing him to sleep didn't work. Like so many times before, I heard our bedroom doorknob turn and held my breath.

He silently walked to my bed, shook my shoulder and gripped my arm, pulling me toward him. I wanted to scream but couldn't wake Julie. Dread made my feet feel like lead and knowing what was ahead, I could barely make them move.

He closed his bedroom door and tipped a chair back beneath doorknob that would crash down and make noise if Julie tried to come in. I hoped she would sleep.

The same as always. Lighting a candle, hands all over me, pulling off my night gown, making me walk around the room without clothes, twisting my delicate pubic hair, sitting on his lap, straddling him, hurting, squeezing me so tight I couldn't breathe or scream. If I pushed him away, he'd slap my buttocks hard, sometimes bruising. I learned long ago I had to let him do what he wanted, bide my time, go away to the river bluff, concentrate on the horizon.

Faraway thoughts would blunt my anguish but not my shame.

That night, when he was done, he fell back, resting till his breathing slowed, all the while gripping my arms, not letting me leave. "I've decided you can enroll Julie in the day-care and work after school." He flung my nightgown at me. "Tell me who to make the check out to and how much each month, now, get out."

I scrubbed my body with a hot soapy washcloth and applied lotion to erase his smells while my brain raced to planning an escape. It had to be soon. I found myself worrying more and more about Julie. I couldn't let him touch her. I'd already failed Mama. I couldn't fail Julie.

Tiptoeing into our room, I looked at Julie's beautiful sleeping face, partially illuminated in moonlight. I had to protect her from his abuse.

Feeling dirty, unclean despite scrubbing, I crawled into my bed and tried to sleep. Lying beneath clean sheets with clean smells reminded me of Tess and how hard she'd tried to teach me to protect myself.

Instead, I ended up in her bed.

Finishing high school and attending community college in Riverside would get me started on the road to independence. I'd have a way to support myself and Julie. In the meantime, I could make a little extra money at the daycare and save some for an escape—and save our souls from the devil.

I started thinking more about Opal and Jimmy as saviors to help me get us out, but we must have money and a place to live, so I had to be patient. I didn't know what Papa would do to them if they helped us escape and exposed his abuse. If he wasn't in jail, I feared he would hurt them to save himself.

In the morning after a troubled sleep with my brain grinding through ways to leave, Papa opened the bedroom door. I hadn't heard his footsteps. My heart stopped. My eyes popped wide open. Fear pulsed my body and I sat straight up like a jack-in-the-box. When I saw he was dressed in work clothes and carrying his grip, I relaxed. He'd be leaving, on the rails and out of our lives for a few days.

Papa scanned the bedroom, focusing on Julie first, then me. "I packed my own lunch bucket and filled the thermos. The crew exchange is in a few minutes, then I'm on the rails. I left a few bucks on the table."

I waited till I heard the freight rattle out of town then fell into a dead sleep, dreaming I was in the train headed back to Montana with my newborn in my arms. When Julie shook me to awaken me, I swung out my arm and hit her chest.

She grabbed my hand. "It's me, Julie. Wake up. It's not a bad dream. It's me. We're okay."

"I'm so sorry. Did I hurt you?" I sat up and hugged her. She was already dressed, her hair combed into cute ponytails, one by each ear.

She laughed. "You surprised me. I'm fine but hungry. It's almost eleven o'clock. I let you sleep in. The beater car isn't here. I think Papa is gone. I'm so glad."

"He's out on the rails again. Let's eat and go for a bike ride." I wasn't sure where I wanted to go but I felt the need to escape from the house. I needed fresh air; the prairie wind always helped. My heart clutched in my chest realizing how sad, at her young age, Julie knows we are better off alone than with Papa.

Chapter 11 - Shopping in Riverside

B icycling through side streets and out River Road, riding up a high point where we could see the horizon refreshed my brain, easing bad thoughts and pain. Out where the pavement ended and few cars traveled, I felt calm. We rode fast along the gravel and reached Mama's bluff, where she and I often watched ducks and big gray pelicans float down the river.

Below us along the steep bank, the Missouri River spilled over rocks. A distant herd of black cattle sprinkled the expansive landscape where few humans ventured. I wished I'd brought peanut butter cookies like Mama did so long ago because today might be the time to talk to Julie like Mama did, trying to protect me at a young age, about the age of Julie.

Of course, Julie was too young to reveal ugly details.

The day was so bright and calming, I decided to avoid negative topics and talk about school instead. Our lives were so isolated, Julie had little contact with other children. I thought she was mature for her age, but I counseled her about accepted behavior and not to talk about our strict homelife. We stayed until the clouds darkened, looking like rain.

In town, we parked our bikes and walked along the sidewalk looking in store windows. It was rare we'd go downtown because I expected a cop to be eyeing us, or someone from church who might stir up Papa by telling him we were roaming the town. Occasionally, we shopped at the Corner Grocery, searching for a recipe ingredient.

Riverside was a nice town with people who said hello in passing, who stopped to let us cross quiet intersections. People smiled at us. We smiled wooden smiles thinking we looked normal, but it was safer to just stay home and avoid Papa's wrath.

How could we trust strangers when we couldn't trust our father?

I had trouble thinking about him as our father. I equated *father* with dirty words, a verb of abuse. He *fathered* us, but he wasn't a father, he was an abuser. A tyrant, a beater, a liar, a rapist, a bad man who people thought was a good family man, a hard worker, a widower, a deacon and a respected railroad engineer.

Papa was not a father.

Julie stopped to look in the dime store window where school supplies were displayed. She wouldn't need much for preschool, but I suggested we go in and buy a notebook and a couple new pencils for her. It was fun walking up and down the aisles like I had with Mama. Now, I was here with my own daughter, Cousin Julie.

The clerk and store owner, a suspicious tall woman, loomed over us, following close, watching every move. I recalled Mama said the woman worried about kids stealing from her. She wore an apron with the words, *Five and Dime,* in an arc over her massive breasts. Her stark appearance with unruly hair and mean eyes pushed Julie closer to me, until the little girl took my hand for reassurance. After we bought her supplies and were safely back on the sidewalk, Julie took a deep breath. "Let's not go in there again. She's scary."

"That's her objective. Frighten little kids so they don't steal from her."

"I don't see how she makes any money scaring people away. But I love my pencils. Thank you."

Down the block, we looked into a clothing store. One window had work clothes like Papa wore to the railyard, heavy dark pants and stiff shirts. In the other window, wooden mannequins modeled printed cotton dresses with buttons up the front. "Tess called those housedresses. She would laugh and say it was a good name for them because you shouldn't leave home dressed like that."

"Did she wear frilly clothes?"

"No. She preferred slacks and T-shirts ordered from a catalog because Papa didn't want her in public flirting with other men."

"Her pictures are so pretty. Why didn't Papa want people to see her?"

"Jealousy."

Julie looked at me, questioning eyes.

"He didn't like other men looking at Mama because she was so pretty. Maybe he thought she'd run off with someone, so he locked her up at home, just like he does to us."

We walked to the end of the block and then back to our bikes. When we took off, I was reminded mine had developed a funny click and squeak. I didn't want to ask Papa to check it so I wondered if I could buy a little can of oil and see if I could fix it myself. I told Julie my plan and she loved the idea of shopping in another store. We stopped while I checked my money. Four dollars, probably enough. We pedaled to the hardware store.

A chubby grandfather clerk wearing a badge with the name "Chuck" pinned to his red apron greeted us. "Hi ladies, how can I help you today. You look like you're on a mission."

Julie smiled at him. "We need some oil for Anna's bike."

"I saw you ride up. Let me take a look at it. Maybe I can help." He headed out the door.

I told him what was happening when I pedaled.

"Take a spin and show me."

I hopped on and rode down the sidewalk, then turned back and rode past them. It made enough noise that when I stopped and wheeled it over to him, he squatted down and moved the pedals. "I hear it and see the problem. I'll get a wrench and some oil. You won't need to buy anything."

The man did his magic, and I took a ride on a silent bike and returned to his grin, hands on his hips. "Purring like a cat, now. No more squeaks. I think I fixed it."

"You did. Thanks so much."

"You're welcome." He nodded to the door. "We have free popcorn for shoppers. I just made some. Why don't you both come in and get a bag."

Julie's eyes widened. "Could we, Anna?"

We followed him inside where he heaped a couple little white bags with delicious smelling popcorn. We wandered around the store munching and shopping. He sat behind the counter whistling and working on a crossword puzzle.

Julie held up the bag. "Thank you. It tastes so good. You have a very nice store."

"Let me know if you need some help. I've worked here a long time, so I pretty much know where everything is."

I stopped at a display of padlocks and wished I could lock Julie and me in our bedroom at night. Next to the padlocks were screws and hooks. Some of the hooks had a screw dangling from one end. The bin said *Hooks with Eye Screws - 69 cents*.

I had seen a similar one on our storage shed in the backyard where we kept rakes and shovels, and on the garage door. Exactly what I needed to install on the inside of our bedroom door. I picked one up along with an extra eye screw and took it to the counter.

Chuck showed us how they worked together and measured the distance, so we'd know where to put the screws into the wood. He placed them in a little bag and counted out the change. "I'm glad you found some useful hardware. Come on back anytime you need some help fixing something or just stop in for a bag of popcorn."

He waved from the doorway and watched us ride off.

We waved. I yelled back, "Thanks for fixing my bike."

When we were about a block away, Julie looked around to be sure no one could hear. "He was so nice. Too bad Papa has stink eyes and no smiles."

Chapter 12 - Enjoying the Calm

During the summer, we visited with Grandma Edith, stopping at her little house a few blocks from ours just to talk when Papa was out of town. On one visit, she had taken a fall a few days earlier and needed help getting back to her easy chair after walking to the kitchen to make lemonade for us. We enjoyed sitting in her screened-in front porch.

Julie liked showing us how she could help. One afternoon she poured milk and made sandwiches for us. She delivered them with a flourish and thanked Edith for teaching her how to make sandwiches cut into fancy little triangles. We both thanked Edith for all the wonderful care she gave us and especially for taking care of Julie when she was a newborn.

During those busy school years with Edith, we never talked much about her life. I guess she was too busy being a mother to both of us. We mostly talked about kid things. She read many books to Julie, some she brought in a big cloth bag slung over one arm. She carried crocheting projects and note paper for letters she wrote to friends, things to fill her time when Julie was sleeping and growing strong.

It turned out Edith had retired after teaching school for many years. She said Tess was one of her students and very bright. She knew Steve, too. I was so sorry I hadn't gotten to know Edith better during all those hours we spent together. Later, on some of our visits, we talked about Tess and her big brother. Edith knew more about our family than anyone other than Opal. She said when Sally died, no one planned a funeral. The preacher and a couple friends said good-bye prayers at her graveside service.

We learned Steve was five years ahead of Mama in school, a good student, too, but ran out of money after one year of college and enlisted in the Navy. On our way home that day, I was quiet and feeling sad for Sally. There was no one to care when she died. Her son didn't even come to the funeral. She had abandoned Tess, and it was as if Tess didn't exist. I would guess Sally had regrets about giving her child to a madman. She probably prayed long and hard, but it would do no good. She should have saved Tess, protected her and forgot about looking like a bad mother in the eyes of the church ladies. I'd learned long ago that prayers don't work, actions do. I would protect Julie as long as I lived.

Later, I asked Edith why Steve wasn't home for the funeral.

"I heard he was at sea and couldn't get leave. One of his high school friends, Buddy Willis, might know where he is now if you want to locate Steve. Buddy's mother goes to the Episcopal church down the street. I'll ask her."

Weeks passed.

When Papa was in town, he wanted food on the table at 12 noon and 5 p.m. He spent most of his time outside working on his two cars but tinkered mostly on the newer Chevy. He kept the beater-car for everyday use but never took us for a drive in either car.

Julie stood by admiring the bright blue Chevy one day as Papa lay on the grass shining the chrome bumper till it looked like a mirror. He asked her to vacuum the car carpet. She told me she felt honored to be asked and did a thorough job as she crawled around cleaning the pretty car. Papa gave her a dollar when she finished, saying it was a tip for good work.

Seeing her big smile and the care she took folding the dollar, then tucking it in her pocket struck fear in me. I knew he was sweetening her for honey sessions because of the way he smiled at the positive effect a little money had on the child.

In the evenings, he'd spruce up, comb his hair, and put on cologne before going out. He never told us where he was going or what he was doing but drove off in the shiny car. The only thing I cared about was that he seldom dragged me to his bedroom. I thought he must have found a new honey.

Overall, life was better for a while because Papa stayed away more and more. We knew when he left with a grip and soon heard a freight leave town that he'd be gone for a few days. When he was home, he dumped dirty clothes in a pile and expected them to be washed and ironed. We were his handmaidens.

When Julie qualified for kindergarten that was a problem because it was half-days and I didn't get out until 3 p.m. Luckily, when I enrolled her, I asked at the daycare near her school if she could stay there in the afternoons.

After school began, I walked her down the street to Sunshine Daycare on my lunch break. The kids were younger than Julie, but at five, she was very mature. The manager said Julie helped with the little ones, feeding and reading to them.

Julie was safe and I was pleased to work there each afternoon from 3-5 p.m. It worked well and we got home by five-thirty each day. In the wintertime, it was starting to get dark by then, but it was just a few blocks to walk home.

As soon as we reached home, we'd flip on the lights and pull the shades. I'd start dinner while Julie practiced piano. It was a nice routine. I did my school assignments while she read or entertained herself. My schoolwork was never late, and I tried to get 100% on everything. Papa never once asked about our grades.

Julie adjusted to school and the daycare situation, and me to my job.

During the winter, there were more disgusting painful honey sessions when he dragged me out of bed in the middle of the night. Sometimes he kept me awake for hours. It was as if he wanted to keep me up so long and beat me down so much that I'd be too tired for school and I'd quit.

That wouldn't happen.

I'd endure anything to educate myself so Julie and I could leave his torture and live on our own.

I loved it when he left town taking my stress with him.

Julie and I studied together. I taught her arithmetic, like Mama taught me as soon as I knew my numbers. I had Julie practice reading out loud to me.

We basically raised ourselves. Papa only spoke if we asked a question. One night when he was gone, Julie snickered when I told her I didn't like to ask him anything because I never knew if he'd blow up and yell at us. She nodded. "Don't poke the bear." Then burst out laughing.

I choked in laughter, too. "Exactly, but where did you hear that?"

"Daycare. The teacher said that when someone was going to wake up a three-year-old boy who was usually wild. She wanted to let him nap."

"I agree, it fits for Papa, too. He's unpredictable." The best way to deal with him was to mind our manners, do our jobs, stay out of his way, and sit quietly in church when he was in town. I made a grocery list. He brought them home and dumped bags on the counter, never putting anything away. He expected us to wait on him.

My senior year went well, and I enjoyed talking to Billy, the driver education student I'd gotten to know. We sat near each other in a few classes. I helped him with math when he was struggling. It was nice sitting near him, noticing a fresh smell, thinking his mother must use Tide to wash his clothes. I hoped he'd grow up to become a good man like Jimmy.

Edith had told me Tide was her favorite, so when Julie was a baby, I asked Papa to buy it for us. Our clothes smelled as fresh as Billy's. He touched my hand after I had explained a math problem after class. "Thanks for the help. I wish I could do math like you."

I laughed. "My mother started me as soon as I could count, so maybe I got a head start. I'd better get going. I have a little part time job. See you tomorrow."

I walked fast to Sunshine Daycare and found Julie singing songs with little kids. It brought me joy to hear her happy voice and to get a hug as soon as she saw me enter. At Christmastime, they sang holiday songs.

Papa was in and out as usual but dressed up one evening and when he returned said he'd attended a deacon meeting at the church. "We will be attending a program on Christmas eve. A children's chorus will be singing."

Julie's eyes lit up. I wondered if she wanted to sing with them.

Papa shook his head. "You can't be in the choir because they practice in the evening. I don't want you out on the streets at night."

That was fine with me, but Julie looked disappointed. I had no interest in attending church at all, let alone singing. We had never celebrated holidays. It was just another day to him but before Mama died, she and I would listen to holiday music on the radio and sing happy songs like "Frosty the Snowman." The winter before she died, we baked sugar cookies and decorated them with green frosting trees. Papa ate the cookies but didn't say thank you and brought us no gifts.

After announcing the church program, he opened the closet door and got out a yardstick.

Julie and I looked at each other. I wondered if he was going to beat us when we'd done nothing wrong.

"Come here and stand by the door casing. I want to see how tall you are."

Julie stood straight with her back against the frame.

He penciled a line on the white painted wood and put a "J" beside it. "You're next, Anna."

I complied.

Papa put an "A" beside my height line and then measured them. "You're both shorties like Tess was. I guess I need a waist size, too." He left the house and returned in a few minutes with a tape measure I thought he got from his tool chest in the garage.

I was first. He measured my waist and chest. I clenched my teeth and stiffened to stop from screaming and shoving his hands away from me. But when he pulled Julie over to do the same, my heart rate skyrocketed. I didn't want him to touch her. I stepped close and offered to do it, trying to stop him.

Papa pushed me. "Get out of my way. If I need your help, I'll ask you."

He gently wrapped the tape around Julie's chest and then her waist, noting our measurements on a slip of paper. "There's a clothing store in my layover town, so on my next trip, I'll buy you new dresses to wear to that church program. Let's measure your feet in case I see some shoes I like." We each stood on the ruler for the measurement. "I never liked Christmas but being a deacon, I have to support the church. I won't allow you to sing with them because I don't want you hitching a ride with anyone. Remember, I have *eyes* on you all the time. If you don't behave, I'll know about it."

When I went to bed that night, it took a long time to fall asleep. I kept seeing his hands on Julie. The next day was Saturday and I got out of bed quietly to avoid awakening Julie. I tiptoed out to the kitchen where I found a five-dollar bill on the table.

He'd left town. I was surprised he didn't get us up to make him breakfast and pack a lunch. We never knew what to expect. Sometimes I felt like an abused dog and wanted to hide under a table until he left the house. This time he left when we weren't even aware of his departure.

My stress generated directly from him like static electricity making my hair stand out. I never knew what to expect so it left me uneasy all of the time. His work was steady, but his schedule varied, so we didn't know when he'd be home. I often wished he'd never return.

Julie and I looked forward to the holiday school break beginning on Wednesday at noon. The half-day meant we'd have all afternoon to ourselves and could take a walk in the snow. Maybe we'd visit Mama. Julie and I would be out of school until after New Year's Day.

The coming year would bring big changes, first grade for Julie, community college for me, inching closer to an escape.

Chapter 13 - Holiday Surprise

J ulie and I sat out of the wind, this time behind the large granite Stanton Family marker. It was about as tall as Julie, so it offered some shelter in the blustery wind. I sat in the same place the night before I left town on that long train ride to Minnesota before Julie's birth. Now, my little girl was sitting beside me. I put my arm around her wishing Mama could meet her. It would be fun to have a photo of the three of us, looking like sisters, our blond curls swirling in a summer breeze. Instead, Julie and I were sitting here shivering, talking to the dead.

It's really not that bad when you have no one else to talk to.

The old oak tree had a few remaining leaves, but most had been taken east on a ride with the wind after the fall freezes turned them pretty colors and sent them to their deaths, carpeting the earth in faraway places. At least for Jimmy's sake, most of them blew away and he didn't have to rake them. He had enough work to do digging graves, but in the winter, the ground was frozen too hard to dig. Mama had told me the bodies waited in a refrigerated morgue in a neighboring town until the spring thaw. I tried not to think about a refrigerator filled with bodies.

I didn't really like the idea of bodies being buried. I'd read about cremation. Maybe that was better. I thought about Mama, and her mother Sally who had let Mama be stolen by a bad man starting this string of Stantons. I wasn't even sure what to call us. From my reading, I knew our family lived in shame, visible to everyone but hiding in plain sight. Pretty girls. A "good father." Church goers. Soon we'd be sitting in church, in our pew on the left side near the front, Papa beside us, all dressed in our Sunday best, wearing new holiday dresses, smiling fake smiles in the light of Christmas trees. Someday, it would be wonderful to have a lighted tree in our house.

After telling Mama about school and how well Julie was reading and doing arithmetic, and about my good grades, we sang, "Joy to the World" before trudging back home.

I never talked to Julie about my dark thoughts. I wanted her spared, like Mama had tried to spare me from Papa but I wasn't smart enough to escape. Now, he had both of us locked in the same house and me locked in his bed. And Tess is forever buried beside a mother who deserted her.

On the way home, we walked through downtown looking at holiday decorations. The town fathers had hung lighted wreaths on streetlamps. Many stores had colored lights in the windows. We passed the ACE hardware windows where snow shovels decorated with red bows stood crisscrossed in fake snow. We were a few steps down the street when we heard a familiar voice. "I have fresh popcorn! Come in out of the cold." It was Chuck, holding the door wide open.

We both smiled and ran back.

"Today we are serving free hot apple cider. Your cheeks are rosy from the cold. Would you each like a cup with your popcorn?"

We nodded. Julie removed her gloves and took his offering. He directed us to a couple chairs where shoppers could try on ice cleats to keep them from slipping. I removed my coat, helped Julie with hers and hung them on the chairbacks. We sat in warmth with delicious cider and popcorn, listening to Christmas music from the overhead speakers.

Chuck helped a shopper then came back to chat and gave us cider refills. After we finished our snacks and were putting on our gear, he stopped by with a couple little cellophane-wrapped candy canes. "Here's something to sweeten you up when you get home. They are good with hot chocolate."

We thanked him and walked away. I felt lighter and happier holding Julie's little hand after our pleasant interlude with Chuck.

When we walked into the house, Julie dumped her coat on the couch. I hung hers and mine in the hall closet. I heard her in the kitchen and found her crouched by a lower cupboard looking at baking supplies. She looked up when I entered. "Anna, do we have cocoa? Could we make some hot chocolate?"

"I've never made it. Let's find a recipe."

I found a can of cocoa then took out our recipe box. Julie placed the sugar container on the counter with two mugs. She read the cocoa label. "Here's a recipe. After we make some, could we make cookies?"

I walked over to Mama's little radio sitting on the counter. "Let's turn on some Christmas music like my mother and I used to. Those recipes are a mess so we could organize them today, too."

The small wooden box looked old, scratched, and even had a little dough of some kind dried in a lump inside the cover. We decided to make dividers to index them. In Julie's fine writing, she laid the dividers on the counter, "Cookies" was the first one, then came: meats, hotdishes, salads, desserts.

She read through the first few cards and put them in the correct piles. She found one she liked that I made for her, my favorite cookie recipe. It's so good, we will share it with you in case you need to bake something special. You can either use raisins or chocolate chips.

Julie loved breaking eggs, so she did that part. We used a little electric hand mixer of Mama's that looked old but worked fine. I let Julie do lots stirring but I used the mixer to make sure she didn't hurt herself.

As she was stirring and humming to the radio, I dumped the rest of the cards out and spread them on the table. Something remained in the bottom of the box. I pulled it out and shrieked.

Julie turned. "What? Is Papa home? Do we have to hurry and clean things up?" Then she saw what I'd found. "Who's in that picture?"

We sat down, side-by-side at the table and looked at a photo of a sailor in uniform. A thin young man. Three more photos paperclipped together showed him at older ages. They were signed: "To Mom, Love, Steve." I cried.

"Anna, what is the matter? Do you know him?"

"No. I only heard about him. It's Tess's older brother who enlisted in the Navy after one year of college. Tess didn't know where he was and remember, Edith told us she knew one of his friends whose mother still lives here. Maybe we can find him."

Julie ran to look out the windows in front and the back of the house. She returned. "What would Papa do? He doesn't like strangers."

"Well, Steve is family, but I know he wouldn't let us see him, so we can't tell Papa anything about this. Let's go talk to Edith. We could bring her some cookies."

I turned on the oven and finished mixing the cookie dough and spooned it onto the cookie sheets. We sipped our delicious hot chocolate while we waited for them to bake and ate two hot ones right out of the oven.

When we were finished and the cookies cool enough, we wrapped a half dozen in waxed paper for Edith, placed them in a bag and rushed out the door. I felt guilty leaving the kitchen in a mess but doubted Papa would be home before Friday.

Edith was delighted to see us and nibbled a cookie while we asked her advice about contacting Steve.

"I think it is only right you get together." She dialed her friend who said she'd ask her son Buddy if he had Steve's address and would call us back in a few minutes.

It seemed like forever to me, but Edith answered it on the first ring. She handed the phone to me. "Here is Buddy Willis. He is home for the holidays and has Steve's address. I'll get you something to write on."

I sat down to write. Buddy sounded cheery and said he always got a Christmas card from Steve. I wrote down the address. San Diego, California. Faraway from Montana, but a possible way to connect.

I thanked Buddy and told him Steve was my uncle. We were so excited to possibly make his acquaintance. After thanking Edith, we ran out the door to buy a Christmas card to send to Steve.

It took the rest of the afternoon to write the letter. When we finished, we decided we couldn't use our own return address because if Steve wrote back, Papa might pick up the mail. He'd probably beat us, and we'd never see the letter. So, we returned to Edith's to get permission to use her address. She agreed and gave us a stamp so we could stop by the post office before heading home.

Chapter 14 - Holiday Confirmation

F riday morning, we got up early to make apple cinnamon muffins, hoping to sweeten up Papa when he arrived. It was a cold day. Still air, unusual for the prairie where the wind blew about thirty miles per hour most of the time. The sky was clear blue, not a cloud to be seen when I stepped outside to sweep the step. The outdoor thermometer read zero.

My heart felt lighter than usual because of the hope of finding Steve.

I went back inside to set the table. We played some duets and heard the freight train whistle at the crossing west of town, so we anticipated his arrival.

Hours later, around noon he stomped in carrying an armful of bags that he dumped on the dining room table. "Sure smells good in here. Whatcha making?"

Julie jumped up and picked up the plate to show him. "We made muffins for you."

"Well, isn't that nice, a treat for Santa. Thanks. I'm hungry." He hung his jacket in the closet and rubbed his hands together as if to warm them. "I hope these fit you okay. I want you to look pretty for the program tonight." He handed us each a bag. "Go in your bedroom and try these on. Come out and model them for me."

We did as we were told.

First, Julie opened her bag and pulled out a long red velvet dress, with white lace around the long sleeve cuffs and V-neckline. Her eyes were huge as she held it up beneath her chin. She placed it on the bed and opened a shoe box. Black pumps with a narrow strap, patent leather. She put them on and fastened the straps. "They fit." Next, she put on her dress with my help.

I tied the velvet belt. "I'd say it's a perfect fit. You look beautiful."

She opened my bag and pulled out a long dark green velvet dress and handed it to me. A row of pearl buttons decorated cuffs on long sleeves and at the neckline resembling a necklace. My shoes were similar to Julie's. I slipped them on. "A perfect fit for me, too. Are you ready to show him?"

We opened the door. He was sitting in a living room chair munching a muffin when we reappeared. "Spin around a couple times. Let me see how they fit."

We turned.

He nodded approvingly. "The woman who helped me did a good job. You will both look great at church tonight. Now I have to sleep. I've been up a long time."

Julie did a pirouette. "I love it. Thank you, Papa."

My wooden smile said everything. "I like mine, too. Thank you."

We tried not to disturb him as we worked in the kitchen making beef stroganoff for dinner as a surprise for him. He had showered when he appeared wearing a white dress shirt and dark pants. His hair was still wet, and the sweet smell of his cologne followed him instead of fried onions when he lifted the cover to see what we had made.

I had the water boiling for noodles, so it only took a few minutes to finish dinner preparation. Papa ate two big helpings and put his own plate in the sink, unusual for him to clean up anything.

We washed the dishes just in time to get ready and walk to the church with him. I felt attractive in the new clothes. Julie skipped along the snowy sidewalk. A brisk wind whipped white powder down the street fogging some of the beautiful lights in neighborhood windows and blew up my dress making the satiny interior feel like ice against my skin.

The sidewalk was bare and slippery. With the wind, no one needed to shovel the walkway. We carried our new shoes and wore snow boots. No one with any sense would go out in this weather without a warm coat and boots. Papa wore a down jacket with a hood. His long stride put him far ahead of us.

Little white lights sparkled on strings wrapping three pine trees near the front of the church. They looked like little stars and, on each treetop, a large star with sparkles around the points shone brightly. The children's choir wearing white robes with big red bows at the neck sat off to the side where the adult choir usually sang during Sunday services.

After Pastor Bob's opening prayer and short reading of the Christmas story from the Bible, our piano teacher flew in like a witch from the darkness from behind the kid choir, her gown flowing as she spun and sat on the seat at the organ and filled the church with a loud rendition of "Joy to the World." The congregation stood and sung loudly. This was followed by "We Three Kings of Orient Are."

I felt pretty in my long-sleeved dress, the prettiest dress I'd ever owned. Julie looked so happy with the lights reflecting in her eyes. When the singing stopped and I turned around to sit down, behind us a few rows back, I saw Penny and Charlene. My eyes met Penny's. We scanned each other's identical dresses. My joy deflated and I felt my heart stutter.

Was Penny Papa's other *honey*? A year younger than me and without a father to take care of her. I swallowed hard to keep a stroganoff surge from spewing out on the beautiful dress.

We listened to a series of four cheery songs and a couple solos from the kid choir. Julie rocked with the music. After the "Merry Christmas" greetings from many of those attending, I saw Papa wave at Penny and Charlene. He walked us home and then drove off in the Chevy.

He didn't come home on Christmas eve or Christmas Day.

Julie and I talked about his behavior. I envisioned him with Charlene and Penny, maybe opening gifts from beneath their brightly colored tree, spending the night and taking them out for a holiday breakfast.

Someday, we'd have a Christmas tree.

Julie and I went to bed. I heard her humming "Jingle Bells" as she drifted off to sleep.

Before I crawled into bed, I touched our soft new dresses hanging in the closet and tried to enjoy the thought of owning such beautiful clothing. I pushed back on thoughts that

Papa really didn't care about us at all, just about looking good in public. I was sad for Charlene and Penny Davidson because now I knew for sure a madman had entered their lives and Rex wasn't there to protect them.

He was in the ground, not far from Mama.

Chapter 15 - Good News

The day after Christmas, Papa returned to pack his grip saying he'd be back after the new year. That was fine with us, he could stay away as long as he liked. This time, he left ten dollars.

I put it in a safe place. We probably had enough food on hand. We could always eat one of Julie's favorite meals, just open a can of beans and boil a hotdog from a stash in the freezer.

I found her flipping pages of the new year calendar and asked what she was thinking about.

"I'm counting the months till the end of school and the beginning of our summer. I like good weather when we can bicycle and go for long walks." She counted December on the current calendar. "The winters are long and cold, but I wanted to count the days since we sent Steve the Christmas card. How long would it take for him to get the card?"

"At least a couple weeks."

Julie looked down, sad. "I hope he'll write to us."

"It's a nice day, not much wind. Let's go for a walk. The fresh air might cheer you up."

She went to the closet and slipped on her boots. "I'd like that. Could we go to the library? Opal cheers me up, too."

We trekked out to the cemetery first where we talked to Tess and told her about our dresses. We didn't feel like singing and I couldn't tell her about my thoughts regarding Charlene and Penny because Julie, at five years old, was too young to hear the story I was imagining.

It was too cold to stay very long so we headed to the library but found it closed for the holiday week. By that time, my feet were freezing, and Julie was hopping to keep hers warm. "If you're as cold as I am, I think it's time to head home and make some hot chocolate."

Julie was happy with that plan and within an hour we were warm, wearing comfortable lounging clothes and wool socks, playing piano duets.

Winter months faded to spring. Warm winds melted the snow bringing buds then pale green leaves back to the trees. Daisies took bloom. School kept us busy. Papa demanded our attention to cleaning the house, windows, and his clothes. Things had been going well. He was distracted, home for shorter periods and for a couple of months, I was thankful there were no honey sessions to endure.

Academically, we were both doing well but Papa paid no attention. If what we did what we were told, went to church with him and were not costing him money, he didn't seem to care. He left a catalogue one morning on his way out of town. "Check through this. You are both looking shabby in your dull old clothes, and you are both growing. Find something colorful for summer."

We were excited at the thought of some new clothes instead of outfits from the thrift store. Looking through the catalogue was a new experience but when we chose a couple outfits, he didn't like them, and ordered nothing for us.

At school, some of the girls in my classes talked about going to the prom and their dates. Those thoughts were not part of my cares. I was pleased and embarrassed when Billy asked me to the prom. I flushed and told him I would like to accept, but my father was so strict I couldn't date or even attend a party.

He shrugged. "I'm sorry, too. You're missing out on a lot of fun. I was hoping you'd come and watch me play sports, but I haven't seen you at any of the games."

"I wish I could go to games, but I have to take care of Cousin Julie. She is little and lives with us. Papa won't let us go out at night." I almost said, our father instead of Papa, and that would have been a huge mistake.

Secrets are hard to keep, they might slip out even when your life depends on not revealing the truth.

Not long after my conversation with Billy, I was called to the principal's office. My heart would not behave as I dragged my feet down the hall to the office at lunchtime. I had no idea what I had done to result in the summons. Maybe Papa was ill somewhere or had an accident. Maybe it was some emergency with Julie. I had the urge to run out to check on her first.

I hoped she was fine, and this wouldn't take long so I could get to the kindergarten and walk her to daycare before my afternoon class started.

I walked into the office and saw Geraldine, a face I knew.

She grinned. "Congratulations, Anna."

I'm sure my confused look surprised her. "I thought I was in trouble."

"Oh, no. The principal has some good news."

I smiled, still afraid to breathe and in a hurry to leave.

Mr. Anderson came out of his office and offered his hand. "Anna, I have two pieces of great news. One, you are at the top of your class. You have been named Valedictorian, and two, the scholarship you applied for came through."

I flushed. Not from embarrassment but shock and joy. I doubted Papa would care except that I'd cost him less money. I sat down. "I am so surprised, I feel faint."

"You only have a couple months left of school. I hope you have plans for college."

"I have an application to attend the community college nursing program here in the fall."

Geraldine said, "They have a good program."

Mr. Anderson agreed. "That's a fine plan. Our office will help you complete the application process and forward your academic record. It's an amazing transcript. I hope you will go on to a four-year college. If you do, the scholarship will pay for all four years."

"I'm so happy because I didn't know how I was going to be able to go to college. My father isn't happy about paying for it." The scholarship was an answer to prayers if I believed in prayers. "I want to go to the university, but right now, I have Cousin Julie to care for. She's in kindergarten, so we'll both be attending school in Riverside for now." I turned to go. "Thank you so much. I have to walk Julie to daycare where she stays till I'm out of school at three. I work there a couple hours a day."

"You are one busy girl. Working and getting straight As. Good for you." Geraldine smiled, "I know your mother would be proud."

"Working there, helping with little kids gave me the idea for nursing. I better run. Thank you so much!"

Mr. Anderson opened the door into the hallway to let me escape. "You did it yourself. We're all proud of you."

When I told Julie my great news, she skipped all the way to daycare. "I am glad you are so smart, and you help me learn. I really like school and daycare. Maybe I can go to college someday. What do you think Papa will say?"

"Hard to know. He should be happy about the scholarship, but he likes us under his thumb and uses money to isolate us. With no money of our own, we're totally under his control like he wants."

Julie stopped. "Don't tell him. It's a good secret."

Chapter 16 - Success

The last couple of months before graduation went fast as I prepared my valedictory speech. Being a mouse in hiding my whole life made the idea of standing in front of so many parents and city folk a frightening prospect. I asked for help from my English teacher. She said the topic should be uplifting and something I believed in.

One evening in early May when we had nearly finished dinner, I told Papa I was valedictorian of my class.

He shrugged.

"I'll be giving a speech at graduation on June 6th. Will you be able to come?"

He went to the wall calendar. "Nope. I'll be on the rails." Papa sat back down and took a sip of his coffee. "You must have brains like your mother. You don't need more schooling."

"I thought you'd be pleased to know I applied to the nursing program at the community college."

He pushed back from the table with his jaws clenched.

"Who do you think you are that you can *tell* me what you are doing? I'm in charge around here."

I stood up and moved out of reach, placing my plate in the sink. "I'll be eighteen soon, a few weeks after graduation. I found a part time summer job." I explained it was at the daycare where I'd been working.

He listened, but the more I said, the more red-in-the-face he got. Veins bulged on his forehead.

I ended with, "Edith said Julie could come over to her house and stay when I'm at work." Papa jumped to his feet overturning the chair sending it crashing to the floor.

Julie cowered, leaning on me for protection.

All five feet and my one hundred pounds stood straight in front of Papa's six-foot-two frame with Julie behind me. I fingered my special ring, bringing me strength. "You promised Mama you'd pay for my education. I'm going to college without you. You should be pleased."

He picked up the chair and sat down, straddling it, arms on the back rest. "I'm not going to let you sit in class and run around with boys, expecting me to pay Edith for Julie's care." Papa glared. "It's time for you to just get a job and take care of her. That's final." Papa walked to his bedroom.

Julie and I said nothing as we cleared the table and washed dishes.

A few minutes later he returned in dress clothes smelling of cologne.

I turned toward him. "You promised Mama you'd pay for my college. Paying for Julie costs less than college."

"Who cares what I promised Tess. She's dead."

He left and slammed the door like an exclamation point.

Julie hugged me. "Don't worry, Anna. We can take care of each other so we can both go to college."

Her little arms and strength infused me with steel. Damn right!

Chapter 17 - Julie's Birthday

School and work meshed well. I had to bide my time, but I was good at that. Years of hiding abuse, fake smiles, perfect in public, perfect in church. Who would suspect my torture?

Mama said I could do anything if I set my mind to it. I twirled my ruby ring to remind me she was always with me.

I watched Edith teach Julie all sorts of things, she even helped me with some of my classes. Soon after Julie was born, she had taught me skills I could adapt to the daycare job. I guess I must have been a help to Bobbie, the owner, because my paycheck after two weeks of work was bigger than expected. I asked if she'd made a mistake.

"I couldn't do this without you, Anna. You are my best employee." Bobbie gave me a hug. "You are terrific with the kids. I thought you'd be able to use the extra money for school in the fall." I thanked her profusely and ran partway to Edith's, anxious to give them the good news.

Edith wouldn't accept any money from me, and Papa hadn't offered to pay her. I knew he'd blow up if I asked him, so I had planned to pay her from my earnings. Like the owner of the daycare, Edith said it was a small contribution to help a star student. Besides, she said loved Julie's company.

Each evening when Papa was on the rails we were relaxed. Sometimes Edith fixed us dinner and we watched television with her for a while before heading home.

Papa returned calmer and more agreeable after he left saying he wasn't appreciated. At least he wasn't as mean and derogatory, but I avoided being in the same room with him whenever I could. Fear and intimidation by his presence was part of his control over us. Always wary, on edge, not knowing when he'd blow up over some seemingly meaningless happening.

I told Edith the date of Julie's birthday in mid-May. We planned a little celebration for turning six. The day before her big day, Julie and Edith baked a birthday cake of Julie's choosing. She decided on angel food with buttercream frosting.

On the Saturday of her birthday, she skipped most of the three blocks to Edith's. My work sped by and I rushed to join them for hotdogs and cake. When I went inside, I'd expected a rush from Julie, but there was no greeting. I heard Edith's voice in the kitchen and found her talking on her wall phone, the coiled red cord snaked to the receiver. She hung up. "Opal hasn't seen them. I'm worried about Julie."

I screamed, "Where is she?"

"Your father picked her up in his fancy car right after you left her. They've been gone for nearly four hours after saying he was taking her for a birthday spin." Edith's eyes teared. "I don't know what to think. Maybe they've been in an accident."

"Where were they going."

"He didn't say."

"I don't trust him."

Edith looked puzzled.

"I'm going to run home and check. I'll be right back."

I ran up to the front door and found it locked. I rattled it and knocked. I was fumbling for my key when Papa unlocked and opened the door. Standing there with his shirt off, behind him I saw Julie spinning around in a dance wearing a frilly tutu. She was laughing and really enjoying herself. The scene made me weak with fear. I stood there speechless not knowing what had been going on. He sat down on the couch.

Julie rushed to me. "Anna, look what Papa bought me for my birthday. He is going to buy me dance lessons. I'm so excited. Watch." She spun around and then sat on his lap, throwing her arms around his neck. "Thank you so much."

His hands encircled her waist. "You are a beautiful dancer. I knew you would be."

She smiled at me. "He wants me to call him, Daddy."

My eyes fixated on his dreamy eyes. He looked like he had gone to some faraway place and time.

I was stone-faced. What was he doing? What had he done to her?

He nudged Julie off his lap and stood up. "I have to leave for a while. I'll be back in a day or so."

He took his packed grip from his bedroom and drove off in the beater car.

Julie stared at me. "Are your sad? Why aren't you happy? I'm sooo happy. I loved the blue car ride almost as much as the dance lesson gift and modeling for Daddy."

"Did he hurt you?" I dreaded her response.

"He told me Daddy's teach their girls about boys, what to do to make them happy and how to dance for them. I love to dance and learn new things." Her face flushed. "I'll change clothes so we can go back to Edith's for my party." She headed into his bedroom.

Julie went in and picked her clothes from the floor including her underwear.

A cold sweat drenched my skin. "Did he watch you change clothes?"

She nodded.

"Why did you take your underwear off."

"He said girls don't wear underpants with dance outfits because they might show."

She spun around and bent over, exposing her little butt. "See, the tutu looks better without pants showing. He also put lotion on my legs to make them look good."

Oh, God. What has he done to her?

I was horrified and weak. I sat down on his bed. "What did he say?"

"He said it was too bad my mother had died, and he'd try to be a better adopted father."

We went to our bedroom where she took off the little dance outfit. "He promised both piano and dance lessons because I was growing up so fast and he wanted me to have both."

She threw on her clothes and grabbed my hand. "Let's run. Edith will be worried because we were supposed to only be gone a little while."

I followed her but felt no joy. Only dread.

She was so young, so naive, so vulnerable.

Edith met us at the door. "I'm relieved to see you. Dave just stopped by. He apologized for being late and delaying Julie's party. Said they were having so much fun together the time got away from them."

Edith led us into the kitchen where she had the table set. "I don't know the man after all these years, but he seemed sincere. Julie, did you enjoy the ride?"

"It was so much fun. He even let me sit on his lap and steer."

Weak knees dropped me to a chair. I tried to keep a stone face, but if anyone had looked into my eyes to my brain, they would have seen nothing but horror. I was glad neither Edith nor Julie seemed to recognize my reaction because it wasn't something I could discuss right then.

Julie needed her day. With sparkling blue eyes, and cheeks aglow, she sat down to her birthday dinner. Edith brought out the cake and lit the six candles. I had trouble even eating one bite because the hotdog had stuck in my throat.

I placed Julie's gifts on the table. She unwrapped a new book I'd bought for her and squealed when she saw Edith's gift. The loving woman had made cooking and baking part of each day. She had written Julie's favorite recipes on multi-colored cards and tied the deck of her favorite recipes with a red bow.

Julie's sixth birthday was memorable for so many reasons.

For her, it seemed as though dreams had come true.

For me, looming nightmares.

Chapter 18 - Accelerated Violence

Julie wore her dance outfit many evenings and tried to pirouette on her toes. She decided she'd probably need special shoes to be able to perform but still had fun wearing the frills around the house. When Papa walked in, dirty and smelly after his trip, Julie was spinning around in the living room as I played the piano. I hadn't anticipated his arrival, or I would have had her dressed in regular clothes.

She ran to him and gave him a quick hug.

"Hey, don't you look terrific. We need to get more of those outfits."

I didn't speak, just looked at him with a stone face.

"Would you like dance lessons, Anna. Both of you could dance for me."

I shook my head. "I'm too old and not a dancer." I moved the piano bench in and straightened the music, hiding my disgust from him.

He spoke to my back. "You could learn, Anna. Tess and I used to dance to radio music. She had rhythm." Papa shrugged. "I'm glad Julie likes it. I'll see if I can find dance lessons for her age." He went in his bedroom, closed the door, showered, and returned smelling clean and wearing fresh pants with a long-sleeved white shirt. "I have a deacon dinner meeting at the church so won't be here to eat with you." He left in the Chevy.

We were asleep when he returned but I was a light sleeper, always on alert. Minor noises awakened me, a passing car, and certainly, trains. The tracks ran through town less than two blocks from our house. I would go right back to sleep most of the time, but a passenger train came through a couple times a day, usually in the afternoon heading east and, about three a.m., heading west. It was the early morning one that often awakened me. It would toot at the edge of town. The whistle was a pleasant tone, recognizable, different from the freights. I often imagined the people on board, experiencing happy trips, not like mine to Minnesota. Someday I'd love a train ride to a faraway place like Mama and I read about. I wish she could have gone with me.

The afternoon train was the one that carried me to the home for girls and reminded me of all his gross honey sessions rocking and rolling along the rails with me trying hard not to throw up because of morning sickness. A nightmare I'd never forget, and always worried when another might occur, like tonight when I barely breathed as I lay waiting for Papa to close his bedroom door and start snoring.

Instead, I heard footsteps cross the living room and down the hall, stopping outside our bedroom. I could hear his breathing, then—the knob turned, and the door opened. His footsteps stopped at Julie's bed, then he approached mine and took my arm, pulling me from bed. A hand clamped over my nose and mouth. I couldn't breathe or scream. He dragged me out into the hallway and closed the door.

I struggled, kicked, and tried to wrench my way out of his grasp, dropping to the floor, only to have him pick me up, carry me over and throw me onto his bed. I couldn't scream and awaken Julie. He closed his door and leaned against it laughing. "Surprised, ya, huh?" He pulled up my nightgown. "I told you before not to wear underwear to bed." He ripped my panties down and forced his fingers inside me.

I bit his arm and scratched at his face. "I hate you. Stop!" I kicked. He grabbed my leg and twisted it, hurting me.

Papa laughed. "You're mine. There's nothing you can do about it. I just had a nice meeting at church and prayed for you." He rubbed my belly. "Getting pregnant was dumb. No one would have known, but you are shamed forever, have a scar on your belly and have Julie to remind you every day. You're a slut. You're not going to college. I won't let another male touch you, ever. I'll kill you first."

I screamed and pushed him away. "I'm going to college, and you can't stop me."

"Your sins are unforgiveable. You're headed for hell. Come here."

I jumped off the bed and ran for the door.

"I like you feisty. Keep it up, bitch." He pushed me to the floor and put a knee on my chest while he unzipped his pants. "I'll spread the word around town that you are screwing any guy who looks at you. I'll just have to lock you up and throw away the keys to keep you here for me."

He put all his weight on me. I couldn't breathe. A hand over my mouth and nose stopped my screams and then wretched pain I felt so many times before. He removed his hand before I passed out this time as he pulsed inside me and left me lying on the floor gasping for breath.

When he went into the shower, I staggered into my bathroom and locked the door, vowing he'd never touch me again. It seemed some switch inside him had flipped. He had become more unpredictable and violent than before.

Before what? I wondered if something had happened. Was the thought of losing control of me and my attending college that led to this?

When I saw him without a shirt, with Julie twirling in a tutu in front of him, I had choked, suspecting the worst. He appeared to have trouble controlling himself around Julie, touching, grabbing. I knew I couldn't leave him alone with her, and this time he traumatized me so much I shook long after I heard him snoring.

Another thing that worried me was he didn't smell like liquor.

He did this to me without being drunk.

Hot water and soap washed away most of his disgusting smells. Bruises were starting to show on my arms, and my chest where he crushed his weight down with his knee. It hurt when I took a deep breath. My dirty nightgown with blood and stains lay on the floor. I threw it in the closet. Maybe I'd need proof to support my story when I finally revealed his abuse.

Chapter 19 - Graduation

Julie lay on her bed reading when I decided to enter our third bedroom. Opening the door where Mama died was like entering a dusty tomb. It's a room I seldom entered. Too many sad memories. Dead flies and dust lined the windowsills, something Papa had complained about when Mama had few breaths left, when he still wanted her to wait on him.

I tried to block rotten memories and, instead, recall her words and last hug. The empty bedroom held such sadness and her dusty dresses had lost her pleasant smell. I looked through some drawers and found a little bottle of her soft powdery perfume I took as my own. I decided to wear it on special occasions and wanted to wear it for graduation.

For the graduation ceremony, I wore one of Mama's dresses. It was one that had looked particularly good on her. I was surprised it fit me so well. She was a little taller, but my five-foot-one, 110 pounds fit it fine. I had washed the delicate fabric by hand and hung it in the fresh air on the backyard clothesline along with Julie's new thrift store dress.

I combed Julie's long hair into ringlets. She wore the sweet little white sundress with black polka dots and Mama's perfume. Edith, Opal and Jimmy sat in the front row with her. My family was there with me. I pictured Mama beside Julie enjoying the fact she looked so much like us and was pleased we were wearing her perfume.

I'd given a few speeches in classes but the thought of standing at a microphone in the gymnasium made my knees weak. I had worked extremely hard on my speech, putting in some of Mama's teachings that were broad and could help anyone. I had practiced it so much with my English teacher, I didn't even need notes.

My theme was to find strength, aim high like being an airplane pilot above the rough terrain of life. Fly your own way through the skies. I also used an analogy to playing the piano, something many people could relate to. I ended with: *It is your life, you must play your own song and not let anyone stop you from making beautiful music.*

When they announced my scholarship, everyone stood and clapped. It was a wonderful evening, an end to difficult years and the beginning of a new life.

Chapter 20 - July Violence

Working at the daycare four days a week with Julie at Edith's worked well but as July, and my eighteenth birthday and Mama's deathday, approached a terrible sadness crushed me. This year I wanted her with me more than any other birthday I could recall except the year she died, the year when I learned I was pregnant with Julie. Now, I needed Mama's direction for my adult life.

Eighteen is a special time, a coming of age, a time to fly on your own but I felt like I had an albatross around my neck.

Papa.

Unable to fly because of the heavy weight.

I had come of age so long ago.

Julie didn't add to the burden. She brought me joy.

My albatross was a combination of concealing abuse and lying to her.

I had dreaded my eighteenth birthday because I had decided I must tell my little Julie *the secret*. I had been living a lie since Mama died and Papa began raping me, and since her birth six years ago when the lie expanded. I believed Julie was old enough to keep a secret and see we were working toward a day when Papa could no longer keep us as prisoners.

She was old enough to understand why we had to continue playing the charade of Cousin Julie until the right time came to tell the world.

The night before my birthday, when Julie was already in bed asleep, Papa came home stumbling and crazy-drunk, demanding I quit my afternoon job. He dragged me into his bedroom. My favorite blouse ripped when he threw me onto his bed and pulled off my clothes. He hurt me bad without lotion. I screamed. He made me bleed. Blood all over the sheets and on him. So much red, I thought I was going to die.

He laughed.

"Clean up the mess." He pulled the sheets off the bed and threw them at me as I stood there with blood running down my legs. "Wash the damn sheets."

To hide his violence.

His sin.

It was the worst of all the times he raped me.

He showered as I sobbed, putting fresh sheets on the bed. I hoped Julie didn't hear what was going on. I feared violence against her.

I put the sheets in a cold-water wash and filled the bathtub with warm water so I could soak. I hurt so bad from damage inside me I took Tylenol. The water made me hurt more at first, but I washed with soap and started feeling better and fell asleep in the tub.

I awakened shivering in cooled water.

I heard no sounds from our bedroom, and I hoped I wouldn't awaken Julie when I slipped into my bed. I lay awake. Furious, scared, knowing I had to stop him but not knowing how.

He was killing me, killing my spirit.

What would he do next? Where could we go without money or a place to live. I wanted to go to the cemetery where no one would hurt us.

PART 2

JULIE

Chapter 21 - Julie Speaks

I'm not very good at telling stories because I'm only six. If I stumble around and make mistakes, I hope you'll understand what I meant. I'll start by telling you what happened last night when Papa came home meaner than usual. I was getting my jammies on for bed, and my bedroom door was closed.

He charged into the house stomping like a mad bull and yelled at Anna. "You're not going to college and that's final. Your thoughts will be tainted by lies. Read the Bible. That is all any girl needs to know."

Anna screamed, "You promised. You don't even have to pay. I earned it!" Then I heard a slap. I pictured that big man hitting her. I looked around the room for something I could use to hit him with. All I saw was a plastic ruler. He'd laugh at me. I peeked out the door. The lights were out. He was still yelling.

I closed the door and lay on the floor under my bed. He wouldn't see me if he came in.

I woke up on the floor. I had to pee, so I sneaked to the bathroom. I hurried really fast and ran back to my room. My bed felt better than the floor. I listened to his mean voice. He yelled bad words, sin words. I tried to read Winnie the Pooh, but Eeyore was sad like me and made me cry.

That night, I woke up in the dark after 12 on the glow-in-the-dark clock on our desk. Anna was in her bed crying. Today was her birthday. Anna should be happy.

I heard Papa walking around. The back door closed and the junker drove away.

Anna stayed in bed with her back to me. When she finally got up in the morning, she looked sick, with tired red eyes and a sad face.

I fixed her cereal for breakfast before our walk. She said she didn't want to see anyone. Wanted to stay away from people. Away from town. Away from the church. Anna was too upset to even have a fake smile.

Cop cars passed us twice. A bald officer with a white mustache waved.

I looked away from him. He went around the block and stopped, making us walk past the car. He hit the siren a jab that made us jump. He was laughing when I looked back.

The wind was so fierce, it blew something into one of my eyes and Anna had to help me. Her hands shook so much she had trouble getting it out.

I felt bad and didn't know how to cheer her up. She really likes peanut butter sandwiches, so when we got back home, I fixed her one but after two bites, she crawled into bed. I snuggled in beside her. I didn't sleep but she did, for a long time.

I got up to make her birthday dinner. Beans and a hot-dog. I had a surprise birthday cake, a cupcake with one candle I made with Edith and hid from Anna in a little bag so I could surprise her. I knew Anna would be pleased with the cupcake because it was her favorite, chocolate.

After dinner, I sang happy birthday to her.

She hugged me and made a silent wish before blowing out the candle on her little cake. She licked some frosting but left the rest, saying she'd save it for later. I think her stomach was upset because she went back to bed.

After washing the dishes, I made sure the shades were drawn and doors locked before going to bed. I thought Anna was sleeping. She faced the wall again, so I slid my pajamas on in the dark and crawled under soft, clean sheets. I lay on my back listening to sounds of the night, then heard her crying. Not hard crying, just sniffles.

"What's the matter, Anna. Why aren't you happy on your birthday? Are you sick?"

She whispered as if Papa might overhear, but he was far-away, working on the rails, driving another freight train. She said, "I miss my mother. I'm so sad. Today is her birthday, too. I wish you had known her."

Anna's bed squeaked when she turned over to talk. "Can you keep a secret?"

I nodded, then realized it was dark and she couldn't see me. "I've never had a real secret, but I know it means not to tell."

"It's very important not to tell or Papa said I would disappear. Not like magic. I think he means he'd kill me if I told anyone this secret."

I cried out and rushed to her bed. "No! Don't disappear. Don't scare me."

"You're safe. I'll always take care of you."

"Things will be the same for us after I tell you a true story, we just can't tell anyone, not Edith, not Opal or Jimmy. Nobody."

I sat up to listen.

Anna lay on her side and slid one arm under her pillow, resting her head down. "This is my mother's story, but it's yours and mine, too. You see, when she was a little girl like you, some of her favorite memories were with her daddy when he'd make her laugh by singing little songs like 'Tessie Lou, I love you.' That was years before a whirling devil-wind swept through their house leaving eleven-year-old Tess married to Papa."

I shook my head. "No way. Girls don't get married. You aren't making sense. Did you have a nightmare?"

"It's real. That's when Mama started wearing fake smiles to protect herself. She didn't dare to make him mad."

I said, "In the photo of you and Tess on the piano, you look like happy teenagers."

"We were just like you and me. Fakes in public and sad at home."

I thought a minute "You taught me about fake smiles, like Halloween masks, hiding feelings."

"We hide from Papa. Kids aren't supposed to be sad and keep secrets about bad things, but we have to. I've been waiting for you to be old enough to keep a secret."

I assured her I was old enough and this is what she told me.

Tess went to the big courthouse with her parents and Dave, we call him Papa now. They stood in front of strangers.

Tess said, "I do," but she didn't.

Dave said, "I do" and meant it.

He married Tess when she was eleven years old and moved her to another county, far away from her home. He wouldn't let her see or call her parents. They didn't even have a phone in their home. We still don't.

Dave trapped her in a dark little house and dressed her in pretty clothes. She was sick and sad, with Anna growing in her belly. He never let Tess go to school. She cried every day because she loved school. Tess knew she had a baby growing in her belly and didn't know how it was going to get out. What would happen to her? Tess had needed Sam, her daddy, and his love she'd felt every day before the stupid wedding.

Months later and a hundred miles from her parents' home, Tess heard a knock at the door. The sound echoed in the empty house. Dave was at work, and no one ever came to visit. She was scared and tiptoed to the door. She peeked through the window.

There stood Steve, her tall teenage brother with his back to her, looking up and down the street.

Tess jerked open the door and pulled him inside. Her belly bumped him when he wrapped his long arms around her.

They sat on the couch, hugging and crying.

Steve told her a trucker friend was passing through and saw her crossing the street here with Dave. He squeezed her tighter and said he was glad he'd finally found her.

Tess was scared Dave would hurt them if he found Steve with her.

Steve said that Tess's dad was so upset after the news that he quit his job and headed out to find her. Her brother cried, "Dad's dead." He hugged Tess and told her the cops found him in a ditch, maybe dead from a heart attack.

Steve tried to make his little sister stop crying and pulled her to the door to take her home with him.

She touched her basketball belly and said, "I can't go home. Mother couldn't face the church ladies and be seen with me. She doesn't want me."

I cried when Anna said that. How could a mother not want her little girl?

Steve left but gave Tess a phone number to call him at college. If she changed her mind, she could come and live with him.

Anna was born on Tess's twelfth birthday.

I cried harder when she told me the rest.

I'm not sure I should tell you, but I have to tell someone, or my heart will explode.

Please don't tell anyone or we might die.

Promise you won't tell.

Chapter 22 - My Secret

After Anna fell asleep, I lay on my bed trying to make sense of everything as shadows streaked across the ceiling when cars passed by. Our old house creaked and squeaked as if little mice lived in the walls. I'd love to snuggle one of them. Maybe they're scared, too.

The shadows went black when I pulled the sheet over my head. A cloud of bleach and laundry soap surrounded me, cleaning the air, calming my heart and pushing fears away into the closet where they waited like ghosts. I wish they'd be gone forever but I know they'll come back. This time they poked me with scary thoughts about being alone and starting first grade.

Our family isn't normal like my neighbor and sort-of-friend Janey's. When I sat around their table eating soup and bread one day when Papa was out of town, they hugged each other and me. Their funny stories made my heart happy like a butterfly.

There are no butterflies in our home.

I have to cover my ears to block the sound of Papa's angry voice spinning through the rooms like bats zooming in a night sky.

Before tonight, I was afraid to be near kids my age because Papa kept us away from everyone except for church. I am very shy.

Today, Anna said she'd walk me to first grade. That helped a lot. But now, I'm afraid of something else, really scared because of a happy secret I can never tell. Never. I can't slip up and make a mistake. No one can know.

After Anna went to sleep, nighthawks screamed outside my window calling me to get out of bed.

I sat up and pulled back the curtain to watch them dive and spin in starlight, doing circles in their playground in the sky. Were their shrill voices tonight trying to warn me of another devil wind? Of Papa?

Seeing them safely zooming in the night sky stopped my trembling. The hawks reminded me of a little bird I once held. Its tiny fluttering heart tickled my hand before it flew away and perched high in the apple tree singing a beautiful song. I wanted to fly away and sing with the birds, but I couldn't fly. Besides, I would never leave Anna.

I lay back down and closed my eyes, listening.

Anna was crying again. Soft noises. Deep zigzag breaths.

It's so strange. I am trying to understand, you see, Anna told me she's my mother, my very own mother.

Are you surprised?

I thought Anna was joking because we don't have a mother in our house because Tess died of cancer when Anna was twelve. Tonight, Anna is crying on her birthday. This should be a happy day.

Why is she crying when I'm so happy to have a mother?

Maybe because she had to grow up too fast.

Papa and Anna have always called me Cousin Julie. Until tonight, I thought I was a baby with no mother. Adopted into this family when my mother died birthing me. Adoption is wonderful, but my secret gift from Anna tonight was to learn my mother didn't die birthing me.

She is alive and right here with me.

I wanted to sing like the little bird that flew away and tell everyone the song in my heart, but Anna says we must keep the secret.

I can tell no one, not even Papa. Especially not Papa or he'll kill Anna like he warned her. No one can know he's her father and my father, and that she is my mother. We are in triple trouble.

He'd lose his job and go to prison because it's wrong to do that to a child.

I crawled into Anna's bed when I could no longer stand to hear her crying. I hugged her and patted her teary cheek. "I love you, Mommy. I'll always love you."

She cried harder and pulled me into her arms. "I thought you'd hate me for lying and telling people we are cousins."

"Oh, no. I'm happy as a baby kitty."

She hugged me so tight I could hardly breathe. "I love you, Julie. I'm sorry you didn't know my mother. Tess was smart and made me happy. She was a good mother who helped me grow up fast even though she was very young and often sad." Anna held her breath. "Everything changed when she died."

I remembered the picture on the piano. "We look like Tess."

Anna rested her head back on the pillow. "Yes, we do."

Soon, Anna's breathing slowed and her arm across my chest felt heavy.

My eyes wouldn't close until the birds chirped and the early sun streamed through the curtains painting lace shadows on the wall. I don't know how long before I finally slept but my eyes popped open when I heard a far-off train whistle.

A freight train would rumble back into town someday soon carrying Papa. We'd hear him park behind the house. The door would slam. He'd stomp in wearing stinky work clothes smelling of diesel fuel.

Always frowning.

Always angry from working on the rails, driving an engine pulling freight cars.

Always the same.

Anna's body stiffened against me. Her bony elbow felt sharp like I imagined our scarecrow's stick arm inside his red plaid shirt would feel as he stood guard shooing crows from our garden.

Maybe she heard the train, too. I touched her. "It's not Papa's train. He just left town. Do you want to get up?"

She sat up with her arms flailing. ".... a train whistle. He's coming." She shook.

I hugged her. "He's not coming. He's far away." I turned back her bedspread. "Wake up, Anna. Don't be afraid."

She fell back. "I guess I was dreaming he was going to hurt me again."

Questions buzzed like hornets in my brain. In the morning light, I saw her bruised arm and mark on her cheek. "What did he do to you? Look at your bruises."

Anna touched her sore arm and closed her eyes.

I patted her hand. "Mother, what do I call you?"

"Anna, like always. He must never know I told you the secret."

Chapter 23 - I'm Not Cousin Julie

Anna let me break some of the eggs and turn the bacon. I think she was hungry after eating so little the day before. After washing dishes, she suggested a walk out to the cemetery. "Let's go talk to Tess."

My lips curled in a little smile, a real smile. "Is she the only one I can tell my secret to."

Anna nodded.

We walked slowly through town carrying fresh cut daisies from the garden.

Our neighborhood in Riverside, on the edge of the prairie looked very safe.

Did anyone suspect our trouble with Papa? Anna said people probably felt sorry for him. The sad man with no wife and two kids to take care of.

Does anyone know?

Do his buddy cop friends know? The ones Anna pointed out driving up and down the street by our house when he was gone.

Cops are supposed to be good and keep us safe. I don't think they know, or they'd arrest him.

We turned at the edge of town onto the narrow dirt road marked by the familiar arch at the entrance and each of us walked along in a rut with a Mohawk of cut grass between them. The road looked like someone dumped lakeshore sand to fill dips.

Anna walked ahead and reached Tess's grave first. I was a little jealous because I wanted to tell Tess the story myself. By the time I got there Anna had placed our flowers in Tess's vase. She sat up on the family marker, so high her feet didn't reach the ground. She held out a hand to help me up. With her arm around me, we stared at her mother's headstone, *Teresa Mae Stanton, Age 23, Born July 14, 1950 – Died July 14, 1973, Rest in Peace.*

I looked at Anna. "Do you really think there is a god? We say, 'God is great, God is good...' but no good god would have let Tess die or let Papa hurt you."

Anna scanned the cemetery where little flags waved over veterans' graves and plastic flowers grew, where bushes decorated graves near family plots, where Tess and her parents rested in peace. "We go to church and pray, but I look around at the congregation and wonder if there are other secrets in there no one will ever tell. But we can tell Tess."

"Can I go first?" I begged. "Please?"

Anna smiled. "It's your story, too. We'll both tell her."

I squeezed Anna's hand. "Tess, I want you to meet my mother." My hand suddenly went weak, and my tongue tied. I'm not sure why, maybe because I said the secret out loud. I looked around. Just then a breeze rocked the oak tree.

Today we were the only alive people in the cemetery, so I knew it was okay to talk out loud. Maybe it was because I realized the responsibility Anna had, taking care of me when she was only twelve. Now, I will help take care of her.

Anna said she'd told Tess where she was going before she took the train to the Catholic Home for Girls, but she just couldn't bear to tell her everything until now. We had come out to talk to Tess many times but never talked about me in particular.

I took a deep breath. "Tess, we never met but Anna told me so much about you, I feel like we know each other. I am actually your granddaughter and so happy to be in your family."

Anna hugged me. "Mama, Julie and I have been out to visit you since my cold November trip to tell you I was leaving town but I my lips couldn't tell the whole story until now, because I finally told Julie I'm her mother. I had to grow up and develop the strength to stand up for myself and for Julie. I've had trouble sleeping for a long time because questions without answers fog my brain. Last night I found an answer. I decided to become a new person and live with the name I chose when I left Minnesota. I have been too weak to do what is right. I am 'Ann.' The old weak Anna is dead."

I nodded. "I like *Ann*. It sounds strong." I turned back to Tess's headstone. "Being called a cousin didn't feel right. People always took us for sisters." I glanced at Ann. "Don't get me wrong. I was glad to be in the Stanton family but now, I have a loving mother and know you are my wonderful grandmother." I smiled. "I'm not an orphan anymore."

"In public, we're still cousins." Ann patted my knee. "We must live a lie. We have our secrets."

"I know." I looked back at the headstone. "Tess, I'm too young to understand everything, but I know why Ann and I look so much alike with curly blond hair and crooked fingers like Papa because we are *double sisters*." I laughed.

Ann raised her eyebrows as if asking a question.

"You know, like the Thompson boys who are double-cousins because their dads are brothers and the mothers are sisters."

Ann nodded. "That sounds good but not quite right. The boys look similar, but we share the same father so I'm your half-sister and your mother, it's called inbreeding and it's illegal."

My brain twisted hearing Ann say it that way. "Are we all going to jail if anyone finds out?" I jumped off the granite perch and straightened some of the flowers in Tess's vase while I tried to straighten my thoughts. "Ann, what do you think Tess would do if she was alive and actually knew?"

"She'd want Papa in jail. If she were alive and found out, Mama would have done everything to save me from him. She wasn't like Sally."

"Back when you were pregnant, why didn't everyone know what happened to you? Couldn't they see your belly getting big like that lady we saw in church last week?"

Ann's eyes teared up. "After you started growing inside me, Papa dragged me onto a passenger train. Rocking on the rails made me throw up half the way to Minneapolis. He left me in the Catholic home where I lived until you were ready to come out, so people here didn't know. There were other unmarried young mothers at the home, but it was scary living with nuns. I'd never met one. Lutherans don't have nuns."

"I thought nuns were good people. Why be afraid?"

"Other girls, older than twelve, some pretty old, like twenty, told me nuns would steal my baby on the night of the birth. I sat in prayer sessions and scrubbed floors each day and cried every night for weeks worrying about you. I couldn't imagine a baby alone without its mother. I was barely able to take care of myself at twelve, but I vowed to keep you and fight everyone who tried to make me give you up to the nuns for adoption."

I hugged her. "I'm glad you saved me."

"It wasn't all bad there at the home. When the nuns had a doctor come to examine the pregnant girls one of them stood by. A nice nun stayed in the room with me. One time a kind chubby one named Sister Grace held my hand. She also prayed with me one time asking for God's help and forgiveness for me."

"For you? Papa's the bad one. She should have prayed for him."

Ann said nothing for a while, lost in thought. "He told them it was the neighbor boy, so she probably prayed for him instead." Ann laughed. "At least you look like me and don't have buck teeth and black hair like Janey's brother."

I pictured myself like him. "I wouldn't mind curly black hair. I like him. He's really nice and looks just like his dad."

Ann hopped down. "Luckily, the nuns taught classes and a tutor helped us, so I didn't get behind in school."

I waved as we walked down the road toward town. "Bye, Tess. We'll be back to visit another day. Love you."

I must call my mother Anna until I can tell everyone our secret. I asked her to tell you the rest of our story.

PART 3
Chapter 24 - More Lies

Papa returned from a rail trip. After that last horrible night before he left town, we were dreading he'd be home before long and cause more trouble. The next morning, Julie and I sat at the kitchen table eating cereal when I heard Papa in his bedroom, his shower running, and then drawers slamming. He walked out of his room and dropped his grip packed with clothing for a work trip. "Anna, help Julie and hurry up. Pack a double lunch and fill my thermos. I'm late."

"Leaving so soon?" I placed his lunch pail on the counter. "You just got home."

"What's it to you?" Veins bulged on his forehead, breath reeking of toothpaste and old alcohol. He stood behind us, watching as Julie buttered bread and placed stacks of bologna and cheese slices on the bread. I quickly wrapped the sandwiches in waxed paper and tucked them in his lunch box hoping we did it well enough so he wouldn't yell.

Julie's sweet face turned. Her innocent blue eyes met his angry bloodshot glare. "Papa we have some bananas. Do you want some in your lunch?"

He squinted at her as if trying to focus and held up two fingers.

Julie placed them in the lunchbox and stepped back not quite out of his reach.

"Come here, girl." He squeezed her arm, fingers pressing into the flesh.

She pulled away and rubbed her arm.

"You did a good job with the sandwiches. You're growing up. Looking more like Anna every day. That's good."

He took the grip and lunch box, heading to work and out of town. I hoped it was for a long, long trip.

After breakfast and vacuuming the house, we refilled a water bowl in the flower garden after seeing the neighbor kitty trying to catch a butterfly nearby. Forget-me-nots were in full bloom, so we picked some for Tess and walked out to the cemetery. It helped me to go out there where the wind ruffled our hair, where we were at no risk of being scolded or bothered. I still hadn't fully recovered from Papa's abuse and hurt too much to ride my bike.

I bent down to place the bouquet of tiny blue flowers on Tess's grave, not really paying attention to what I was doing. Julie grabbed my arm. "Look!" She pointed at a simple collection of flowers in a fruit jar sitting next to the stone vase we usually used.

We looked around and saw no one.

"Who do you think left flowers for Tess?" Julie asked.

I was dumbfounded. "I don't know. Mama didn't have any friends. Papa wouldn't let her work or socialize. When she was on her deathbed, she talked about being alone and sad except for the joy of being with me."

"Couldn't she invite friends over to visit when Papa was gone?"

I shook my head. "Mama talked over the fence to Lila, Janey's mom, but she was afraid to go anywhere, even when Papa was out of town. His cop friends watched her when he was gone, like they watch us now. They probably tell him we come out to the cemetery, too."

"Why didn't she fight back?"

"She was trapped like we are, no money, no rights. Papa gave her a small allowance for emergencies just like he gives us. Without a telephone in the house, she couldn't even call for help."

Julie frowned. "I'm sorry for her. It's like we are in a play, acting out her story. Two more blond girls locked up with a mean man."

I sat on the grass and beckoned Julie to sit beside me. "Tess never drove a car. Can you keep another secret?"

Julie nodded.

"I took driver training and have a license."

Julie jumped up and spun around in a dance. "That's wonderful. Is it fun?"

"It was fun learning. Don't say a word to anyone, not even Edith or Opal."

"I wonder where Jimmy is today." Julie looked around. "Maybe he left the flowers."

"Maybe. I think he did. Sometimes, when Mama and I came out here to put flowers on graves, he'd sit with us beneath the trees. It was so peaceful."

Julie kneeled by Tess's headstone and ran her little fingers in the grooves of her name. "So, you and your mom would talk to Sally just like we're talking to Tess today?"

"Yes. It was nice. We'd also bicycle along the river trail where the wind swept along the wide part and out across miles of ripening wheat that looked like waves on a golden lake."

Julie clapped her hands. "Let's go there today."

We walked along the dirt trail and met some of the girls in my high school class acting like toddlers, running in circles and laughing. When we stopped on the bluff, I explained to Julie I had nothing in common with them and would rather be with her.

Julie stretched out on the grass above the river lying on her belly, chin in her hands. She turned, "Anna, I was so happy when you said you'd walk me to school. I'm afraid of first grade in the big school." She stared at me, looking so small, so young. "I'm worried about college taking you away from me."

"Not a chance that would ever happen." Julie seemed satisfied and lay on her back for a while watching white clouds track across the sky. When she was ready, we headed back through town. I stopped half a block from Mack's Shack on Main and pointed.

A breeze carried delicious smells of grilled onions and sizzling meat. Music rolled out into the street. Papa's blue Chevy Malibu sat in front.

I signaled for Julie to follow me. We walked fast, crossing the street before passing the beer joint in hopes he wouldn't see us. "Didn't he say he was leaving town on that morning freight and that he was running late?"

"Maybe he missed it."

I hesitated, "Or was he lying? Maybe he had other plans."

We stopped at the park near home where we sometimes went to swing. We were swinging high when I dragged my feet to a sudden stop to watch a blue car pass.

Papa's Chevy.

Where was he going? Headed west. Not much that direction except Falls City. I had thoughts of my experience with the grimy old doctor in that town who would have killed Julie with an abortion if she had been smaller at the time.

Papa wouldn't let anyone borrow the Chevy. I knew he would never let me drive it, yet there was a girl driving. Her long reddish hair blew in the wind.

Julie shielded her eyes from the sun. "He's in the passenger seat."

Feeling jealous because I would love to drive that car, my eyes followed it heading out of town. "I think it was Penny Davidson. Her mother works at Mack's Shack." My legs shook. What did she do to deserve the honor of driving Papa's treasured car? "Papa lied to us about going to work. If he was in the passenger seat, Penny must have gotten her learner's permit and he's giving her driving lessons."

Julie frowned. "Why is he treating her better than he treats his own children?"

"Because he's evil and controlling. Penny will be sorry."

"Where is her mother?"

Chapter 25 - Painful Truths

After seeing that Papa was actually in town and had lied about leaving meant that we had to be on guard. He could walk in at any moment. I talked to Julie about the importance of keeping the house in order. That afternoon, I walked her to Edith's before going to my job. Working from noon to four p.m. three days a week was a light schedule. Those hours allowed me to help with feeding the kids which was a chore with a couple dozen kids under the age of six. There were four of us working, so things went well, and I enjoyed the time I spent there, especially when I received my first paycheck.

I showed it to Julie. She was excited and went with me to the bank to open an account. I deposited it and felt wonderful. It was a steppingstone to freedom. I used Opal's P.O. Box address so Papa wouldn't find out I had a bank account. I thought it might provoke an outburst and he'd try to steal my money. I would have asked Edith but figured if there was a problem and Papa blew up, Jimmy would be there to defend Opal.

Julie and I spent time at the library, and I told Opal things were not going well at home. Papa was drinking too much.

She said Jimmy told her Papa's car was at the beer joint so much he wondered if he'd lost his railroad job.

I was shocked. If he wasn't working, that would explain why he was lying. But, without his money, we'd have trouble buying groceries and paying the electric bill.

Opal saw my panic and looked concerned. "He might be spending time with Charlene. Her daughter is in the Riverside hospital. She had some sort of surgery complications, not sure what."

We didn't see Papa for about a week and when he showed up, he'd been drinking again. We were both frightened because drinking made him meaner than usual. He didn't speak to us, just showered, changed clothes, and left. It was hard to know what to think.

We went about our schedule. I was glad Julie could stay with Edith in her comfortable house smelling of her good cooking. Crocheted doilies decorated tables and beautiful plants sat in the windows. Julie enjoyed helping with vacuuming because Edith's knees still gave her trouble.

We were about out of milk and bread because Papa hadn't brought groceries home lately, so after work, I picked Julie up from Edith's house and we walked to the Corner Grocery. We came around the end of the canned vegetable shelves and ran into Charlene. I'd only seen her around town and in church. I didn't really know her but recognized her frizzy ponytail and horn-rimmed glasses. She walked right past us, trailing the smell of cigarette smoke then stopped short, and turned around.

I was surprised when she spoke.

Her raspy words were friendly. "Hi, girls. Are you having a good summer?"

We nodded in unison. "Julie and I are enjoying ourselves. Bicycling, going on walks and I'm working part time at the daycare." I couldn't stop myself for asking. "How's Penny? I heard she was sick?"

"Had an infection in her blood, but she is getting better. I guess it was appendicitis." Charlene put a few items in her cart. "My car is leaking oil and I didn't want to drive all the way to Falls City to get her. I might not make it and they're discharging her today."

"I'm glad she is better."

"Yeah. Dave is giving her a ride home from the hospital. See ya later."

We headed to checkout. After we were outside the store and headed toward home, I looked back to see Charlene come out with her arms full of groceries. She drove off in an older car spewing stinky exhaust.

"What are you thinking, Anna? Is Papa sweet on Charlene, or her daughter?"

"Maybe he's just being friendly." I doubted my own words.

My little girl was probably right, maybe both of them. Charlene was about forty and had a beautiful daughter my age.

Chapter 26 - Enslaved

On Wednesday, Julie and I arrived home about 4:30 after getting off work, looking forward to a good evening at home with the next few free days. We found Papa had returned. He was coming in the back door carrying groceries when we came through the front. I knew he'd been home to shower and change a few days earlier after I had found a heap of dirty clothes on the floor of his bedroom. I wondered if he was avoiding me after his horrible behavior.

I doubted that. He considered us his slaves.

He sat down at the kitchen table. "Don't I even get a greeting?"

Julie said, "We're afraid to talk because we don't want to make you mad. Are you happy today?"

"You might say so. I even brought you ladies some treats. There some ice cream in the freezer for you. The house looks good."

I just looked at him and had no words after what he did to me the night before he left.

Julie started emptying the grocery bags and putting things away. "Thank you for bringing food. We were getting short on milk and bread."

"Charlene Davidson said she saw you in the grocery store, so I thought I'd better fill the cupboards again."

I helped Julie put groceries away. "We saw your car around town a few days ago and wondered what was going on."

"I hurt myself on the job and was off work but I'm going on a run tomorrow."

Julie the peacekeeper was being nice. "Could I make sandwiches for your lunchbox?"

"Sure. Two bolognas with cheese and include two of those apples I just bought. There is a big bag of them over on the counter."

My suspicious eyes drilled him. "How was your trip to Falls City?"

"None of your damn business."

I couldn't stop myself. I had to know if he impregnated Penny and then got her a botched back-alley abortion like he tried with me. "Charlene said you went to give her daughter a ride home from the hospital. If it was appendicitis, why wasn't she hospitalized here instead of Falls City? Did she run into complications with your old doctor buddy?"

Papa slammed a fist on the table. "You bitch. Keep your nose out of my business."

"Hmm. Am I psychic?" I must be right based on his behavior.

Papa left the table saying he'd be leaving as soon as he packed some clothes since we didn't appreciate his presence.

I rolled my eyes at Julie.

She smirked, put her head down and kept making sandwiches after we decided to have bologna sandwiches for dinner with tomato soup. Julie finished packing his lunch and

put it in the refrigerator. I set the table with bowls and silverware. She served our sandwiches. "I'm starved. Thanks,
Julie."

Papa stomped through the kitchen and without saying
goodbye, took his lunch from the fridge on his way out the
back door.

I took a sip of the hot soup. "Maybe I have Papa worried.
I hope to keep it that way."

"He's acting like that spoiled kid in the daycare. Papa
needs a time-out."

Because of his recent behavior, not coming home, no appar-
ent railroad schedule and more drinking, I wasn't sure what
to expect from him. I tried not to think about it because
there was nothing I could do except try to plan our escape
and take good care of Julie. With a couple months left before school ended for both of us, I hoped there would be no
blowups with Papa.

I wanted us to have a good summer. With Edith's help
and positive influence on Julie my stress level decreased. But,
that internal gnawing of being afraid of Papa never went
away. It would show up at any moment with thoughts of him
ruining our lives more than he had already.

The night he screamed at me about all sorts of things and
hurt me so bad, he threatened to tell his friends and the deacons that he was having a terrible time with me, lying about
everything. Maybe he had sensed my rising anger and hate
for him and feared someday I'd expose his behavior. I think
he has been setting things up so no one would believe me if I

told them what he had been doing for years. I've researched a few things. Testing Julie's blood would support my claim and possibly confirm he is her father.

I was hoping to get my education and no longer be forced to depend on him. Then, I could take Julie and run. He had already threatened to kick me out and keep Julie. I guess by law, he could do that because I turned eighteen and without proving I am her mother, I'd have no rights. I have to bide my time to do this right.

After he left, I nearly told Julie my long-term plans but then decided not to burden such a small girl with such big secrets. Our situation was dire, but I shouldn't make her share the burden. Observing a few short interactions between Papa and Julie made me think he was looking at her in a special way. I had to protect her from his ugly thoughts and acts.

Julie and I had already talked about not letting him touch her, but it made me cringe the way he gently moved her blond curls when he wrapped the measuring tape around her chest. The way he "measured her" for the Christmas dress appeared the innocent act of a loving father if you didn't know him. I hated seeing his hands around her waist and touching her chest.

Julie loves that dress and thinks kindly about him because of the gift.

Of course, I couldn't tell Julie the terrible truth that he demanded sex from me. I was so afraid of him I felt trapped and helpless. I hated myself more every time I took another one of those damn birth control pills. Someone in his right mind would not rape his own child. That says it all.

I have to face him month after month, year after year, looking *good on the outside* in public but knowing our family was filled with sin, shame and lies. Even with the shades down, the doors locked, and the house clean, I felt dirty, and that people were watching us.

Sometimes I wondered if they could read my thoughts.

Chapter 27 - Penny

"We have a project before we walk over to Edith's." I finished dressing and combed our hair thinking we'd both look good. No one would suspect my horrible sins.

I took the little hook we bought at the hardware and measured the distance with a string, then made a couple pencil marks on the door and molding where the screws would go.

"What are you doing? I thought that was for the garage door."

"I don't want Papa to come into our room. I hope this will keep him out."

Julie shook her head. "He's very strong. I think we'd need a hook about a foot long to keep him out." She laughed.

"This is very serious. I suppose when he discovers the lock, he'll be furious."

Julie nodded. "He likes to be in charge of everything."

Getting the screw started was difficult. I had to pound a nail in to make a hole, then pull the nail out before I could first screw the one with the hook hanging on it into the molding and then the little one with the "eye" on it into the door. My arms hurt worse by the time I finished.

We tried the lock. Julie stood outside the room and turned the knob. She pushed in on the door.

I watched from inside the bedroom. The hook made a noise but held when she rattled the door and tried to enter.

I opened the door for her. "We got it in the right place. I think it works the way it's supposed to."

Edith greeted us and already had some plans for Julie including a short walk. I told them I had an errand after work so I'd be a little late. Before we left home, I looked in a desk drawer in Papa's bedroom where I'd seen a spare key to the Chevy. I took the key on a little chain with a Chevrolet emblem dangling on it and put it deep in my jeans pocket where I knew I wouldn't lose it.

After work I raced to the bank first to deposit my latest check but kept one-hundred dollars in escape money and a few dollars for incidentals. Then, went to the hardware store. I was happy to see Chuck working. I removed the key from its chain before I asked him to make a spare.

He was cheery like before, whistling as he worked and made sure I had popcorn to eat while I wandered around the store, mostly staying out of sight. I didn't want anyone to see me nor see anyone I'd have to speak to. Plus, I wanted to get back to Edith's without anyone but Chuck knowing about the spare key.

When I left with treasures in both pockets, money in one and a key in the other, I hurried up the street toward Edith's and ran straight into Charlene Davidson.

Not wanting to talk to her, I smiled and walked on past. She caught up with me and stepped in front, blocking me, frowning, tears in her eyes.

"What's wrong Charlene?"

"I'm sure you know. Don't fake it."

I shook my head, confused by her words and behavior.

She gripped my upper arm where the bruise was darkening. I winced and pulled back.

"Your dad's been messing with Penny."

Blood rushed to my face. I was right. "Oh, no. What happened?"

"He's been helping us out since Rex got killed. You saw me and Penny at church on Christmas eve. I think he bought you the same dress he bought for Penny. She loved it." Charlene pulled me over to a parking area just off the sidewalk.

I felt very uncomfortable with her telling me this and the fact that someone passing by might overhear. "He's been good to us. Buys a few groceries. You know, helping with some car repairs, the stuff I can't do." She wiped a tear. A cigarette rasp slowed her words. "I thought I knew him pretty well after all the time I've spent bartending at Mack's. I thought he was sweet on me. It turns out a fifty-year-old-man would rather screw a teenager."

"I'm so sorry. Is Penny okay?"

"She wouldn't talk. Depressed. Laying around the house, crying. I finally got her to tell me what was wrong." Charlene glanced around. "I know I shouldn't have done it but saw his car parked outside Mack's Shack this morning and walked in. I shocked everybody sitting at the bar including him. I screamed bloody hell and told him to keep his hands off my little girl or I'd call the cops on him."

I hugged her. "You did the right thing. I think you should report him to the police. Rex is not here to protect her."

Charlene trembled, looking at her feet. "Dave spun around on the barstool and grabbed my shoulders. He shook me and said Penny was lying. I almost lost my footing and caught myself near an old duffer in bib-overalls sitting at the end of the bar. He said, 'Believe the girl, Char. He's done it before. Too bad you can't ask his dead wife.'"

She looked up at me. "I was speechless when Dave walked over, struck the old man and screamed at him to shut up, then stormed out and drove off. I helped doctor up the old man's lip. I gave him an ice bag and a free beer."

I looked at my watch. "I have to go pick up Julie. She's at a friend's house. I'm sorry I have to leave and so sorry about Penny." I hugged her. "This is horrible. I think you should call the cops."

I tried to hide my emotions as I walked Charlene to her car. "What are you going to do?"

She got behind the wheel and sat with the door ajar. "I don't know. I'm afraid of him now." Charlene rested her head on the steering wheel. "I saw him flip out once before in the bar. Not a pretty sight and today he hit that old man."

"Do you have anyone to call who can stay with you?"

Charlene looked old and exhausted. Deep facial wrinkles grooved her face. "My sister'll come over, but I have to try to talk to Penny first." Sad eyes looked at me. "Penny lied to me about everything. It wasn't appendicitis." She burst into tears and handed me a hospital bill. "I just came from the Post Office."

Thousands of dollars. Diagnosis: *post abortion sepsis*.

Charlene started the car. "She almost died, and Dave did it."

"You have the evidence. Report him." I closed the door.

Charlene backed out and drove off in a car spewing dark exhaust.

I felt terrible for both of them and worried about what Papa would do when Charlene went to his cop buddies. When I got to Edith's it was nearly five o'clock. They were happy and Edith was taking a hotdish out of the oven. She placed the bowl on a hot pad in the center of the table. I dropped into a kitchen chair smelling the delicious food.

"You look tired out. Did you have a bad day?" Julie smiled. "Did you poke the bear?"

I laughed. "You can make me smile even when I'm exhausted."

"Edith showed me how to make rice-hamburger hotdish." Julie smiled as she dished each of us a helping. "Now I can cook more than canned beans and hotdogs for you."

Edith passed a canister of Parmesan cheese. "It tastes even better if you sprinkle a little of this on top."

They filled me in on their day and I talked a little about work but said nothing about my errands or Charlene's story. The events weighed heavy on my thoughts but time with Julie and her exuberance about learning more cooking skills improved my mood.

At home, I quickly stashed my money in the safe place with my driver license in the lower bookcase and placed the original car key on its chain back in Papa's desk drawer.

After a couple duets, we read awhile before turning out the lights.

I lay awake thinking about Penny and the confirmation of my worst fear about Papa's abuse. She'd had an abortion. Did he pay a lot of money for it? I had enough money for essentials with my job, but he hadn't given us any emergency allowance for weeks. After hearing Charlene had accused him in front of a bunch of his drinking buddies worried me.

Penny is under-age. Would the local police believe her?

With his behavior out in the open, gossip would get to the church and board of deacons.

His life would change and, with luck, so would ours.

Chapter 28 - Devil Wind

Papa's railroad schedule was not as regular as it had been, and we didn't know when to expect him. Sometimes he told us he was going on a run. Sometimes he took a grip and lunch, sometimes he didn't. Our next few days were free of the daycare schedule giving us time to do a little yard work, weed the garden and take some bike rides. One nice day, we packed lunches and brought bottles of water for a ride way out along River Road beyond where the pavement ended.

I loved the prairie way out there, the peace of the cows mooing, and fields of golden grain waving in late July sun. River Road followed the railroad tracks, so we often counted the box cars when freights rattled by and waved if the passenger train passed. I told Julie that someday we would take a long ride on that train and people would be waving to us as we sped past.

Prairie winds blew us along when we were riding. Some days it howled off the Rocky Mountain east slope and barreled across the flatland. When we arrived at our special picnic area, we climbed up on a heap of big rocks to look around. A doe with twin fawns grazed in the field across the tracks, paying us no attention.

In the fall, that's when the tumbleweeds bounced and rolled down the road ahead of us. I couldn't recall a day when there was no wind. Some people don't like the wind, but I didn't really mind rushes of clean fresh air. But on those blustery days when dust devils rose and sped across the landscape, I thought of Papa. An evil wind. Like Mama's story when her peaceful home was destroyed by a devil wind that swept through her house and carried her far away with me in her belly.

Papa wouldn't be marrying Penny, but his evil ways had harmed another family, a woman and her daughter, without someone to protect them. He targeted them knowing they were sad, poor, and needed help. Providing friendship and help gave him the excuse to be close and sweet-talk Charlene and the vulnerable teen crying for her father.

I wished the devil wind would take Papa faraway so he couldn't hurt anyone else. I was fearful for Julie's safety. How could he look at her as a sexual target?

She is still a baby, my baby and I had to protect her.

Julie is so adorable and unfortunately, he had found how needy she was for his attention and how little it took to sway her his way. I know she heard me telling her not to be alone with him but probably didn't understand the importance. Out here on the prairie was a good place to talk. No one around and the place Mama had chosen to talk to me when I was so young.

I didn't understand then either.

Julie was lying on her back eating a sandwich watching a magpie fly overhead, its iridescent blue-black feathers shining in the sun. I lay down beside her. The ground was sandy and warm from the sun with tufts of grass poking up in clumps. A very pleasant place to be nestled behind a boulder out of the wind. I hated to approach an ugly topic but had to do it.

It was as if she was reading my mind. "Anna, why don't you want me to be with Papa when he is being so nice to me?"

Her eyes wandered to my arms where the bruises were fading. "Why did he hurt you?"

"Well, it's difficult to talk about it but I'm glad you asked. Remember, I told you the big secret we can't tell? I am your mother, and he is your father. If anyone knew, he would be in prison."

She finished her sandwich and turned over. Her blue eyes bright, inquisitive, but tearing up. "He can't go to prison." She pounded her little fist on her leg and sat up straight. "He is a good person. Only bad people go to prison."

"There are certain rules that can never be broken. Any man who looks to a child for sex is a bad person. At your age, sex isn't something you should hear or think about. Sex between a man and woman is an act that makes babies. I wouldn't be talking to you about this if I wasn't worried about you."

She sat up. Her face flushed. "He showed me his honey. Is that sex? It was ugly and I wouldn't touch it. When I took off my panties to put on the tutu, he touched me with it between my legs. It tickled."

I screamed, "Damn him." I hugged her, shaking. "I knew it. He's started."

Julie wailed. "He was happy I let him do it and said I couldn't tell anyone, and he'd bring me tutus and toys. I was so happy, and it was my birthday."

"Oh, my god. Don't go anywhere with him, ever."

We walked around the area and down the embankment to the river where we threw stones and watched them splash. Julie threw hers way out and stomped her little foot. Angry. "I'm scared because I told you. What will he do to me, now?" She turned toward me crying. "Why can't we have a nice daddy like that grandpa at the hardware store named Charlie, or like Jimmy. They like us and smile. We need a daddy who smiles." She sat down hard on a rock. "Let's run away."

I told her we had to bide our time, but I felt the same way she did.

Chapter 29 - Telling

About a week later, one afternoon Papa strolled in the front door dressed in dark slacks and a white shirt, the way he dressed for church. I knew he'd been in the house and changed clothes because the worn ones were on the floor waiting for me to pick them up.

I think he'd been in town for three days before we saw him. Julie and I had walked past Mack's Shack a few times. I didn't think he'd be in there after what happened when Charlene confronted him, and I wondered where he was hanging out. What was he doing? All I knew for sure was, I was glad he hadn't been bothering us.

We gave him wide berth, no greeting.

He disappeared into his bedroom, closed the door and I heard the bed squeak, so thought he was probably lying down.

Julie quickly made peanut butter sandwiches for a picnic, and we left on our bikes, wanting to avoid contact if possible. Maybe he'd be gone when we returned. This time, we went to the cemetery, a place of escape. We hadn't been to the cemetery for weeks, nor to the library.

The sturdy old oak tree near the Inman's and Stanton family's plots had seen a lot of sorrow in our family and I'm sure it heard my wailing stories when I came out to talk to

Mama. I mostly cried about not seeing her but couldn't bring myself to tell her how I'd failed to keep Papa away from me until the night before I left town, pregnant, on that train headed east.

Julie settled on the grass beneath the oak and unwrapped our sandwiches. She handed me one. "I put some of Edith's strawberry jam on them this time. I'm glad she showed me how to make jam. Cooking is easy now that I can read."

I sat beside Julie and took my sandwich from her. "It's so nice we have her. She is a combination of a mother and grandmother we never had."

"Don't say that. You're my mother, and you are a very good mother. Edith is our grandmother because your wonderful mom died too young."

"That's true. Our lives are a little mixed up, but we have each other. I think starting first grade for you and college for me will be wonderful. In about two weeks, we'll be walking to school."

"Can we get some new clothes?"

"From the thrift store, sure. I think I'll wear jeans and sweaters. I have enough, but you have been growing. I'm glad Tess made sure I went to school. I love learning."

"Me, too. Let's go see Opal and check out some books."

We walked up the cement steps to the small-town library, a small log building with beautiful stone decorating the front. Based on the cars in the parking lot, I thought there would be a lot of people inside.

Julie and I joined them between lines and lines of book-cases. I heard Opal's laugh, so I knew she was working. After the place cleared out, Julie and I went to visit her.

"Oh, I'm so glad to see you girls. I haven't seen you in a long time. Edith filled told me things were going well, and Julie was becoming quite the cook."

Opal took Julie's hand. "Come with me. I have some-thing to show you. We rearranged the children's section. We even have some comfortable chairs and a rack of new books." She returned a few minutes later smiling and without Julie. "She's settled into a chair with one of the new books."

I sat with Opal in her office behind the counter where she could keep an eye out for people ready to check out books. Concern wrinkled her brow. "I wanted to talk to you about something without Julie. Are you and Julie okay? I heard some gossip I found hard to believe."

I stiffened. "We are okay. What did you hear?"

"Dave got kicked off the church council board of dea-cons after Charlene reported him to them for messing with Penny. It caused a big stir."

Flushed and ashamed. "He's a horrible man. Charlene told me. I said to call the cops on him. Guess she didn't do that. You know, Penny is younger than I am."

"Jimmy and I were horrified. If you ever need help, like we told you when your mom died, come to us immediately. Is he treating you alright?"

I slowly shook my head and took a deep breath, afraid to say anything. I just pulled up my sleeves where bruises on my arms were faded to an ugly yellow-green color.

Opal gasped. "Oh, no. What can we do?"

"I don't know. He's very strict, mean, and will kick me out if I say anything. So, don't tell anyone or I won't have a place to live."

Julie rushed in with two new books she wanted to check out. While Opal was helping her, I scanned books in a section familiar to me and found a reference book on sex abuse counseling.

Opal's eyes met mine, but she said nothing about my choice.

Julie went out ahead of me.

"Thanks for the offer. I'll ask if I need help."

She walked us to the library door and gave me a strength-infusing hug that would last a long while, at least I thought so at the time. But, when we arrived home, things didn't look right. Papa was gone, his bedroom, a mess. An old leather suitcase I'd seen in his closet for years was missing, along with his leather jacket and a blank part of his closet showed missing shirts and pants. I called Julie.

Julie walked into his bedroom.

I pointed to the closet.

"What?" She walked in and looked around, peering into a dresser drawer. "Looks like he took a bunch of his clothes. Where did he go?" She teared up. "He didn't even say good-bye."

I hugged her. "Don't cry yet. Maybe it's for the good but we can't depend on him for much of anything."

I looked in his desk drawers. The checkbook was missing. A key to his favorite car was there. "I don't know where he might have gone. Did he leave us a note?"

On the kitchen table we found five twenty-dollar bills beside a tablet with a scrawled note. *I'll be gone a month or so. Behave yourselves. I may be away, but my eyes will be on you. Papa*

We looked at each other. Julie shrugged. "At least he left us a little money."

The counters were heaped with bags and boxes of food. "Yes, and he bought a bunch of groceries." I looked in a couple of the large bags. "This is more than we need for a month."

I sat down feeling depressed, uneasy, wondering where he went and exactly what happened. Did he lose his job? I pulled Julie to my lap. "I think this is a good sign. I have no idea where he is but at least, he left us some money and food, so he cares a little. Plus, he'll be gone when we start school, so we don't have to stress out knowing he will walk in at any time and be mad about something."

Julie pulled my sleeve. "It's a sad day when your kids are happy that you're gone. Anna, come on! I'm happy, now. Let's go get an ice cream to celebrate."

Chapter 30 - Prayers for a Pervert

We went out to get our bicycles and saw the junker parked beside the garage. The Chevy sat inside beneath a cover to keep dust from collecting on the shiny paint. I scanned Papa's work bench where every tool was clean and in its place. Even a greasy rag was folded neatly. Some parts of his life were organized, other parts, chaotic like when he's here and we jump around like monkeys on a string to please him and avoid his wrath.

I backed my bike from its resting place and followed Julie out the side door. "Let's enjoy just being together in peace without picking up his clothes and worrying about being yelled at when he shows up without warning."

I hooked the door before riding off and checked in my pocket to be sure I had one of his twenties for ice cream. We loved The Parlor, a plain old place with a fancy name. Black and white tile covered the floor in a chicken wire pattern. Some of the tiles were cracked and missing, but we didn't care. The ice cream was scooped, and really hard. We waved at Chuck and bicycled across the tracks and a mile farther heading west toward Falls City.

We usually bought a single scoop cone and sat outside, hiding in plain sight.

It's funny how after living so long in a house with little contact with anyone except Papa and talking to the dead, I almost felt invisible. I wore dull clothes, and the thrift store clothing didn't always look that great. I never wore anything flashy that might attract attention. I hoped we'd get some real deals at the thrift store on our way home.

Julie looked sparkling happy, smiley, rocking back and forth in anticipation of placing her ice cream order. I decided this was going to be a special time for us. A little freedom. I whispered in her ear. "Let's have a sundae."

Julie frowned, questioning eyes.

"You know, a couple scoops with toppings. We have enough money."

She jumped at the idea and scanned the list of options on a menu board on the wall beside a giant mirror behind the cash register. "I'm having vanilla with strawberries and marshmallow creme."

I laughed. "Papa would croak at the thought of allowing you all those sweets. I'm having hot fudge with whipped cream and a cherry on the top. I'll give you a taste, if you'd like."

We placed our orders and sat at a corner table where we could watch other customers. It was sort of our own television show since we didn't have one. We could watch people for real, from a corner where we were most comfortable away from prying eyes.

Julie talked about thrift shopping and buying school shoes. I hoped we'd find a hooded winter coat for her because the walk to school at times would be windy and cold.

Once we were served, we didn't talk much, just savored every bite and shared with each other. We decided both choices were delicious. Her strawberries were especially good and tasted like fresh berries, not jam. They served fries and burgers, but the ice cream was a perfect treat for us. I needed the calories because I often had little appetite and stayed skinny like Tess.

Worrying about Papa's unpredictable behavior kept me on edge, roiling my stomach, but I tried to hide my stress from Julie. I teased her and made her laugh like my mother did for me. I gave her lots of praise for doing well writing and reading. Papa never once admired my good grades or achievements. Spending so much wonderful time with Tess gave me a role model, a good start and some self-confidence. But she could never have prepared me for what I'd endure after her death. She tried, but I failed her.

I couldn't fail Julie. I'd already come way too close.

When we walked into Pay Day Thrift, the waft of an odd mixture of odors made me queasy. It was like moldy sweet perfume blended with Lysol. That smell brought my senses back to shopping for baby clothes, when I first came here with Papa and bought clothing for my newborn. I had no idea what I was doing. A sweet old lady shopper had peeked at Julie, wrapped in a blanket in my arms. "You are such a good girl, taking care of the baby."

Julie went straight to the shoe racks and found a great pair of snow boots. We were discussing coming back later in the fall for a winter coat when they might have more coats on display as Charlene and Penny entered and saw us.

I felt uncomfortable, not knowing if I should pretend I didn't see them, or just be friendly and nonchalant. I didn't have to decide because Charlene walked right over to me. "Is he gone, yet?"

Penny headed to the shoes, ignoring my presence but I flushed, uncomfortable not knowing what her mother meant. Charlene braced herself against a rack of blouses. "Thanks for talking to me the other day downtown when I was so upset. I was sure the cops in this town wouldn't do anything, so I went to the preacher and spilled the beans." She coughed and took a raspy breath. "Pastor Bob about pissed his pants. He sat down in a sweat and called a deacon. The three of us talked and I told them the dirty truth and said they better do something about Dave, or my next stop would be the police and would look bad for the Church Board. I mentioned front page news."

I pictured the tense scene and was glad Charlene had the courage to talk to them and expose his pervert behavior. His lies. "Yes. He's gone. Do you know where he is. He just left a note that he'd be gone for a month."

"Yeah, and I demanded he pay all the bills and pay for counseling for Penny and me and never come near her again."

"I'm glad you found a counselor."

She dug in her purse and brought out a key. "My car died on top of all the other trouble. Dave gave us a new one." She pointed to a red four-door in front of the store. "Used, but in great shape and new to us."

All I could think was, Dave was sweetening them up for later.

Charlene continued. "Pastor Bob prayed over me and Penny, and later called to tell me the deacons raked Dave over the coals of hell. One of them drove him to a Billings Christian inpatient therapy unit. They said he'd come back a new man."

"Now, I know where he is. I hope the therapy does some good. Thanks for telling me." After Charlene went about her shopping, I joined Julie. We both found pants and sweaters that looked like new. Julie rode off ahead of me with the loot in her basket. "Thanks, Anna. We made quite the haul for $12."

Riding home, my mind whirred like our wheels. Spinning endlessly. Would Papa tell the counselors about his life of raping and impregnating me? Continuing the abuse over years? And now molesting Julie? I doubted it.

I wondered if the counselor would be required to report the information to authorities if he did confess.

It seemed he had done this over a lifetime and four weeks of praying wouldn't cure him. Oh, he might be forgiven by some, but he would never, ever, ever gain my forgiveness. What he had done to our family was unforgiveable.

His behavior with Penny was disgusting, illegal and could have killed her. Not his daughter but she's a child, too young to consent to sex with a 50-year-old man. How could the deacons think a little counseling and prayer could fix a pervert? That's what the books I've read call men like Papa and they are incurable.

Pervert Papa. That's what I should call him to his face.

It's the truth.

Chapter 31 - Escape Plans

We gathered up our new thrift purchases and dirty clothes, including Papa's. I sorted them into piles of dark and light to wash while Julie practiced the piano.

My thoughts fixated on Papa's perversion, and I wondered how many girls he had harmed. The church solution gave him an easy pass. No prison time. No public exposure and shame. I felt even more compelled to stop him since it looked like he was getting off Scot free.

I had saved my semen-stained nightgown. You may find it disgusting but I decided to place it and a pair of his stained underwear in a bag. I hid it in my closet. From my reading, the science of DNA was used beginning about ten years ago. It was magical in identifying perverts. Maybe someday I'd need the evidence to stop him. I hoped not, but my escape plan had many facets. Our lives depended on careful planning, including transportation.

If I had to drive in an emergency, I wanted to try out the Chevy. I don't mean drive it. That would be foolhardy because if his cop buddies stopped me, they might not give me a ticket, but they'd tell him. That would be worse than a ticket.

His car meant more to him than Julie or me. Because Papa was hundreds of miles away in Billings, it was a perfect time to familiarize myself with the car.

After Julie was asleep, I took my key from its hiding place and quietly left the house through the kitchen. I didn't turn on the porch light. I sneaked out the back door and made my way in darkness along the walkway to the garage. I raised the garage door and slipped behind the wheel. With the car door ajar and interior light on, I inserted the key after making sure the automatic was in park. It would be a disaster if I made the mistake of accelerating right through the garage wall.

My legs shook so much I could hardly keep my foot on the brake. I turned the key and held my breath. It started on first try and purred. I felt around, making sure I knew where the headlights were and how to change beams. Next time I would have to bring a booster to sit on. I found I was too short to reach the pedals and see over the dash.

Satisfied I'd know what to do, I closed the garage door, returned to the house and stashed my car key in its hiding place. I made sure the doors were locked and crawled into my twin bed next to Julie's where she lay curled, breathing like a purring kitty.

We slept long after our usual time to get up. It was a luxury to lie in bed with no likelihood of Papa coming home any time soon. Of course, we had little real control, but formulating an escape plan brought me some comfort in our unstable existence. Maybe Papa would return home in better control, but I had no confidence prayer or counseling would change his behavior.

After breakfast, we left home to do a dry-run timing our walk to the elementary school and the community college. Fifteen minutes to Julie's school and another fifteen to mine, would be easy daily trips. Edith's house was only two blocks from Julie's new school so she could walk there by herself if needed, but I planned to escort her. We entered the college and walked the long halls and from my campus map, we located classrooms, the library and lunchroom.

I had one more week of work, three days, then a five-day break before the first day of college. Based on the date Papa left, we'd have a couple weeks of school completed by the time he returned.

Julie wanted another notebook, a few pencils and ruler so we walked to the Five and Dime. "I'm surprised you want to go back here after our last experience." I held the door for her.

"I'm older now and I don't think she'll scare me so much. I was only five last time when I was really scared. Could I have money so I can pay for it myself?"

I handed her three dollars, not knowing how much she might need. The big gruff owner followed us around like she did the previous time. Julie made her choices and walked to the checkout.

"That will be a dollar-fifty." The woman placed her purchases in a bag.

Julie laid two dollars on the counter, received her change and thanked the woman.

"You are very welcome. I must compliment your behavior. Please return any time. Here, take these two pieces of bubble gum. Study hard. School is very important."

We thanked her and left.

Outside, Julie said, "That was a surprise. She's nicer than I thought."

A knock on the front door late in the afternoon stabbed my heart. I stood statue-still. No one knocked on our door. Julie lifted her hands from the piano and froze. She shot a look at me and came to my side, pressed tight. Her little hand on my leg trembled. She whispered, "Maybe we should hide and wait until they leave."

Another knock.

I took her hand. "I wonder who it is. Let's go together."

I looked through the peep hole window in the door. "Church women."

Julie opened the door. "Hi, I was just practicing the piano. Hope you weren't waiting long."

For being so young, she was quick-thinking and sounded perfect, not like a frightened daughter of a pervert.

I gave them a fake smile.

One stout lady with pink cheeks who smelled of sweet lotion thrust forward a wicker basket heaped with fresh bread, cookies and a hotdish. "Pastor Bob said your father was called out of town on business. We put together a little basket of things for you."

Julie took the gift, her eyes wide, smiling. "Thank you so much, now we don't have to figure out what to make for dinner."

A tall thin woman towering over her friend pushed forward and peered into our perfect house.

Not a thing out of place. I thought *cleanliness is next to godliness* was probably looping through her mind. But my thoughts were, we're good on the outside, but our home is filled with shame. Don't come in or we'll taint your purity.

I didn't invite them in. The only time I recalled anyone in our house was on Mama's deathday, when Pastor Bob prayed for her and the mortician took her away, then when Jimmy and Opal came to check on me.

I thanked the ladies.

Julie announced, "We are pretty good cooks, but thank you very much. I'll return your basket and casserole dish to the church.

The women walked away talking to each other. I hoped they were satisfied with what they saw and would leave us alone. It was thoughtful of them to come by, and we would enjoy the tasty meal with homemade bread, but I wanted them to keep their prying eyes away from us.

Chapter 32 - Starting College

Julie and I were remote control robots under Papa's fingers. I always felt him looking over my shoulder, even when I was reading. Especially if I read something he probably wouldn't approve of. His control was so pervasive, even shopping in a damn thrift store I found myself thinking he would balk at the cost of a two-dollar blouse or rip something off me if the neckline was too low. I knew turtlenecks, and loose skirts or pants were unlikely to bring his wrath so that's what I wore most of the time. I had to be sure they were at least one size bigger than I should wear. Nothing formfitting or he'd explode.

Another shopping trip before our schools started was successful when we both found comfortable lace-up walking shoes. It was less than a mile to school, much shorter than our leisurely walks in the country. We had our clothing pressed and ready. Books in my bag and Julie's supplies by the door.

On the first day of school Julie awakened early and showered. She was ready long before our planned departure time. On the route, my emotions ping ponged between having a dream come true and terror. I had achieved what Mama said I might have to do, attend college without Papa's help. I earned my dream scholarship through hard work. She was right. We could never depend on Papa to keep his word. Terror followed me like a bad friend, reminding me he might somehow ruin everything. I dreaded his return.

After the first week's trial of meshing schedules and adjusting to school, we were convinced our plan would work. My college classes were easier than I thought, and I completed homework in a couple of hours. Julie loved her teacher who placed her name on a desk in the front row.

We stopped by the day care where I had worked to see if she would need me part time during the school year. I brought my schedule for reference. Friday afternoon and Saturday morning were the best time for her. I told her I could confirm as soon as I discussed it with Edith, but she said Julie was welcome to be there with me. She didn't need to be with a babysitter because she was so good helping the little ones. "I'd like to pay her, but I'd get in trouble. I'll give you a raise and you can share some of it with her. The daycare would be closed from December 22-January 2nd giving us a real Christmas break after my final exams.

Biology turned out to be my favorite, anatomy was second. After reading some nursing books, I wished I had known more when I was pregnant so I wouldn't have been so scared. Second semester, we would start studying physiology and psychology along with beginning medical terminology and healthcare skills using manikins.

It all seemed foreign to me, but I thought of the girls' home in Minneapolis and how the nuns taught us to take care of babies. The nun instructors used little tutorials, showing us a skill and then we repeated it under supervision.

Feeding a baby and changing a diaper were not comparable to caring for an adult, but the manikins were just big practice dolls, so nothing to be concerned about.

I was so busy learning, reading and taking quizzes I didn't think much about Papa's return until one evening after Julie handed me a letter addressed to Miss Anna Stanton and Miss Julie Stanton. "I wonder who this is from. Maybe it's from Tess's brother."

No return address.

The penmanship was recognizable.

Papa.

Just seeing his handwriting made the tasty macaroni and cheese in my stomach turn into a baseball.

Dear Girls, I hope you have been well behaved. I'll be home on the last day of September. My deacon training has been help-ful. Papa

"The church paid him to go away for deacon training?" Julie looked incredulous. "Why are you shaking?"

I sat back and tried to relax. "He's an evil sweet talker and people believe him. Papa is lying to hide his bad behavior from us."

Julie frowned. "He can be so dear and bad at the same time."

"Remember what I said. Don't trust him and don't go anywhere with him unless I'm there." I slapped the table. "I wish he'd never come home."

She looked sad.

I pulled her over to sit on my lap. "Julie, Charlene Davidson told me he raped her daughter. He sweet-talked both of them."

"You mean he pulled her clothes off?"

I nodded. "He should be in prison, but Charlene didn't think his cop friends would arrest him, so she went to the church. His deacon friends sent him to a counselling clinic. That's where he is."

Julie cried hard. She shook her curls. "He wouldn't do that."

"Remember the day he had you take off your clothes and dance for him? That's the beginning." I cried, hugging my crying child. "Don't ever let him touch you."

Julie went to bed early and when she was sleeping, I sneaked in and took my Chevy key and carried a couch pillow out to the garage. I decided not to start the car and just test the cushion fit. It was perfect after I adjusted the seat forward.

I tested the key putting it in and pulling it out a few times to practice the procedure quickly. The transmission shift positions were easy to read. I was careful to put the seat back into the exact position I'd found it so he'd never suspect. I'd done nothing wrong but went back in the house feeling very guilty for sneaking around. But I was ready.

Chapter 33 - Temporary Peace

The last week of September, school and our first two daycare work sessions ended at noon on the Saturday before Papa returned. We cleaned and dusted the house, making sure everything was in its place with his clothes clean and pressed. Julie wiped the last dish and placed it in the cabinet. "Do you see anything he could yell at us about?"

I made a quick round of the single floor simple home with three small bedrooms and two baths. I arranged the couch pillows, and when straightening the piano music I looked up at the photo of Tess and me. Based on my appearance today and Julie's, it could be us, wearing the same plastic smiles.

Julie came behind me and said what I was thinking. "It looks like you and me."

"It sure does. At least sometimes, we have real smiles."

"Yeah, when Papa is out of town." Julie sat down at the piano. "I think we have everything in order, so let's play some duets before bed."

In Sunday morning darkness, glowing green clock numbers told me 4:30 was too early to get up. I felt exhausted despite being in bed for more than eight hours. I listened to every freight and the 3 a.m. passenger train. Crossing horns sounded at the edge of our sparsely populated northeastern portion of Riverside, and soon I heard the familiar noise of wheels on numerous cars rolling along endless rails. Someday, I hoped to be riding the rails on the passenger train on a long vacation with Julie, going somewhere fun and far away from Riverside.

I finally fell back to sleep.

When I awakened, the sun was barely bright enough to provide light for Julie. She lay curled on her side facing me, reading *Winnie-the-Pooh*. Her eyes peered over the top of the page. "I'm feeling like Eeyore today, glum and sad."

"I'm sorry. Sometimes I feel like him, too. Come lie with me and maybe we can find a sunny place in the book, something to cheer you up."

Julie snuggled in with me and read aloud for a while and then flipped a couple pages ahead. "I marked this when I read it before because I like Christopher Robin and you sort of say this to me all the time, 'You're braver than you believe, stronger than you seem and smarter than you think.' You know what, I think we both are."

I laughed. "I think we make each other stronger and smarter because we help and love each other. That's the way it should be."

It was so comfortable lying together, so safe with nothing pressing to do. We fell back to sleep and got up about noon. We had no idea when Papa was going to arrive and had no reason to greet him as he usually said nothing or yelled at us, so we went for a walk. This time, around town with a stop at Edith's to say hello and discuss having Julie stay with her on Friday afternoons and Saturday mornings.

She was very happy to see us and invited us in for cookies and milk. I felt safe in her little home with the shades high, sunlight beaming in all the windows and delicate lacy doilies covering many surfaces. I asked her about a photo in an oval frame sitting on a bookcase. It pictured old people dressed in formal clothing.

"My grandparents, my mother's family, that's her on the right. She was thirteen in that picture. They lived in eastern Montana on a farm, immigrants from Germany."

We talked about early life, farming using horses, and about her mother's education in a one room school, with all ages of kids from the surrounding area.

Julie said, "Walking a few blocks to school here is a lot easier than walking miles in the winter wind on the prairie."

Edith agreed and said her mother was instrumental in her desire to become a teacher. "I'm sorry you girls lost your mothers. It makes life more difficult."

Julie hugged her. "You are sort of our mother and helped us a lot."

Edith's eyes teared. "You are the daughters I never had. I love you very much. Please come to visit any time."

We stayed for another cookie and then headed to the park to swing. I found swinging swished my stress away. The up and down, up and down, seemed to slow my heartbeat when I felt the dread of Papa's return. Swinging brought peace. If we had a swing in our yard I'd be out there often, just to reset my mind.

Swinging helped me think. Plans swung through my thoughts, forward positive thoughts about the future, backward thoughts of failing tests, forward to reassuring myself I'd do well in college, back to Papa's abuse, forward to escaping him, back to the bad life, in the end finding a safe new life.

Finishing a basic nursing associate degree was the first ticket to freedom with a nursing job. Then, when possible, to attend a four-year program to finish an advanced degree with my scholarship money and the ability to make more money.

Classes during the first month were not difficult. The hardest part would be dealing with Papa. Always a stress, not knowing what he'd do next.

When we arrived home, we found he'd come and gone leaving his suitcase in his room and dirty clothes heaped on the laundry room floor. We ate our hot dish with ground beef and macaroni in peace. Dinner was over and the dishes done by the time he walked in reeking of beer and found us sitting on each end of the couch reading with the radio playing music in the background.

"How did the counselling go?" I looked at him over the edge of my book.

His eyes stabbed me. "What the hell are you talking about?"

I let him stew for a minute. "Charlene told me your deacon friends sent you off for a cure so you'd keep your hands off Penny."

He sat down. "She's a damn liar. It was a training program for church deacons. I'm glad I went. Hope you didn't get into trouble with me not around to keep an eye on you."

"We were good. I love first grade." Julie the peacekeeper smiled.

"Glad to hear it. Some guys at Mack's told me there's been trouble around town, some break-ins. I don't want you out on the streets at night."

"We're home by 4 o'clock most days." Julie closed her book. "Do you want some leftover hotdish?"

"Not hungry. Ate my favorite burger with fried onions at Mack's. I leave early tomorrow morning for a run. What time do you leave for school?"

"Before eight." I expected him to demand breakfast or some form of waiting on him that would make us late.

"I'll be long gone by then." He got up and went to his bedroom.

We tip-toed around hoping he'd stay in his room.

I turned off the radio, checked the locks and hooked the lock inside our room before going to bed.

Chapter 34 - No Merry Christmas

In the weeks leading up to Thanksgiving and then Christmas break our home seemed normal. No yelling. Church on Sundays when Papa was in town where we sang hymns, and he gave us each a dollar to put in the collection plate. At home, civil discussions about food and groceries. Before Christmas break, Julie left her report card with all As on the table for him to see. He signed it without a comment. I didn't bother sharing my grades. Seeing me doing well in college would probably rile him.

After being off work for a month, he took longer shifts. His absence pleased us. My Friday afternoons and Saturday mornings at daycare brought in a few more dollars. Papa left us money, but I went easy on it, sometimes using some of my own for us to do a little thrift shopping and buy ice cream treats.

When the snow came, we were ready with hooded coats, boots, hats and warm gloves for our daily walks. Some days I wished we could drive to school in the Chevy, but I had no experience on ice. We saw cars sliding around corners and I wasn't prepared for winter driving, besides, it was out of the question.

We hadn't worn our Christmas dresses for a year. Julie tried hers on and examined herself in the door mirror. "I sure hope we we'll get to go to the Christmas eve service so I can wear this. It still fits fine. If I don't wear it this year, I might grow out of it."

"Papa hasn't said anything about attending a holiday service. I guess we should ask him. I saw it posted on the bulletin board the last time we went to church."

Julie hung up the velvet dress. "I'll ask him when he comes back."

Saturday afternoon we walked down to the Five and Dime. Julie wanted to bring the woman some cookies. I thought it was a nice holiday idea, so we made sugar cookies with frosting and sprinkles when we got home. I put cookies on a paper plate and covered them with plastic wrap for her.

The owner of the store was so pleased when Julie came in with the plate of cookies that she wiped a tear. Profuse thanks and a free candy cane for each sent us out the door smiling. We had made her and us happy. I told Julie we were doing things Mama would have done, only we have a little more freedom than she had. We bought a Christmas card to send to Steve Inman, hoping we might hear from him this year.

Before writing the card, we stopped by to visit Edith and bring her a plate of cookies. She was thrilled and asked us in for hot chocolate.

When we left, she sent home two identically wrapped gifts with us. "Now, don't peak inside. Open them Christmas morning." She waved good-bye from the doorway.

Walking in the crisp winter air under sunny skies with Christmas lights in windows and having finished my first semester of school, I felt happy. My decision to become Ann, with a mind of my own and a plan for freedom, made me feel stronger and able to stand up to Papa, at least a little. Anna still had to be Anna, the submissive daughter with the plastic smile, but Ann became stronger and stronger.

In the meantime, I remained Anna, his victim and hated myself for failing to expose his behavior and torture. Biding my time with a plan gave me the strength to fight.

I didn't think there was any real hope of Steve rescuing us. He didn't answer our card from the last Christmas. Maybe he didn't get it, or maybe he was still in the military and traveling abroad.

Maybe he was dead.

I wrote a friendly note about our schools. I included Julie's school picture and a small graduation photo of me, so he'd recognize us if he came to town. I gave him Edith's address and phone number saying not to come to our home as Dave had not changed since he'd married Tess. I'd told him in the first Christmas card that Tess died.

This time, I didn't ask him to come to visit, just that I wanted him to know we existed and that we hoped to include him in our family someday when we escaped from Dave's control. We both signed the card: *With* love, *Ann and Julie.*

I didn't want him to think we were begging him to come and save us. What military guy wants to be saddled with a couple of young relatives?

Chapter 35 - A Holiday Death

Completing introductory courses including basic anatomy and physiology were milestones in my nursing education. I loved both. Finishing the first set of final exams left me with a feeling of great accomplishment. My feet were light when I picked Julie up from school starting our Christmas vacation. I had purchased books for the next semester and already scanned the courses. Medical terminology interested me almost as much as psychology. Learning words like *nephrology*, the study of kidneys, was fun. I was sorry *Abnormal Psych,* was a higher-level class, but taking basic psychology the next semester was a beginning. I bought both textbooks because I wanted to know why Papa was so abnormal with such a crazy streak.

When Papa returned, Julie asked him if we could attend the Christmas eve gathering at church. He said it was a fine idea. He offered to pay for a trip to the hair salon as a Christmas gift, so we'd look spiffy that night.

Over the years, I had trimmed our hair but we both wore our hair long, and sometimes tied the curls back. The thought of a hair appointment had never crossed my mind.

Julie jumped up and down at the prospect.

"Go ahead and make appointments for both of you on the 24th in the morning. Better do it today because I would guess they get busy during the holidays." Papa handed me ten dollars. "I think this will cover it. You can have your hair trimmed a little, but not short. I like my girls to look like Goldilocks."

His words made my heart stumble. Mama had said that he likes young girls. For him *like* had a special meaning. A disgusting meaning.

"We love our holiday dresses from last year." Julie smiled. "I tried mine on and it fits fine. Thank you for the hair appointment."

After he drove off, we went to the kitchen for breakfast. Julie put cereal and milk on the table. I poured small glasses of juice for each of us. "I think he's behaving better."

"He's not drinking as much so he's not as mean to us." Julie ran to the closet and grabbed our coats. "Let's run to Edith's to use her phone to call and get our appointments."

We took an afternoon appointment, just after lunch. Julie and I had a great experience, being pampered, lying back in the chair with warm water streaming through our long hair making it curl more. Daisy Jo massaged my scalp, and it was so relaxing I nearly fell asleep. She told us we were beautiful and could be models.

It was nice to hear kind words and feel good on the inside, but as we walked home my thoughts drifted to the dark secrets hidden in my soul.

Julie skipped ahead in her bulky boots. Neither of us wore scarves or hats that would disturb our beautiful hairdos.

Papa was home when we stomped snow outside and entered. I thought we'd hear kind words about our hair. Instead, the smell of diesel fuel, onions and beer met us and we found him sitting at the kitchen table snoring, his head resting on folded arms.

We tiptoed into our bedroom to get ready for Christmas eve church. I whispered, "I hope he goes to bed for a while before we go to church. It starts at seven, so we have about four hours for him to sober up."

Julie placed her dress on the foot of her bed, then lay down beside it being careful not to mess up her hair. "I hope he's nice tonight."

"Me, too. I want to make hamburger hot dish for dinner. Let's just stay in here and hope he'll go to bed."

Within minutes, I heard him cough, then footsteps outside our room.

Slam! Our door struck the wall when he threw it open and stood glowering at us. "I've been waiting for you. Where the hell have you been?"

Julie scrambled away from him to the head of her bed, frightened. Her voice trembled. "We went to get our hair done." She turned her head to show him. "See."

"You should have left a note. Had a rough trip. A damn truck stalled on the tracks. I couldn't stop the train. Killed the driver. I'm going to bed." He walked away and closed the bedroom door.

I held my breath, thoughts spinning, trying to analyze the situation and wondered what the future held. "That's horrible. Someone died."

Julie came and sat on the bed beside me. "Will they put him in jail?"

I knew prayers and counseling wouldn't cure him. Now, he has killed someone. "I don't know. Maybe, and if he was drunk driving a train, he'll get fired."

Chapter 36 - More Worries

Julie placed a red cloth on the kitchen table. She added plates and silverware while I boiled rice and fried hamburger. Three place settings. We didn't know if Papa would get up and eat with us or not. Or what his mood would be. Would he go to church? We had better not rile him.

I served the food, a big bowl in the center of the table and whispered, "Let's walk to the church and sing carols even if he doesn't come with us.

Julie smiled. "Goodie. We need to sing. Christmas is supposed to be happy even if we don't exchange presents. We can make it fun."

About six, after we finished eating and washed our dishes, leaving Papa's on the table in case he wanted to eat. We dressed for church. I zipped Julie's dress and fluffed her hair. "You look beautiful."

She put on her black patent leather shoes. "These are tight, but I love them. I know I will have to wear boots, but I'll wear these around the house till we leave."

When we were ready, we sat on the couch waiting for time to leave. It only took about ten minutes to walk there. I turned on the radio to play Christmas songs.

About six-thirty, Papa appeared dressed in dark pants and a white shirt. His showered hair still wet and perfectly combed. "Well, isn't this festive. Two beautiful girls waiting for me."

Julie jumped up. "Do you want me to heat up the dinner for you?"

"No thanks. The burger at Mack's Shack is still stuck in my stomach. I'm not hungry. Let's go."

Papa walked ahead of us, too fast for Julie to keep up. She had to run at times, but I held her hand. She looked up at me, eyes sparkling beneath a streetlight. An angel with snowflakes falling on her lashes.

People greeted us. Some of the deacons nodded to Papa and said he was looking good. Lots of Merry Christmas greetings followed us as we walked down the aisle to our pew. We always sat in the same place, like others in the church. It was as if each family claimed a special place to sit and never gave it up. When someone didn't come, their absence was obvious to everyone. It usually meant they were out of town or someone was sick. I had wondered what they thought when I was missing for so many months, living at the Catholic home for girls.

Julie went in ahead of me and settled onto the bench. Papa next to me. I didn't want her to even sit beside him.

As I removed my coat and let it slump around me, I scanned the people filling the church. I spied Charlene and her daughter. My eyes locked on Penny, shocked by her appearance.

She stared back. Her beautiful red waist-length hair was gone, cut like a boy's, shaved on the sides. Hoop earrings as big a canning jar rings sparkled in a flickering line of candles in a towering candelabra near them.

Charlene smiled at me, her arm around Penny who wore a black turtleneck sweater. I hoped they were doing okay. I wondered if Penny cut her hair to repulse Papa. He liked his girls with long hair.

I turned back and hugged Julie. We waited for the music to begin.

Near the front of the church, the organist again swept in wearing a black robe with a red banner draped around her neck. She settled on the bench like a fat raven and after a few adjustments to the settings on the organ and wiggled to get her plump body positioned exactly right and feet on the pedals, her fingers struck the keyboard. Bam! "Joy to the World" filled the church with a booming sound so abrupt people startled, then jumped to their feet in song.

Julie giggled and stood with me and Papa as we all joined in singing.

Songs filled most of the hour. Preacher Bob's voice warbled above others at times, but later, his words shocked me. He told the Christmas story, led more songs, then his short sermon devolved from Christmas to prayers of thanks, and prayers for the soul of the deceased who suffered an untimely death that occurred, ending with, "Dave Stanton's train struck a stalled vehicle. Please pray for the family and for Dave. Amen." He led us in the Lord's Prayer and then we all sang "Silent Night."

On our way out, many of the parishioners hugged Papa and said, "You're in our prayers."

Little did they know how much he needed their prayers when his daughter prayed he would burn in hell.

We walked home without speaking. Papa strode through the house and out the back door to the garage. Minutes later, I heard the Chevy leave.

We didn't see him until the next afternoon but on Christmas morning we fixed scrambled eggs and toast before opening our gifts from Edith. We received beautiful matching doilies crocheted by Edith's loving gnarled fingers.

Julie held hers up to a window to examine the intricate pattern. "This is so beautiful. We need to go and see her to thank her in person."

Later in the day, the wind let up and we decided to brave the weather and walk the three blocks to Edith's. We looked forward to seeing her. I wanted to be sure she was doing okay. "With her knees aching in the bad weather, maybe we can help her with something."

Julie said, "We could clear her sidewalk if the wind hasn't blown the snow away already."

Edith invited us in for a wonderful visit. Julie decided to sweep the front sidewalk. She came back inside with rosy cheeks. We had steamy cocoa with tiny floating marshmallows waiting for her. I sat at the table with them sipping the delicious drink and noticed the local newspaper. The railroad accident was headlined. My stomach lurched. "This is horrible. It's about Papa's train accident." I picked up the paper and looked at a photo showing a crushed delivery truck and a jack-knifed derailed boxcar. "He said it was a rough trip and a man died when the diesel engine struck a stalled truck. Will he go to jail for this?"

Edith said, "I don't think so. The article says nothing about the engineer being impaired. It's hard for trains barreling down the tracks to stop. Is he home now?"

"He came home yesterday, drunk. We went to church, then he left and didn't come home last night. We don't know where he is." I shrugged feeling like I'd already said too much.

Edith hugged Julie. "I worry about you girls. If you ever want to come and stay with me, come over day or night. I have a spare bedroom upstairs."

Julie sipped her drink. "Thanks so much for the cocoa. Could we do a sleep-over sometime when Papa is out of town?" Julie beamed. "It would be so much fun. I'll help make dinner."

I thanked Edith and emphasized how thankful I was for the offer of refuge if we needed her help.

Back home again, we found a note on the kitchen table with a ten-dollar bill. Julie read, "Dear girls, I was proud to be with you last night at church. I packed my gear for another road trip. The railroad asked me to work an extra holiday run. I'll be gone at least a week, probably longer."

She looked at me, concern in her eyes. "Do you think this is the truth?"

"I don't know. He's drinking again. Let's try not to worry about his behavior and just concentrate on our classes."

Julie's downturned mouth showed her sadness. "It's stupid for kids to worry about a parent. I wish we had a normal family."

"I'm sorry. I try to be a good mother. I hope you don't worry about me."

"Oh, I never worry about you." She smiled. "You have two big jobs being a mother and a sister. You are the best Christmas gift ever, a mother who loves me."

Chapter 37 - New Year

The New Year came in with bitter cold blizzard conditions. Prairie winds swept through town drifting snow to the rooftops of backyard sheds and burying cars. Snowplows couldn't get through and ranchers were out trying to save their herds. Schools were closed until the weather improved and the roads re-opened. It gave us a few more days of vacation. Julie and I stayed home, well-fed, happily sipping hot chocolate and reading beneath warm blankets.

I wondered how things were going out on the rail line. There was no way to hear except by listening to the radio. Papa wouldn't pay for a telephone, so we had to walk somewhere to get help if we needed some. We didn't. We were safe. Happy to be alone. Happy he was gone.

We never knew what route Papa would take on his runs, but he had mentioned driving grain cars over the mountains to the West Coast on some trips. I had seen photographs in a news article about disastrous accidents in the Rockies in previous years. So, I knew part of his rail route over portions of the mountainous terrain during the winter could be hazardous. The railroad constructed sheds called snowslips over the tracks in high-risk avalanche areas.

Eastward from Marias Pass flatland stretched to the horizon. It was there that high winds swept off the east range and derailed strings of empty box cars being pulled along the Montana High Line across the flat northern stretch where wind blew unobstructed. So his route across the flat prairie land to the East could be treacherous because of winds and drifting snow. Driving a train sounds safe and easy but my thoughts carried me along the High Line rail route, never knowing where our father would be. Without his income, we'd be doomed. I worried whether he was home or working. Always uneasy. Not knowing what to expect. An untrustworthy angry adult who made our lives miserable, generating fear and sometimes restless nights but safer alone in a creaking house than to have him inside causing chaos.

When school finally opened, Papa had not yet returned. At the end of the first day back in college for me, and back in first grade for Julie, we were both excited to be learning. I had read the two psychology texts cover to cover but didn't find any information to help me understand our father's behavior. The texts steered away from covering perverts. I read all of my textbooks over the vacation to be prepared for classes.

Mama was a fast reader and taught me at age three to pick out words and begin spelling games. I'd done the same with Julie, so at six she excelled and was proud of her report card. I hoped we both would do well this semester and with Papa gone so much, our minds were less troubled and open to learning. As soon as he walked in one evening, doom and tension swept through the house like some sort of electric shock. I could see from Julie's stone-faced expression and stiff spine that she felt the same way I did.

Papa said little, as if he'd been gone a day or two instead of almost two full weeks. He dumped a pile of dirty clothing on the floor of his bedroom where I had dutifully picked them up and washed them since the age of ten. Washing clothes was a chore, but I loved the fresh smell when the job was done and was quick with the iron. He liked creases in his pants and in the long sleeves of his dress shirts. Except when he walked in stinking of railroad fumes or with beer joint odors clinging to his clothes, he looked and smelled like a good clean church-going man. Good on the part people could see.

Too bad they couldn't see into his soul.

For dinner, we all ate leftovers of our favorite rice hot-dish with hamburger, mixed vegetables and tomato sauce. Papa said grace, praying for all sorts of blessings, then served himself and took one bite. He pushed himself away from the table. "Anna, you can do better than this tasteless crap. Julie, you should start cooking and show your cousin how it's done."

Julie's expression remained frozen. She took a big bite, chewed slowly and swallowed. "Papa this is my favorite. I love it and helped Anna make it. What would you suggest we add to make it better to your taste?"

I was proud of her for being neutral and unemotional. I waited for his response.

He snapped. "Chopped onions and peppers. You should get the recipe Charlene and Penny use. They're good cooks." He took another bite, then got up and made himself a peanut butter sandwich he ate while donning his jacket. "I'm going to meet with the men at church."

We finished our first helpings and took more. Julie smiled. "I hope they teach him some manners. This is delicious. Let him go eat Charlene's cooking or PB sandwiches."

We were in bed by nine after a little piano playing and completion of school assignments. Before crawling into bed, we laid out our clothes for the next day.

The house was quiet but for a few noises from passing cars. I didn't even hear a train going through town before I drifted off to sleep.

Papa wasn't up when we left for school that morning in mid-January. At the end of each day, we carried mail in from the delivery box near our front door and placed it in a box on Papa's desk. This time, he had quite a stack from letters accumulating before the holidays. We added to the collection during the nearly two weeks in his absence.

Surprisingly, Papa returned in the afternoon after we returned from school. He had a fresh haircut and brought a huge load of groceries into the house including a box of oranges. He sat down at his desk to write checks to pay bills. Then drove off saying he was going to the bank and the post office. He wasn't back for dinner.

We put the groceries away, then fixed a simple dinner of toast and scrambled eggs before finishing our schoolwork. It was a simple day. No drama. Was this the new image of our father?

Chapter 38 - Springtime on the Prairie

After six days home with us, seldom speaking but on good behavior most of the time, he left on another work run. Weather was improving with more warming days and brighter sun. Our walks to school were easier without drifting snow and harsh winds. Weeks passed, good grades came in and our spring break from school was perfectly timed. Papa left town just before school ended so Julie and I were alone.

Late March breezes melted the remaining snow, and we got our bikes out. Some of our favorite trails like the one along the river bluff were still muddy but we didn't mind, we just hosed off the bikes on our return.

The break and good weather gave us the freedom to visit Edith and to see Opal at the library. They both commented on how much Julie had grown and were anxious to hear how college and school were going. Edith had a good connection with a medical clinic where her doctor worked, and she suggested I look for a summer job there. I loved the idea. I told her my nursing program adviser had previously suggested I should look for some sort of job in a medical setting.

Before school break ended, I showed up at an interview with trepidation. Not only would this be my first real employment, but it was also important for my future as an RN. Working at the daycare was just glorified babysitting but I could use it as a job reference.

The clinic manager talked with me first and then introduced me to a nurse who walked me through the clinic on a little tour. Three doctors and a few nurses worked there. They typically hired a couple extra people for summertime assistance to help cover vacations and increased volume.

My main job would be registering patients and seeing them back to the correct offices for their appointments. Hours were noon to five, five days a week. She asked me to wear black slacks and a white blouse, they would provide a name badge on a lanyard.

As I walked back to Edith's where Julie was waiting, I left feeling positive and anxious for their call to offer me the job. Julie heard me and ran to the door. "How did it go?" Edith stood behind her, listening.

"I think it went great, but my knees are still shaking." I collapsed in an easy chair.

Edith smiled. "I just hung up after talking to my cousin Sue. She's the manager you talked to. Based on what she said, your chances for being hired are good."

Julie looked worried. "I wonder what Papa will say. I'll do some of the housework, so you won't have so much to do."

"Thank you. We can manage the house together, but he hates not having us under his control."

Edith hobbled over and sat on the arm of my chair. "This is the right thing to do for your future." She squeezed by shoulder. "It's important clinic exposure and learning how to talk to sick folk."

I looked at her sweet face, crevassed by years of smiles. "I am so excited. I gave them your phone number since we don't have a phone. Sue said she'd call you. I didn't know you and Sue were related."

Edith nodded. "A distant cousin. They have a couple other applicants and will make a decision soon, maybe within two weeks."

At the library, we both checked out books and had a long talk with Opal. My book was about train travel across America. Papa's work provided free rail passes for us, but we had never used them except for the trip to Minneapolis for Julie's birth. I hoped we could have a wonderful trip someday, just the two of us, another one of my escape plans.

I found it stabilizing to look into the future, to better days away from Papa. He hadn't touched me since the deacons sent him away. It was such a relief, but I couldn't let my guard down after so many years of abuse, I didn't trust him.

I lived on the edge of a cliff. One false step and I'd fall over the edge and die. I believed Papa would kill me if I told anyone. Every day, I watched my footing and tried to remain safe, not sure what would make Papa fly off the handle and go berserk over some dumb thing.

I had to protect Julie. After my discussions with her following the tutu episode, I felt confident she knew the importance of never being alone with him. But I worried. She was so vulnerable and sweet, I had to talk to her again to reassure myself she'd scream, get help or run from him.

I still worked for the daycare on Friday afternoon and Saturday, but the rest of the afternoons following school, we'd work on schoolwork for an hour, eat a snack and then go for a bike ride. It was great getting outside with the wind in our hair after the long winter. As soon as the first crocus popped up, we waited for a few more before carefully clipping them off and placing them in a little jar to decorate Tess's grave. It had been months since we'd been out to visit her. Julie was excited to go for the bike ride and carefully placed the flowers.

The grass between the graves was greening but still short. Julie rested, leaning against the Stanton family stone, looking around the cemetery. "It looks like Jimmy has been out here raking and flattening that new grave we passed. It's nice he has a peaceful job."

"Yes. He is a calm man. I doubt he ever raises his voice, kind of like Chuck at the hardware." I looked at her. "We don't have much exposure to good men. It's nice to know they aren't all like Papa."

Julie's eyes turned cold. "Anna, how do you know? Papa acts nice and looks good in public, but he is a horrible man, like someone in a play, acting two parts, one good, one very bad, maybe all men are like him."

Such a comment from a six-year-old hit me like a cold wind, raising goosebumps on my arms. "Julie, you're right. I'm sad. You're young but see the picture so clearly. You do remember what I said about never being alone with Papa, right?"

Julie looked at her little clenched fists. "I won't let him hurt me."

Chapter 39 - Prayers Didn't Work

I was so excited about a possible nursing related job that Julie and I often stopped by to visit Edith on our way home from school. She almost always had a treat for us and when Papa was on the rails, we sometimes stayed for dinner. We'd cook together. She taught us new recipes and skills every time we visited. In late April, Edith answered our knock with the great news that the call from the clinic manager came through. Sue told Edith to have me stop to get details about my job and confirm a schedule.

Julie and I talked about the best time to tell Papa about my new job and defend my decision when he'd demand I quit school because Julie's care would cost him too much. We'd have the solution. She'd be staying with Edith. Instead of solving the problem, he became more demanding and abusive.

I think it was because he realized I was taking more control. His tirades included slamming doors and tossing whatever was within reach, mostly magazines or books. Lies spewed from his mouth about me running around with boys, that his friends would be watching me, that I'd never amount to anything, that I was a worthless slut. On and on.

Julie stood back, out of his reach trembling at his anger. I tried to block his words and thought of peacefulness, sitting on the bluff with the rushing river below. My escape thoughts were pierced by his painful words and his ugly acts when he dragged me from my bed, my lips sealed so Julie wouldn't awaken. My mind helped me survive. It split my body in two, one being abused and one flying away focused on my physical escape with Julie. But the escape side filled with more rage each day.

When we could get away from him, we'd go to the cemetery where in my mind Mama whispered encouragement to be strong and do well in college.

Two weeks before Memorial Day when school would end, we told Papa our summer plans over breakfast. He'd been home for two days and had come home drunk both days. That morning his bloodshot eyes wavered when I exclaimed about my good grades and how great college was going, - and that I'd gotten the clinic job.

Julie looked at me, holding her breath. She moved away from him likely fearing an outburst.

We waited for his response. It took him awhile.

"Good to hear." His words chosen, voice calm. "You'll be making so much money, Anna, you won't need to live here with me and Julie anymore. You can be out on your own, making your own rules without a care." He pushed back from the table. "I expect you to move out the day you get your first check."

I moved closer to him, daring him to strike me. "You're threatening me instead of supporting my efforts to become a nurse. I'll tell your deacon friends you're doing this to us."

"Ha. They'd never believe a worthless teenager." He laughed.

Julie stood behind me, her little hands on my shoulders. "Papa, you said lying was not allowed in our house. That's a lie!"

He pounded the table near her. "Julie, you're a child with a bad mouth. Don't talk back to me."

She moved to my side. "Anna and I take care of the house, cook, wash your clothes and even iron them. You never say thank you. That's bad manners."

"I'll thank you for staying out of my business. I want Anna out of my sight!"

Julie cringed. "Papa, you're not acting like a loving father."

He glowered at her. "Shut your mouth." His hand moved so fast she didn't have time to duck. He backhanded her striking her cheek and mouth.

She shrieked and ran from the room, crying.

I stood and pushed the table toward him, screaming. "Abuser! The deacons know you're a sinner. They'll believe me."

I ran from the kitchen. "Julie! Julie! Where are you?" I found her in our bedroom looking in the mirror at a red welt rising and swelling lips.

The back door slammed. The junker revved and sped away.

I hugged her. "I'm so sorry I couldn't stop him." I cried, my tears dripping on her blond hair. "I'm so sorry. Are you okay?"

She looked at the ceiling, wiping her tears with shaking hands. "I told you I wouldn't let him hurt me. He did but it's my fault. We'll be okay together. Please don't move out and leave me with him."

"Never. We better tell Edith about this in case we have to move in with her."

Julie stiffened. "Would he hurt her? She is so old."

"She has good locks on her doors. You can stay there when I am working this summer. I have to work so we have money to escape."

Julie left the room and returned holding a cold wet washcloth to her face. She took a stuttering sobby breath, trying to control her tears. "I have to tell Tess. Please, let's go to the cemetery. Maybe we should tell Pastor Bob the prayers and deacon classes didn't cure him."

Chapter 40 - Trying to Hide

I sat on the bed thinking through what had just happened, my arm around Julie, not knowing what we should do. Kids don't have many rights. It's legal for parents to strike kids to make them behave. But this time he injured a six-year-old, my baby. Damn him. I had to document the injury for a police report that might be sooner than I had previously thought. I had to save the evidence and my need for a camera had come true.

In the fall, when Julie was with Edith, I had walked downtown to the Post Office and stopped in the drugstore for menstrual pads. It was then I saw a display of small disposable Kodak cameras. We have so few photos, I thought it would be fun to take some pictures of Julie. As I was paying for my purchases a dark thought came to me. I might need it to document Papa's behavior when the time came to get help and report him.

We had taken a couple pictures by the river bluff, but this was a time to use it for something else. I explained to Julie that I needed a picture of her injuries to prove Papa struck her and cause the injury to show police evidence of his abuse.

Having the evidence would help to prevent Papa from taking her away from me and gaining custody. I took three pictures and then hid the camera with my Chevy key.

Julie held ice to her lips to decrease the swelling. After holding a cold wet cloth to her red cheek, the swelling decreased. From Mama's little make-up kit I got from her bedroom dresser drawer. I patted face powder over the red marks to hide them from snooping eyes. We hung around the house hoping Papa wouldn't return, and then, in the late afternoon, we headed to the cemetery with PB sandwiches for a dinner picnic with Tess. We avoided downtown and rode our bikes along side streets where we'd be less likely to meet someone who might see Julie and ask what happened. We would have had to lie.

Crossing beneath the metal arch at the entrance of the cemetery seemed to have magical powers, like entering a magnetic field that lowered stress and steadied my flipping heart. Tense muscles relaxed after a few minutes of sitting beneath the big oak near Tess's headstone. Our bicycles lay nearby beneath a leafy lilac bush with large buds beginning to open.

I looked at Julie's marred face. "I'm glad we brought something to eat. My stomach has been upset. Maybe we can eat out here. How are you feeling?"

"Scared." Julie touched her puffy lip. "This shouldn't happen to kids."

"We have to stop him." I looked down in sadness at my mother's headstone. "I know Tess would support us running away, but we have to be ready with a plan on where to go and what to do."

"Edith said we could stay with her. She told me she doesn't like us staying alone when Papa's out of town."

"She doesn't realize we're in more danger when he's home."

Julie dug in her jacket pocket. "Here's a cookie. I thought we needed treats after the kind of morning we had." She smiled.

I took a bite. "Thanks. We live a strange life, going to the cemetery to talk to the dead."

"It's simple. They don't tell." Julie turned her cheek toward me. "How bad does this look, now?"

"Better. Just being out in a cool breeze might have helped and the makeup covers most of it."

"Thanks for fixing it."

"I wish it was fixed. He had never hurt you before. This worries me."

Julie took a bite of her cookie. "I'm afraid."

We sat in silence until the familiar sound of an old car motor in the distance caught my attention. "Hide, quick. It's Papa. Long ago, he forbade me to come here."

We crouched down and slid beneath the big lilac bush, pulling our bikes under the branches with us. I whispered, "I don't know what he'd do if he found us." We huddled together, trying to be small.

The car slowly came up the rutted narrow road, closer and closer.

I held my breath.

He stopped near the Stanton plot, within feet of us.

Exhaust fumes reached my nose, mixing with lilac smells making me want to sneeze.

We didn't move.

After minutes that seemed like hours, the gears ground and the car inched away. I sneaked a peeked and glimpsed Papa's head moving back and forth as if scanning the cemetery until he slowly drove out of sight. The car came back into view on the next cemetery crossroad where he turned away from us, heading toward the entrance. The rusted dark green junker then turned left at the highway and sped toward town.

Julie trembled in my arms. A few minutes after her shaking subsided, I sat up and stretched my cramped muscles. "We can breathe again."

She got up and walked around Tess's grave. "Grandma Tess, it's been a long winter. Now that it's spring, we'll come out more often. Today was a terrible day. We need to tell you and maybe make a plan to leave home. But we won't leave you, we'll be back."

I let Julie explain what happened to her and added a few comments including the photos.

If Mama knew, she would be heartbroken. Long after her damaged existence with him, Papa continued to smash her dreams and harm her children. He would never stop. I knew talking to the dead was foolish, but it helped to say the words out loud to someone, even to a dead person.

Chapter 41 - Violence

Papa's grip was gone when we got home, so we assumed he'd left town on another rail run. We couldn't be sure. When we placed our bicycles back in the garage, his junker, usually parked outside next to the garage was missing, and the Chevy sat safely inside beneath its dust cover.

Two days later, on Monday morning, Julie's face looked almost normal. No one would ask her what happened. I picked her up at school carrying an armful of books I'd checked out from the school library. On our way home, we decided to talk to Edith, ask her advice about Papa.

We knocked on the door and found no answer, so we walked around to the back door and knocked again. "I don't hear anything inside." Julie cupped her hands around her eyes and looked into the kitchen from the porch. She jumped back. "Oh no! There's blood everywhere." She shrieked, tears pouring down her cheeks. "He killed her. Maybe he killed her. Now, he'll kill us. Let's run away."

I looked inside. Blood drips and red streaks trailed to the sink where a bloody towel draped, hanging off the counter. I didn't see Edith. I shook the door. Locked. She always kept them locked.

I grabbed Julie's hand and pulled her around to the front door. Locked, too. "Come on. Let's go to the library and get help from Opal."

We ran most of the three blocks then up the steps and through the door. We were out of breath when we reached the back office. Opal jumped up from her desk. "What's wrong?"

Julie's eyes filled with tears. "Something happened to Edith. The doors are locked and there's blood everywhere."

Opal grabbed her phone and dialed.

The phone rang and rang. "It could be serious. Let's close up the library."

Did she die? I couldn't take a deep breath. Edith was a grandma by age but a loving mother to us. I'd always felt we could count on her. She had helped me through troubled times as a twelve-year-old with a newborn baby and scarcely able to change a diaper. I had counted on her to calm Julie if she had a fever or earache. Now, when Papa was getting more abusive, and we might need her help in an emergency, what would be do without her?

Would Papa kill her to stop her from taking care of Julie and stop me from attending college? I felt weak and had to sit down.

Edith might be dead.

Opal interrupted my dark thoughts. "I'll leave a note on the door. Let's go." After she made sure no one was quietly reading in a nook or among the bookshelves, she taped her note to the door and locked up. We ran down the back steps to her car. She sped to Edith's house.

I watched her skills and decided she'd make a good getaway driver.

We stood at Edith's door knocking when a car drove up. The driver opened the back door and helped Edith get out. We rushed to help her.

"Lordy, lordy, why are you all here?"

Opal took Edith's arm. "You weren't home and there's blood everywhere. We thought something terrible happened."

The tall thin taxi driver, a young-looking grandpa with a trimmed white mustache, took Edith's other arm and helped her to the door.

Edith waved a hand wrapped in bandages with a spot of oozing bright red blood. "I have to keep this up with an ice bag on it."

Julie looked pale as she held the door letting them pass. "What happened?"

"I did what I taught you not to do. I was chopping onions and not paying attention. Chopped one finger right to the bone. It squirted so much blood it made me feel faint, so I wrapped it in a dishtowel and called my ambulance driver. This is Ted. He always helps me in a pinch."

Ted walked her to the easy chair.

She took a ten-dollar bill from her handbag and gave it to him. "Buy some gas and lunch on me. Sure, appreciate the help."

"Glad you're doing better, Edie. Let me know when you're ready to play cards again." He waved from the doorway and left.

Opal was in the kitchen. She stood in the doorway and called, "Glad you called Ted for help. You sure left a bloody mess in here. I tossed out all the onions and washed everything in hot soapy water."

"I was making hotdish. Guess that was a bad idea. The girls like it and I was hoping to have them stay for dinner."

Julie sat on the arm of the overstuffed chair beside Edith. "I'll make a hotdish for you, okay?"

Opal heard Julie. "Edith, what do you think of us cooking together and calling Jimmy to join us. He can bring the pie I baked this morning."

This arrangement turned out to be a wonderful ending to a tough day. Edith would be fine. After stitches and ice, the bleeding stopped. We put her to bed with her hand up on a pillow. Before we left, she gave me a spare key to her front door so we could always come inside if she didn't answer when we knocked. If she was away, she'd leave a note for us on her kitchen table. And - I thought, if we needed to suddenly get away from Papa, we could let ourselves in even if she was gone.

We didn't get to share our concerns with any of them. The scare with her was enough for one day. They didn't need any more stress.

Jimmy dropped Julie and me off at home. We locked the door behind us, then decided to go out back and see if the junker was still gone. Had Papa really left town? Was the junker parked in the railyard?

The car wasn't by the garage and I hoped he was gone.

We locked the doors and checked the windows before going to bed behind our own locked bedroom door.

Julie fell asleep quickly and I lay looking at the shadows flitting across the ceiling as cars passed on the side street. I listened to freights sounding their horns in the distance and then rattling through town. The characteristic passenger train horn was more musical than the freights. I found it pleasant, meshed with thoughts of someday being on the train waving at little girls on roads, like Julie and I waved from the river bluff road east of town. Finally, I fell into a restless sleep that carried me to dreamland where Julie and I stood on a railroad platform dressed in long white gowns blowing in a light warm breeze. A passenger train approached. Its musical horn coming closer and closer. I had our tickets. We were ready to board. My view was hazy. We ran closer.

The diesel, dented in the front, passed by. The engineer waved and beckoned to me. Signaling to come join them.

I froze.

It was Papa.

Brakes screeched. The train slowed. The baggage car passed, then the diner. The second passenger car stopped in front of us. One woman in the window looked like Tess with long red tinged curls ... or was it Penny? She waved and encouraged me to board.

Tess stood in the breezeway between cars. Yes, definitely, my mother shooing us away. Mouthing, "Run. Run. Go away. Go away." Next to her, hanging over the railing was a dead man, his head crushed, face purple.

Someone waved inside the passenger car. An old woman with a white face and red lips with straight white hair, stringing out from beneath a spring hat with a pink band and a flower as big as a man's fist. Both her hands waved as if trying to pull me toward her. Tess's dead mother, Sally Inman. Next to her stood Rex, Charlene's dead husband. His sad face blood stained.

A man ran toward Julie and me.

Papa.

I screamed and screamed. "We are not going. We are not going on the death train."

Edith shuffled past us, headed toward the train with a little suitcase.

"No! You can't go on that train." I grabbed her arm pulling her with me. She hurried with us away from the train, stumbling because of her crippled knee, but all three of us escaped.

Papa couldn't catch us. He ran back as the train pulled away with him hanging onto a handrail while climbing aboard.

Someone shook me. "Anna, Anna, it's okay. Wake up. Wake up."

Julie turned the lights on and sat on my bed, trying to calm me.

I cried and hugged her. Confused by the nightmare. Trying to figure out what it meant.

Dead relatives and friends beckoned us to join them.

Papa driving a smashed diesel pulling a death train even the dead man he killed hung over the railing.

Was it a warning? Is Papa going to kill us? Take us for a ride on his death train?

Julie patted my shoulder. "Lie back and rest. I'll bring you some warm milk. It will help you calm down and go back to sleep. I'll stay with you."

A few minutes later, she returned with a mug of warmed milk. "Sit up so you can drink this without slopping."

I followed her instructions.

Julie took the empty mug back to the kitchen. I heard water running, presumably rinsing it and placing the cup in the dish drainer. She followed Papa's rules even under these circumstances. *Leave no dirty dishes or you will be punished.*

She returned and crawled into bed with me. I fell asleep with her little body snuggled against mine. Breathing in cadence, I listened to trains in the distance, real trains, not death trains.

Chapter 42 - Reprieve Above the River

A week passed before Papa showed up on Saturday afternoon. Julie and I reached home after I walked to Edith's to pick her up after my last day of work at the daycare. I had put my last check securely in my pocket before leaving and thanked her for the reference for my application to work at the medical clinic. I was happy and looking forward to no work for the two weeks before the end of the school year.

You would think I might be sad leaving the nice job with the kids, but it was a relief. Without the daycare job, I had a couple of weeks to focus on finals, another step toward our freedom. Summer break from school would occur after Memorial Day, just a couple weeks away.

Papa's presence sitting in the kitchen as if waiting for our return stopped us cold. He didn't give us time to even say hello before tearing into us about being insubordinate and talking back to him after his last lapse of civility. "I expect respect. I pay for this damn house and your food. I even pay for piano lessons, but that is going to stop. You know enough to continue without my help." He slammed a fist on the table next to a small paper sack. "I just had coffee with my cop friends. They tell me you have been bicycling all over hell and gone, even out to the cemetery. You're venturing too far from home."

I wanted to slam his words with mine but thought better of it and stared at Julie's stone face.

Papa yelled. "Say something, dammit. What are you, statues?"

Julie stiffened. "You hit me and bruised by face and lips the last time I spoke to you. I'm afraid you'll hit me." She backed away, her eyes fearful.

He stood, took a step and grabbed her arm and pulled her toward him as he sat back down on the kitchen chair.

Julie gasped. A little scream escaped her lips.

I stepped forward. "Let go. You're hurting her. I'll go to the cops this time."

Papa shoved me away and pulled her to his lap, wrapping an arm around her.

My thoughts shot back to him naked, making me sit on his lap. I jerked his arm away from her. "Don't touch her, dammit, or I'll tell your friends."

A laugh erupted. "You sound so tough. I told you before, my cop buddies wouldn't believe you."

I pulled Julie off his lap and behind me. "I'll keep going to the station until they do believe me. There will be a record and eventually they'll stop you from torturing us."

Papa laughed again. "No way. Chief Carl's a good friend." He pulled a spray can from the bag. "He just gave me a can of their latest weapon. Mace." He shook the can as if getting ready to spray. "It's small and handy. Disables the creeps they have to deal with. Makes them cough and go blind with pain until they get them cuffed. It works on kids, too." He put his finger on the trigger and aimed at me. "Maybe I'll use it on you if you don't behave."

Julie and I rushed out the front door and stood away from the house breathing heavy beneath a tall pine tree near the street. "I'm not sure what to do." I hugged Julie.

"Let's take a walk." She pulled me toward town. "He scares me."

"I have my last check in my pocket. We can go cash it so we have some money in case we need to leave home." We walked downtown to the bank. A cop car came toward us and parked along the sidewalk. We kept on walking and looked the other way, then ducked inside the bank. I felt intimidated even though I had no idea why the officer had stopped. Maybe Papa called him.

When I pulled the check from the envelope a note fell to the floor. Julie picked up the paper and held it while I cashed the $100 check, asking for small bills.

I tucked the bills into the envelop and walked out with Julie. She read the note aloud. "Dear Anna, Thank you for all the kind care to the children. Have a great summer. You will be a wonderful nurse. Love, Doris."

Julie hugged me. "This is a very nice note. Doris likes you."

The note helped blunt the dismay I felt after our confrontation with Papa. We stood on an empty sidewalk outside the bank. "I think we should tell someone about Papa, but I'm afraid of what he would do. He said he'd kill me and keep you if I told anyone about him really being your father."

Her sweet face looked up at me. "It's a long walk, but I think we need an ice cream cone."

Protecting her gave me strength. I took her hand. We turned down the street toward our destination located about a mile away and across the railroad tracks. We usually bicycled but this was a terrific day for a long walk and ice cream to settle our stomachs. At the railroad crossing, the long wooden arms came down, bells rang, and the red warning lights flashed.

Julie clapped her hands. "Oh goody! It's the passenger train. We can wave at them."

My thoughts spun to the death train dream, but I wanted to say something positive for Julie's sake after facing Papa. "Every time we see the train, let's think about where we want to go when we don't have to worry about Papa anymore. I think we should go to the Pacific Ocean. Where do you want to go?"

"That's easy. With you, anywhere. We'll be happy together."

With all the money in my pocket, I treated us to sundaes. Julie ordered her favorite, strawberry, and I got hot fudge. Feeling much better after eating, we walked toward home and had to pass by the thrift store. Charlene's car, the one Papa bought for her, sat at the curb in front.

We walked inside to look around and spotted Penny in the back of the store trying on a purple mini skirt. Her long legs and thin body looked terrific in the style. Papa would scream "slut" at me if I put one on. When she saw us, Penny turned around in the triple mirror checking her backside. I stopped to admire her. "Penny, that looks terrific on you. Is your mom with you?"

"No. I got my driver's license, and she lets me take the car. Payback for what your father did to me." She scowled.

"I'm sorry for you." I flushed. "He's a terrible man."

Julie stood mask faced. Her eyes on Penny. "You look pretty." Then sadly looked at her own plain jeans, dull blue shirt and feet in scuffed play shoes.

Penny crouched down to Julie's level. "You are a beautiful girl. Let's go find you a bright frilly blouse. We can all look together."

I was shocked by Penny's friendly gesture. If the situation were reversed, I sure wouldn't want to be near a pervert's kids, but she seemed sincere.

We had a wonderful time choosing pedal pushers and bright shirts. Julie found a pink shirt trimmed in lace. She also found a pair of shiny black patent shoes to replace the pair she'd outgrown.

We walked out together, and Penny offered us a ride home. She was a particularly good driver. I watched her every move thinking it might help me when I began driving or had to get behind the wheel of a getaway car.

Papa was in the backyard washing the Chevy when Penny drove up and dropped us off.

He looked up, shut off the hose and walked toward us. "Where the hell have you been?" He watched Penny make a U-turn and head back toward town.

We said nothing. I turned to go into the house.

"Answer me, bitch!"

Julie stopped and glared. "Don't talk to Anna like that. You need to stand in a corner and have your mouth washed out with soap."

Julie and I walked up the front steps. "We were talking to Penny. Why do you ask?" I stared at him, out of reach. "I know what you did to her. The deacons saved you that time."

His eyes widened and face morphed to rage as he spun around and stomped toward the backyard.

I surprised myself when the words spewed out of my mouth. They clearly bothered him. I wondered what he'd do to make me pay.

A few minutes later when I looked out the kitchen window into the yard, he was sitting on a lawn chair staring into space. I hoped he was worried.

Our pleasant encounter with Penny gave me hope she would talk to the police when Julie and I found the right time to get help. I kept a detailed diary hidden in my room with all the dates. What he did. Penny's terrible experiences. The deacons sending him off for repentance and now his lapse into violence.

We busied ourselves in the house washing our new clothes from the thrift shop, then hung them outside instead of using the dryer. I told Julie about the delicious fresh smells when Mama and I used to take the sheets off the lines. She even hung them out in winter. The white sheets would freeze stiff and then usually after a day or so, the moisture would evaporate, and the cloth would hang limp instead of stiff like sailboat sails. Sometimes we ironed the sheets when they were still damp.

For weeks after Mama died, I walked around like a zombie missing being by her side doing everything together. I even hung the laundry outside and would hug the bundle of clothes I removed from the line and smell the freshness, reminding me of her. I was very lonely but grew up knowing about keeping a home because we did lots of work together. It was horrible without her. But now, I wasn't lonely because I had Julie and we did things together.

Sometimes I felt like I was living in a mirror world, an alternate world of some kind. Repeating an existence that seemed like a dream. Living in a mirror with no end.

Mama's picture with me that sits on top of the piano is a painful reality. Julie and I look like that, only younger with empty eyes. My constant fear was that papa would kill me and take Julie for his honey, repeating another generation of torture.

Somehow, I had to escape his control and abuse. Instead of the silence of fear, I would someday end the silence and expose the truth. But I couldn't until I had a plan for survival without our dependence on him. I feared authorities would separate us and put us into abusive foster homes. I wanted us to walk out of the mirror into a new life, no longer invisible to the world, hiding and muted.

When I looked outside, Papa and the Chevy were gone. What a relief.

Julie took the clothespin bag and a folding chair to stand on so she could hang the new clothes by herself. She came back inside to help me fix dinner. We made three hamburger patties with chopped onions mixed in, then cooked them over low heat. One remained for Papa in case he came home later and wanted to eat something. I don't know why we were ever nice to him at all, but he occasionally made a positive comment. We were always hungry for a kind word from him.

By the time we finished eating and cleaned up the house, our clothes had dried in the warm May breeze. I touched them up with the iron before we dressed in the new outfits and went for a bike ride out along the river bluff where we could see to the horizon, Rocky Mountains to the west and prairieland to the east. I brought a light blanket for us to sit on.

The orange sun melted behind the distant mountains streaking layers of high stacked clouds a brilliant apricot color. We sat in silence after climbing over a rocky area out of the wind. I hid our bikes, so no one would see us.

I wondered what my little girl was thinking after such an ugly day. I had to protect her from harm, the words a little girl should never hear, and awful things she should never see.

Papa had become meaner and less predictable, stabbing me with fear. When he struck Julie, it reminded me of how helpless I had felt when I was thirteen and baby Julie was asleep in the next room. I had to protect her and endure whatever he handed out.

Papa's violence toward a six-year-old brought back the raw fear that had paralyzed me for years. I saw myself on the floor in a corner of his bedroom, naked, crying, bleeding, afraid I might die from what he had done to me. I was hopeless and helpless.

Then he laughed, threw a blanket to me, walked into his bathroom, and turned on the shower.

When I was sure he was in the shower, I crept to my bathroom, locked the door and lay in the tub with water running on me. Hot water, too hot. My skin turned red. I scrubbed and scrubbed but knew I'd never be clean.

His violence and mace were ominous. Every day brought more concern.

I leaned against a large warm rock and watched clouds move eastward. Julie lay against me. After she fell asleep, I laid her across my lap. We had found peace beneath the big Montana skies.

A distant train whistle awakened her. We pedaled back to town, arriving home before dark. The house was empty, but that was no real relief because I knew he was still in town.

Chapter 43 - Telling

A car door slammed in the dead of night. A few minutes later, I heard him at the back door fumbling with keys. The door finally opened and closed. Footsteps crossed the living room and stopped. Floorboards creaked outside our bedroom door.

I held my breath as flashbacks of his torture pulsed my thoughts. Dreading he'd try to drag me to his room or keep me up all night yelling and telling me how sinful I am.

If he entered, this time I would scream and fight him. When he struck Julie in the face, I reached my breaking point.

I had to protect her, and I'd rather have her see a fight than for her to become his next victim.

Scanning the dark room illuminated only by streaks from the back porch light, I saw no weapon to use against him if he entered. The small hook locked us inside.

I heard his breathing as he stood just outside our door. Then – the doorknob turned.

The door opened a fraction of an inch. The hook held.

Another rattle of the door.

Then, crash! The door casing splintered, the hook and eye dangled, useless. I don't know what I had been thinking to believe such a tiny lock would keep him out. He was on me in an instant, screaming obscenities. With a fistful of my long hair, he jerked me out of bed, slapped me and shoved me backwards. I fell striking my head on Julie's bed.

She screamed. "Stop it. You hurt her!"

Julie was on her knees on the floor beside me, touching my face. "Mommy, oh, Mommy are you okay? Don't let him kill us." She wailed.

I felt stunned. Confused. And then paralyzed after realizing what Julie had said, not knowing what he'd do with the secret out. He knows she knows. What will he do now?

He flipped on the bright ceiling light. His distorted angry face and with a strange twist of fear in his eyes, he turned to look at the hook and splintered wood. "Bitch! Stupid bitch. You told her."

He laughed out loud, a wicked laugh. "A couple of stupid kids thought they'd lock me out of my own house. What a laugh. I control you. Remember, you are mine. Without me you are nothing."

He took a step toward us.

We couldn't move fast enough, and his boot connected with my thigh. I cried out in pain.

"Shut your mouth. You deserve worse. If I didn't have to work to support this goddamn household, I would stay home tonight and torture both of you, but I have to hit the rails on a long trip. Don't do anything stupid. My buddies know to watch you. Stay home!"

His bedroom door slammed.

+

Julie helped me up. She pulled up my nightgown and looked at my leg. A dark bruise was already spreading, and I had trouble standing. "You need ice on that. It looks awful."

I grabbed her arm. "Don't leave the room. Stay with me."

We both got into my bed, sitting bolt upright, leaning against the headboard.

As soon as his shower turned on and he was busy, we scrambled to get dressed. It was a hot sticky summer night. Julie wore shorts and a shirt but after seeing how awful my leg looked, I wore jeans to cover it. Julie ran to get a bag of ice cubes for my leg and returned with the ice pack and the broom. I thought under these circumstances, it was strange for her to want to clean up the little mess of splinters on the floor.

When I asked her why, she shook her head. "It's the only thing I could see we could use to hit him with if he comes back."

I was trying to decide if he was really leaving, if we should stay, or if we should run away in the darkness, get away and then decide. There was no time to worry about the decision because he appeared in the doorway dressed in work clothing, his grip of clothes in hand. "Get in the kitchen and make me some sandwiches. Make it fast. I can't stand being around you after what you've done. I'll see you pay."

We were too afraid not to comply and jumped around like monkeys again, following his orders. Julie made coffee for his thermos, and I wrapped a stack of his usual sandwiches for the lunch pail. He stood over us watching between pacing back and forth across the kitchen. When I closed the lunchbox lid, he snatched it and Julie opened the door for him to leave. He stomped out with his hands full and drove off in the junker.

We clung to each other crying. Julie sobbed. "Our secret came out. I didn't mean to tell. Now he will kill us." Her little body trembled. She sat on the kitchen floor crying. "What are we going to do?"

I sat down beside her. "He's gone. He can't hurt us now." I took a deep breath trying to think and calm myself. "It's Sunday morning. We can do anything we want."

"Let's bake a cake and bring it with us to visit Edith."

"Perfect. How about angel food."

"Oh, good. I like it plain without frosting."

After bathing and shampooing our hair, we let it dry and curl naturally. It felt good to be clean. Like washing away some of the terrible things our father had said and done to us. I talked about doing something nice to help erase all the sadness and fear Papa caused.

After eggs for breakfast, we went to work baking. While the cake was in the oven, Julie vacuumed and dusted. By the time it was done, the house was so clean it would have made Papa smile, - maybe.

Edith greeted us with open arms, accepted the cake with a big smile and set about thawing some frozen strawberries. We particularly liked sitting on her bench swing on the back porch in the sunshine. We relaxed there talking after eating. I hated to break the happy feelings but decided it was probably a good time to bring up fears about Papa's behavior, not knowing how much I should divulge.

Julie took our dishes inside, and I could hear her working in the kitchen washing them. With her out of earshot I talked about my new job and how my first year of college was coming to an end. Edith assured me Julie was great help and company, so she was looking forward to the end of the school year and when she'd be staying with Edith each afternoon when I worked.

"That is perfect. I won't worry about her staying with you. The job is so important, I want to be sure I can concentrate." I hesitated to say more. Exposing Papa's behavior carried terrible consequences and I wasn't sure how Edith would react.

"Why would you worry about Julie?"

"I don't know what I would do without your help. She's too young to leave alone and I don't trust Papa, so I never, ever, leave her with him." I slumped back in the swing and set it in motion with my foot.

"He's never struck me as a very loving father, but I remember your reaction when he picked her up from here a on her birthday last year. You never told me why, you just ran out of here like a maniac to find her."

"Edith, he's an abuser." My voice trembled.

"What do you mean?" She took my hand. "Is he hurting you girls?"

I looked at Edith's gnarled fingers gripping mine. "Since Mama died, he's done bad things to me. He drives around town like he's a hardworking church goer. He's a deacon. Everyone thinks he's a good father because he looks like one. It's an act."

Edith listened, still squeezing my hand.

"No one would believe me if I called the cops. They're his friends." Tears filled my eyes. My chin quivered as I tried to say the words. "He said he'll kill me and keep Julie if I told anyone how he treats us." I couldn't bring myself to tell her the whole truth.

"My god, child," Edith cried out. "That's horrible. Where is he?"

"Gone for a week. Working."

Edith looked around as if hoping Julie wouldn't return and hear our conversation. "We need to get you out of that house and get help."

"It's okay. She knows. Julie and I have a plan to leave. We are biding our time but thought we should tell you in case things get worse. Could we stay here with you in an emergency?"

She stood up. "Move here now! Before he gets back!"

I tried to calm her down and reassure her that things were tolerable right now but said he had been acting worse and recently struck Julie.

Julie walked in and sat beside Edith. "You both look upset. Did you tell Edith about Papa?"

I nodded.

She put her arm around Edith's shaking shoulders, tears running down the old woman's cheeks.

Edith wailed, hugging Julie and whimpering. "My babies. Oh, my babies. Why didn't I see it and save you? Oh my god. I'm so sorry."

Julie hugged Edith and patted her face. "Don't be sad." Julie looked at me, eyebrows raised as though wondering if she should reveal *the secret*.

I shook my head. "We are going to move away from Papa when we have enough money to leave. That will be one year from now when I can get a nursing job to support us, if we last that long."

After we had all calmed down, I told her I was saving money and had secretly learned to drive. That way, I could take a car to leave, maybe go to Falls City to report him when the time was right. I explained he threatened to kick me out after I turned eighteen. I could be on my own and he didn't want me in college. He said he would cut off the money and would never let me take Julie.

Edith sat there shaking her head. "Sweety, I won't sleep a wink with you in that house. I want you to move in now. Come upstairs and see your bedroom." We followed her up the stairs, her old knees making it a slow journey.

The sunny bedroom on the top floor with a slanty roof had dormer windows with rag dolls sitting on each window still. She fluffed the pillows on the twin beds and opened the closet door. "See, everything is waiting for you to move in. It's a big closet, ready for your clothes."

We sat on the beds and talked some more. I suggested, "How about moving a few sets of clothes and shoes, so if we have to escape in the night, we'd have something to wear the next day."

Edith liked that idea and opened bureau drawers to show us there was room for underclothing and socks. "It's yours. I wish you'd stay here tonight. Try out the beds."

Julie lay down on one, being sure to keep her shoes off the flowered quilt. "This is super comfortable." Her eyes twinkled and a real smile spread across her lips.

Before we left that afternoon, Edith bagged a loaf of homemade bread and a container of egg salad for sandwiches. We had to reassure her again and again that we were safe, Papa was gone, and now that she understood our situation, we felt safer.

Edith's eyes still showed worry. "So, Anna. If either of you are at risk, promise me you will come here day or night."

We promised.

Chapter 44 - Our Bedroom at Edith's

Later in the day, we made our sandwiches and ate outside at the picnic table that was rarely used. Mama and I used to sit there to read, and drink iced tea together in the shade. Now that Julie is older, we do the same on occasion, one of those mirror images with us looking just alike and repeating what Mama and I did.

But I hoped we would end the cycle and make sure Julie and I would be the last of Papa's girls, and never add to that line of girls that reflected in the three-way mirror where there was no end. We had to break that image forever.

Mosquitoes chased us indoors and Julie set about packing clothes to deliver to Edith's house while I cleaned up the kitchen. Then, I joined her and laid out some things on my bed, including a pair of tennis shoes and a sweater. She suggested we both bring at least one pair of shorts in case it was hot.

I found two large paper grocery bags in the back porch cabinet to carry our belongings. I added lotion, extra toothbrushes, and a comb. "I'm sure Edith would let us borrow things we don't have."

Julie nodded as she carefully folded our clothing and slid them into the bags. "Let's bring these to Edith's tomorrow. It will make her feel better to know we haven't forgotten our promise."

I walked Julie to school the following morning. We left a little early to make time for a stop at Edith's to leave the bags there on the way. She was already up and just called for us to come in after we knocked at the door. She was grateful we'd stopped by with our clothes and sent each of us off with a cookie.

At the college I went to the large library to study. I felt comfortable and safe in a soft overstuffed chair in a corner near a window that looked out across the campus. Actually, some days I felt as though Mama was reading over my shoulder and approving my plans.

After memorizing medical terminology, I studied anatomy. Both important tests I'd be taking in a few days. I picked up a schedule of summer classes, not because I wanted to attend while working but I liked to survey options because I loved school. The catalog of courses available and the requirements for my nursing program for the following year looked interesting. I was especially anxious to begin the clinical patient care work.

The law enforcement curriculum stopped me. I had no idea the college offered those classes. Crime Scene Evaluation sounded intriguing, but I knew I was a better fit for nursing than being a cop. On my way to an afternoon physiology class, I bought a drink from a vending machine and ate the peanut butter sandwich I'd brought in my book bag.

After class, I returned to the library to kill time until I needed to leave to pick up Julie when her school day ended. I scanned a couple nursing journals and thumbed through a law enforcement magazine, stopping on an article about mace. I read a second one about the use of stun guns. Both made me worry. I hoped the Chief wouldn't give Papa a stun gun. It would be terrible to be awake and paralyzed, unable to run from him.

I took a tear-out ad from the center of the magazine to order a catalog for police gear and requested it be mailed to Edith's address. Maybe I'd be ready the next time Papa came to my room at night. But I had another thought, could I buy mace or pepper spray in Riverside? The article mentioned hunters could carry it to prevent a bear attack. I checked the clock. I had plenty of time to rush downtown to a sporting goods store and see what they had.

The spray can cost more than ten dollars, but I had the money and decided it might help us. I didn't tell Julie because I didn't want her to worry. I read the pamphlet on its use as I walked to Edith's, then closed the paper bag and tucked it in with my books.

I forced brighter thoughts about long peaceful walks and being without Papa in town for the next week. Julie was in great spirits and skipped half the way downtown to buy a bunch of groceries. We had a lot to carry but enjoyed fresh bananas as a dessert after dinner of delicious bologna sandwiches with cheese.

The rest of the week passed quickly but waiting for him proved ominous. We didn't know if he'd be mean, drunk or both. Days with him being friendly had been fewer than during the winter. Good weather didn't bring a good mood, leaving us uneasy. We dreaded his return after the last confrontation, splintered door, violence and threats.

From past experience, his schedule would have him home a few days and then gone over Memorial Day weekend. We'd be alone, out of school and free for the summer, except for my afternoon shifts at the clinic a few blocks from Edith's house. That sounded wonderful.

On a bike ride before dinner, Julie and I rode along side-by-side talking about the next weekend and Memorial Day. On that Saturday, we decided to put flowers on Mama's grave and on her mother's. So far, the only flowers ready for picking were daisies and Forget-Me-Nots.

Last year's parade in our small town consisted of the high school marching band with a tall guy playing a piccolo, the military veterans carrying flags, a couple cop cars, a firetruck and some farm machinery followed by a string of cowboys and cowgirls on prancing horses. Maybe Edith would like to go to the parade with us. It would be a struggle for her to walk downtown with her bad knee. I hoped someday soon, I'd be able to drive her.

We turned around at the west end of town after hearing a freight train whistle. Julie pedaled fast. "Maybe that's Papa. We could warm up leftovers and share it with him."

We put our bikes away and she set the table while I put the rice and hamburger hotdish on the stove to heat. "Just put out two plates, he usually shows up earlier than this."

"You're right but he's usually drunk, so no telling when his shift ends. He might be at Mack's Shack with his buddies already."

Julie helped herself to the hotdish. "Let's eat fast and go for another ride so we won't be here if he is getting off that train. Hurry."

I liked her idea but ate two helpings of my favorite rice dish with Parmesan cheese sprinkled on the top. We washed the dishes and grabbed our bikes. Riding along side streets, we pedaled west again after Julie suggested a stop to visit Opal and Jimmy. They weren't home and there wasn't much to do in a small town on a Friday night, so we went to a playground to swing until dark.

He didn't show up that night, or on the weekend.

On Saturday, Julie and I sat by Mama's grave and talked after placing flowers in her grave for Memorial Day. The wind picked up, flapping small American flags placed in a row along the road near the entrance and on the soldier graves. Later, we rode out to sit on the bluff overlooking the prairie and wheatland where dust devils rose over plowed fields. From there, we went to Edith's for a visit and to see if she wanted to go to the parade. She decided to stay home with an ice pack on her arthritic knee, so we walked downtown without her.

The parade passed us where we sat on a cement stair in front of the bank. Julie loved the marching band and drummer. The marching piccolo player waved and gave her a big smile.

We walked home talking about summer and how well school had gone for both of us. Better than we could have imagined. The parade was fun but didn't seem to be enough of a celebration for the two of us.

Julie finished first grade with all As and I completed my first year of the two-year nursing program with high scores, but Papa wasn't home to share the great news with him.

The next day I'd start my new job, another step in the road to freedom.

We reached home exhausted but feeling good with our accomplishments. I unlocked the door and held it for her. She smiled, "Papa may not care, but I know Tess would be proud of us."

We left our grades on the kitchen table for Papa to see in case he returned during the night. I hoped he'd be pleased but based on his behavior when I got the little job at daycare, I worried he'd be furious and see the clinic job as a loss of control over me.

Chapter 45 - House Hunting

Tuesday, following the holiday weekend, Papa's bed was empty, so we still didn't have to deal with him. After a breakfast of French toast, we cleaned up the house and left about 11:30 for our walk to Edith's, allowing me to reach work on time.

At home, we left a note on the table beside our grades, reminding Papa that Julie would be with Edith and my new job hours would be noon to 5:00, so we'd be home about half an hour later.

The sunny day added to our spirits. I noticed Julie appeared truly excited about our plans for the summer. Her blue eyes twinkled and had lost that vacant look I'd seen too many times. She flashed the same fake smile I had when we had to talk to people. The smile I had learned from Mama. A plastic smile and empty eyes looked at people who touched our existence, as we disguised our deep fears and concerns. I would have to work on real smiles at work when I greeted the patients.

I stayed a few minutes to talk to Edith. She said their afternoon would be busy, washing the inside windows and washing the kitchen and bathroom curtains. Some spring cleaning, she called it.

The small medical clinic was a couple blocks off Main Street about four blocks or so from Edith's. It sat on a corner, a nice single story brick building with the choice of a ramp or a few steps up to the front door. Sue, the manager, met me and introduced the staff of two doctors, four nurses and a couple secretaries. The staff was all female except one physician, a proper gray-haired guy with a trimmed beard and a pleasant smile, they called him Dr. Joe.

I smiled and shook his hand. "Nice to meet you, Dr. Joe."

"Sue tells me you're in the college nursing program. That's great. We'll be sure to give you lots of experience here at the clinic. I hope you enjoy the job."

Each one of the staff greeted me in a friendly way except one of the RNs, a chunky lady named Arbutus about fifty who walked with a limp and looked like she was having a bad day helping a deaf elderly man into a wheelchair. She grimaced and grunted lifting him. "Hi, Anna. Good to meet you. I hope you are ready to work. We're getting busy."

I assured her I was ready, but was glad when Sue told me she had assigned me to registration on my first day. I thought it sounded less stressful than helping with sick patients. I liked the idea of helping those with appointments reach their proper doctors or to the lab for a blood draw, and then making appointments when people were checking out. Sue said, "You'll be here for a few days until you see how things work. I will gradually rotate you to other positions, eventually taking vital signs and recording information for the doctors before escorting patients to the exam rooms."

Sue complimented me on my outfit and handed me a short white professional jacket and an ID on a string to wear around my neck. Patients streamed in, sometimes filling the small waiting alcove where educational medical fliers and magazines helped them pass the time. I felt very professional in my jacket helping people as they came in for care.

On my fifteen-minute break, I rested in the staff lounge, and read a nursing magazine. I found my first day, at least the first few hours were positive, a great step into the future. Before closing time, Sue had me sign some employment papers and said I'd done a perfect job.

I reached Edith's a little late because of the time it took to check out with Sue and found them sitting on the bench swing on the back porch reading. "The windows look terrific, curtains, too. It sure smells good in the kitchen."

"Julie ironed the curtains. She's a great help." Edith got up and went to the refrigerator. "We boiled a chicken and made some great soup." She handed me a Tupperware container. "I thought you might like some as part of your dinner."

"I'd love some. We'd better get going, Julie. We left that note for Papa." Julie gave Edith a big hug and followed me to the door.

Edith looked worried.

Julie explained, "He hasn't been home all week, but we thought he might be back and wonder where we were."

We waved goodbye and I hurried, trying not to slop the soup, hoping he wouldn't be waiting for us.

We were eating dinner in the early evening on Friday after our week when we heard the noisy motor of the junker stop in the backyard. Soon the kitchen door opened. Papa stared at the two of us finishing our hotdogs and beans. Not the most creative meal, but I asked if he'd like to join us.

I already knew the answer based on the onion breath trailing behind him when he walked through the kitchen and into the living room doorway where he turned and spoke. "I got into town about noon and came home. It would have been appropriate for you to leave me a note, so I'd know where you were.

Julie moved a stack of papers that rested near the salt and pepper shakers toward him. "We left these for you on Tuesday morning since you didn't tell us when you were coming home."

He snatched the papers, scanned the grades, and read our note. He threw them down on the table. "Good job, Julie. As for you, Anna, I suppose you are making so much money you're ready to move out. There's a nice spot under a bridge where you can hang out with the bums until you finish college. Julie and I will live in our comfortable home." He patted her shoulder. "She's big enough and smart enough to take care of herself when I'm on the rails. We don't need you anymore. You're worthless."

Julie screamed and jumped up to my side. "If you kick her out, I'm leaving, too. You're no father. You don't even love us."

Papa reached for Julie.

I pulled her my way, knocking over my glass of water and slopping it onto his pants.

In a swoop, he backhanded me, knocking my head to the side.

Julie cried out. "Oh no! You hurt her again! Stop it!"

Papa grabbed my hair and jerked my face toward his. "It's just a little bruise on your ugly face. Don't bother calling the cops. I'll tell them you sassed me and deserved it." He walked into his bedroom and slammed the door.

Julie looked closely at my face. I could feel it swelling and hurting. Tears stung my eyes.

"Anna, it's red. I'll get some ice for you and do the dishes. Go lie down."

I took the ice cube in a plastic bag and went to our bedroom, feeling distressed by his volatile behavior and violence against me again. He seemed more unstable and unpredictable. What would he do next?

I closed my eyes, holding the ice to the swelling and listened to my sweet young daughter working in the kitchen like an adult. Papa remained in his bedroom. Soon Julie joined me and closed the door. We stayed quiet as little mice, hoping he'd stay away.

After Julie fell asleep, I gathered some important items and placed them in my book bag and hung it on a hook just inside the closet. I'd included my small purse with extra cash, my driver license, earlier photos showing Julie's injuries and the Chevy keys. I tucked my nightgown with the ugly dried blood stains and Papa's underwear in the bottom, thinking the stains would prove I wasn't lying. The last item I added was the pepper spray, on top and easy to grab.

I put on my ruby ring knowing Mama's presence would provide strength if we ended up in the final fight.

I didn't sleep at all.

I thought about slipping out in the night to hide at Edith's. Maybe I was being an alarmist, but I knew what he could do when he lost control. He had struck both of us and that hadn't happened in many months. I had to protect Julie from much worse.

Saturday morning, he roused us out of bed and said we were going for a ride in the Chevy. Julie's innocent excitement filled me with fear. He never took us for a ride. We got dressed and while we ate a simple breakfast of cereal, he explained his intentions.

"I want to take you out west of town to see a place I have been thinking of buying." The house is bigger than this and I might let you have a dog or cat."

I wanted to be excited but had learned never to trust him. I immediately panicked at the thought of being out of town, way out where we couldn't walk to school, or to my new job. Way out where we couldn't get help.

My hands shook so much I could barely eat. Julie didn't notice. She gulped down her glass of milk and collected our dishes. We quickly washed them. Papa was already in the car with the motor running, waiting for us.

On our way out to the car, I whispered, "Don't be too happy. I don't believe him."

Julie scowled. He motioned her into the front seat and me in back. I sat behind Julie and scanned the dashboard, noting the mileage. I wanted to know how far out he was taking us.

It was a sunny day and under different circumstances I might have enjoyed taking a ride in his treasured car. He turned up the radio and played jazzy music with the windows down. What a nice day to take a ride with a loving father. Hmm.

We passed the turnoff to the cemetery located about two miles from downtown, three miles further he turned north toward the river and then took a right at a For Sale sign onto a short dirt road ending at a collection of small buildings and a large faded red barn. A one-story house that looked like it hadn't been lived in for years sat beside a covered walkway to a single car garage. Both buildings with peeling yellow siding and cracked windows, I hesitated to walk up the rickety wooden steps with grass growing up between the boards. The best thing about the place was a yard covered with white daisies beneath a collection of towering Lombardy Poplars and cottonwoods.

Julie and I cupped our hands and looked inside through the grimy windows. A mouse scampered through a sunbeam smearing a shadow across worn out cracked linoleum. Julie looked at Papa. "This is ugly. That poor little mouse." She turned to leave. "I don't want to go in."

"It's a fixer-upper." Papa unlocked the door and pulled Julie in with him. "I'm good at repairs and there is a lot of room for cars with a garage and a barn."

He opened the door wide. "The ad listed three bedrooms. You'd each have your own."

That thought filled me with dread. How could I protect her from him? I looked into three small rooms, one without windows looked like a cage.

Julie's footsteps echoed on the wooden floors as she walked around. "Where is the bathroom."

Papa laughed. "I saw the outhouse when we drove up. You'll be taking sponge baths at the kitchen sink while I watch."

I shuddered at his words and walked out in the yard where the prairie wind whipped the daisies. A sharp gust scattered driveway dust then spun into a dust devil skipping across the road as it picked up speed and rose over an adjacent field. A bad omen.

Julie came up behind me. The wind muffled her whisper. "It's scary out here."

Papa suddenly appeared behind her. "Let's go see the barn."

We followed him, dreading the next experience.

He opened a side door revealing a tiny beam of light from a couple high windows. The smell of moldy grass and manure clung to my nostrils. The dirt floor was cushioned by scattered straw. Pigeons fluttered when he walked over and looked in a stall. Dust rose with each step. "Looks like a perfect place to lock up kids."

We backed out into fresh air and bright sun. Julie coughed. "Papa. this place would give me asthma and nightmares."

"No wonder it's so cheap. I wouldn't even park my Chevy in a barn like this or that garage." He closed the door. "We can go now if you take off your shoes before you get in the car. I don't want you dragging in a pile of dirt."

We sat with the car doors open and removed our shoes, brushing dust from them. Then put them on and tied the laces inside the car. Papa just clicked his heels together to knock off the sand.

I looked back as we drove away, never wanting to enter another house like that. It looked sad and lonely, not even fit for mice.

Chapter 46 - More Trouble

Papa dropped us off at home and sped away, not saying where he was going or when he'd be back. We sat on the back porch. I felt dejected, sad, and worried about what he was going to do now.

Julie seemed to read my mind or at least had similar feelings. "What will he think of next?"

I shrugged. "Who knows? Sometimes, he acts like a mean kid with no manners and no brains. I'd be afraid to get a kitty or dog. We can't trust him not to hurt it."

Julie's little whisper, "Or us."

About half an hour later, he pulled in and showed us a newspaper ad. "Look at this. It's a better house, a little more money and the other direction along the river East of town. I picked up the keys so we can go look at it." He headed back to the car. "Get a move on. Let's go."

When he turned off the highway, the odometer read three miles from our house. Julie's eyes drilled Papa. "This is way too far. We couldn't walk to school every day."

His voice was light, a forced happy tone. "It's on the bus route. You could take it, but Anna would have to walk."

Before I could say anything, Julie said, "No! She'd freeze to death in the snow and wind."

He slammed on the brakes, skidding to a stop. His face red with fury. "It's time you learn how to speak to your father. Anna should quit college and homeschool you, so you don't get so many big ideas." Papa pounded the steering wheel and spun gravel when he accelerated, driving too fast and skidding to a stop about a mile later.

Flat land marked with a few rounded hills and sage brush stretched for miles. Wind whipped the grass and slammed the car door as soon as he stepped out.

Julie turned to me. "I'm not going to even look. He can't make us move out here."

Papa walked toward the white single-story home with red shutters but turned back when he realized we weren't following him. He jerked our doors open. "Get out."

I shook my head. "We won't move here. You can't make us."

Julie closed her door and locked it.

He pounded on the window. Saliva spewing as he yelled, "Open the damn door and get out."

I remained sitting in the back seat. "Look, Papa. We like the house in town. There is no reason to move."

He walked around the back of the car and entered the driver side. Without a word, he drove back to the highways and turned toward town. He drove like a madman, passing cars and finally stopping at our house. "Get out of my sight."

Julie got out and closed the door.

I opened the door and got out. "You could have killed us driving like that." I closed the car door, expecting him to drive off.

Instead, he struck the steering wheel and yelled, "Bitch! I'll kill you with my bare hands if you don't shape up and do what I say."

Tears poured down Julie's cheeks. She grabbed my hand. "Hurry, come on."

We went in the front door. I locked it behind us.

Julie ran to the back door to check the lock. "I'm afraid he'll hurt us when he comes back. What can we do?"

Papa didn't come home that Saturday night. We were both awake half the night not knowing what to expect. I felt better when the sun came up and the house was empty. I had just dressed, and Julie was still asleep when a police car parked near the front door.

I stood out of view, wondering why the car had stopped. Then, a uniformed officer got out and helped Papa out of the front seat. I held the front door opened and noticed Papa was limping as he walked up the sidewalk.

I just looked at them, stone faced, waiting for an explanation.

Papa's bloodshot eyes glared at us.

I stared. "What happened?"

A Band-Aid on his forehead, tangled hair and bloody shirt looked like trouble.

The cop helped him up the steps to the screen porch entry to the house. "He had a little trouble last night."

The officer looked at Papa as if expecting him to say something. The young man I'd never seen before said, "Dave got himself a drunk driving and reckless charge from the Highway Patrol. Had to tow the car away."

Papa snarled. "Where is it?"

"Bob's in Falls City."

"Appreciate the help." He shook the officer's hand. "Thank the Chief for offering to put in a good word for me with the judge."

The policeman left.

Papa walked into his bedroom and slammed the door.

We stood there looking at each other. I motioned for Julie to follow me to the kitchen, out of earshot to talk. "It'll be expensive to fix the car."

Julie nodded. "I'm glad. It might stop him from house hunting."

After breakfast, we left him a note and stayed away most of the day, bicycling. Miles from home and tired, we rested at our favorite ice cream shop, sitting on a park bench outside the front of the store. Watching happy kids with smiling parents coming and going. I noticed Julie sat silent. Her eyes blank, ice cream melting. No smiles.

I hoped she'd be happy and safe someday. I worried about unknowns, what lay ahead for us.

Julie looked up, tears glistening.

I put an arm around her. "Why are you sad?"

"I'm scared. I want a new house far away from Papa."

I agreed. "We're in a bad situation that no one sees. Everyone thinks he's a good father."

"Sometimes he's nice but I want to leave home."

"Run away?"

Julie nodded. "But I wouldn't leave you. We have to go together."

"We can't. If he found us, the police would let him take us back home. Kids have no rights."

I thought for a while knowing I had no answer but to wait until I could support us on an RN salary.

Julie looked hopeful and licked the drips before they escaped the cone. "We have Edith."

"I'm afraid he might hurt her. It's an emergency escape."

"Would Opal and Jimmy help us?"

"When Mama died, they offered to let me stay with them when Papa was on the rails. They didn't realize I was in more danger when he was home."

Happy families passed us. At first glance, I'm sure we looked like two normal sisters enjoying ice cream. Some of them looked away quickly, maybe when they saw our blue eyes as cold as ice, living in our own world, faces frozen.

They didn't see our pain.

We looked good, hair combed, nice clothes, enough money for bikes and ice cream, but bound by invisible ties, threats and secrets. There was no escape.

A familiar loud car engine approached. I held my breath and looked down, hoping it wasn't Papa but if he was looking for us, he might not notice us. Unfortunately, the junker drove past and then circled back.

Papa parked in front of us and got out. "You're a long way from home. I've been looking for you." He threw open the back car door. "Get in." He grabbed both bikes. "I'll put them in the trunk." He lifted the bikes in, leaving the front wheels spinning, hanging out.

We got in.

He drove off. "We are going to look at the Chevy in broad daylight."

We passed many businesses and a large hospital before driving through Falls City, the next town, about five miles south. He stopped at Bob's Body Shop and went inside. Soon he signaled us from the door to follow him. A man led us into a high fenced yard next to the store lined with a dozen crashed vehicles.

I spotted Papa's. The driver's door and front end showed scrapes and dents, the windshield spider webbed.

Papa walked around the car and pointed to his bruised forehead where he'd removed the bandage from a two-inch stitched gash. "Guess my head broke the windshield. I swerved to miss a deer and ran into the ditch and sideswiped a tree. Should've just killed the damn deer."

The shopman opened the passenger door. "Anything you want to get out of the car before we get to work on it?"

From the glove compartment, Papa removed his pepper spray can along with some papers. He handed them to me. Then, he took a toolbox from the trunk. "I guess that's all I need. How long before it's done?"

"We'll put it in line. I'd guess about a week." He scanned a paper. "Superficial damage and a new windshield won't set you back too much."

"I'll stop back in a week with the cash to pay the bill. Thanks."

I put the items I was carrying into the trunk with his toolbox. He closed the lid and ordered Julie to sit by him in the front seat. I watched her stoneface as she climbed in. She fastened her seatbelt and leaned toward her door as far away as possible from him. When he got in, she said, "You weren't wearing your seatbelt last night."

He glared at her. "How would you know?"

"Your head hit the windshield."

"Guess I forgot." He fastened his belt with a flourish. "Glad to see you have yours on. I wouldn't want you to bump your pretty face on something if I stopped too fast." He rubbed his head. "Bad headache. Maybe a hang-over. I need more sleep."

At home, he went to his room and closed the door.

A couple hours later, he staggered into the sunlit living room, squinting. "What time is it? I forgot to call dispatch."

Julie walked to the doorway to see the kitchen clock. "Ten after three."

"Damn. I have to hurry. I can't go out on the rails tomorrow because I have to appear in court. I need to make some phone calls." He showered, dressed, and left.

Julie looked worried. "Court? Will they throw him in jail?"

"I doubt it, but we don't really know what happened. That cop said nothing about a deer."

After pulling a few weeds in the flower garden, we cut bouquets for graves. The cemetery always calmed me.

We decided to take our time and walk after our long bike ride in the morning. We each carried flowers and a bottle of water for the vases at the graves. As we neared the cemetery after very little conversation, Julie looked around before talking. Then whispered, "I wish Papa would run away from home."

I smiled. "We wouldn't send the cops out to get him and bring him back, would we?"

"No, but we need him to pay for stuff. I wish they'd keep him in jail. It's like making him sit in a corner for being bad."

After arranging the flowers on Tess's and Sally's graves, we sat in the shade, silent. Julie got up and walked around the graves. She read grandpa's head stone. "It's too bad Tess's father didn't save her. Was he an awful man like Dave?"

"Oh, no. Tess told me he was loving."

Julie's mouth turned down. "But he let her go. I bet that broke Tess's heart."

"Sometimes, we make mistakes. He died trying to fix it."

She sat with her little arm around my waist. "Papa could never fix what he did to Tess and you. I hope he doesn't get me too."

"I'll keep you safe." I took her hand. "Come on, let's go and do something to cheer you up. I'm starving. How does pizza sound?"

"I love pizza. Are we going to buy a frozen one and bake it at home?"

"We could, but I was thinking about going to the Whistle Stop. Some of my college classmates go there. I hope we don't see Papa. It's close to the station where the passenger train stops."

We found a dark corner in the back and settled in to watch the other people. A teenager in blue jeans, cowboy boots and a red shirt waited on us. "Hey, ladies, you look like twins! Whatcha want to drink. I'll be back to get your order while you sip something icy." She handed us menus.

Julie pointed to one choice. "This looks good, Canadian bacon and pineapple."

The waitress brought our cokes. Julie asked her, "What size should we get?"

"Medium. You'll have a couple slices to take home. That Hawaiian one is my favorite. I'll ask the cook to add extra mozzarella for you." She walked away, her single long braid swaying.

"She's pretty. I like her." Julie leaned back in the booth sipping her drink. "I'm feeling better. It's nice to see happy people."

We stayed at least an hour and enjoyed every bite. Like the waitress said, we had leftovers that would be good later.

It was almost seven by the time we reached the empty house and went to bed early after a long day.

The slamming refrigerator door awakened me, then Papa swearing. Our bedroom door swung open and struck the wall. He flipped the wall switch, turning on the lights. Julie sat straight up.

"What the hell are you girls doing eating out?" He held up a pizza slice. "With all the bills, we don't have money for this." He took a big bite of one of our slices. "I hope you enjoyed it. You won't be going out again anytime soon."

He sat on Julie's bed. She moved away from him.

He moved closer. "Where do you think you're going?"

Julie looked at me, fear in her eyes.

"You're scaring her. Yelling. Eating our pizza. Why are you doing this?"

"Because I can. I own you. There is nothing you can do about it. I hold the purse strings."

I stood up, my bed between me and where he sat on Julie's bed. "I used my own money to buy that pizza."

"I don't like you working. You're getting high and mighty. Quit the damn job."

"No. It's training for my nursing degree. I need it."

"You both better shape up or you'll be out on the street. I'll be in court in the morning. I need some sleep." He walked out leaving our door open.

I closed it and looked at the splintered door casing where he'd forced his way into the bedroom breaking out the little lock I'd put on the inside. It sure didn't keep him out. It just made him mad. I kissed Julie on my way to bed. "I hope you can sleep now. If you can't, crawl in with me."

Chapter 47 - We Need Help

I heard Julie in the kitchen when I awakened. I dressed in my work outfit and joined her. She looked up when I walked in. "I want to go live with Edith, so he doesn't come home and hurt us." Her little hands shook as she held the gallon jug and poured milk on her cereal. The full jug was heavy for her, but she liked to show me she was strong and could do adult jobs. Today was different, her fear from the night before showed. Tears ran down her cheeks when she sat down.

"I wish we could live with Edith, but we have to talk about it." I ate my cereal quickly. "We can go as soon as I make three mayo, cheese and bologna sandwiches, one to share with Edith. She always feeds us. I think we should pay her back."

We locked up and fearing he might see us on the street, hurried to reach Edith's as soon as possible. She answered our knock wearing a nightgown, her silver hair still in pin curls. "Oh my! I thought it might be the paper boy. Are you okay?"

Julie burst into tears. "Papa's home and he's being mean."

"Come on in." She closed and locked the door.

Hugging Julie, Edith looked to me for an explanation.

I grimaced. "I hope you don't mind we came early."

"Sit down with me. What's going on?"

Both of us explained what had happened the night before.

Edith asked, "What about the car accident?"

Her question surprised me because we hadn't told her.

"Opal said Jimmy saw his crashed car being towed through town towards Falls City. It was a mess."

I told her what we knew of the incident and thought it might be why he was so angry and taking it out on us. "He's in court today and had to cancel a railroad trip, so he's missing work because of the accident."

"This has to stop. I don't know what to do." She patted Julie. "I don't want you out of my sight."

"I think he'll leave for work after court, maybe not until tomorrow. We'll be okay when he's gone."

"Can't you stay here with me tonight?"

"I don't want him to be suspicious. If he thought we had any plan of leaving, we'd be in real trouble."

Julie looked my way. "We didn't tell her about house hunting. They were ugly houses out of town."

I added, "He's looking for a place to isolate us and make me quit my job."

"We can't let him do that." When I left for work about 11:30, Edith assured me she and Julie would stay home with the doors locked.

My day working with the registered nurses was very busy with lots of distractions. They taught me to take temperatures and blood pressures. I had wondered if I really wanted to be a nurse because I wasn't even sure what they did except from stories I'd read. Papa rarely took us to see a doctor and we'd never been really sick. I had little experience with doctors or nurses except when I birthed Julie.

By five o'clock I was exhausted but satisfied that nursing would be a job I could enjoy.

Edith and Julie had a delicious dinner ready when I reached the house. When we were eating biscuits with hamburger gravy, Julie said, "Papa drove past many times. I stood behind the curtains watching. I don't think he saw me."

"He knows you stay here, but we didn't tell him where I work. I hope he doesn't cause more trouble."

We had to reassure Edith we'd return if there was any problem at home. She stood in the doorway looking sad when we walked away. I wished we had a telephone so we could call her.

Julie read Papa's note and handed it to me: "I got off with an $85.00 fine for speeding and caught a ride to join a crew down the line tonight. Won't be back till next weekend. STAY HOME!"

I put the note back on the table. "I hope he learned a lesson. From what that cop who brought him home said, he was drunk driving, too."

Julie made a face. "Can you drive a train when you're drunk?"

"I think he'd lose his job if they knew. I guess the Chief got them to drop that charge."

"Let's fix dinner, something good." Julie opened the refrigerator and rummaged around. "There isn't much in here. I guess we could make macaroni and cheese. Is that okay with you?"

"I'll help after I change clothes. I need to save these for work tomorrow."

The next four days were busy, and time passed quickly. Edith and Julie were a good match. Edith said she needed the company and they enjoyed cooking together. Edith's neighbor had grandchildren visiting so Julie had the opportunity to meet and play with some new acquaintances.

With Papa gone, it was a nice reprieve from worrying about what he'd do next, and it set me thinking about a life away from him. Unless they put him in prison for what he did to me, I was concerned I'd be afraid of him showing up at unexpected times for the rest of our lives, no matter where we went.

In desperation, I decided I'd try one more time to get in touch with my mother's brother Steve. He really cared about Tess, I wondered why he hadn't written to me and Julie. Maybe he was afraid of Papa, too.

I wrote to him late one night when Julie was asleep. I didn't know what to say but decided to invite him to visit us. This time I provided both Edith's and Opal's addresses and phone numbers. I explained that Dave had isolated us, we were without a phone at home, and hoping to escape his control soon. I told him I was sorry if I sounded crazy but thought he might have some ideas to help us.

Later, I told both Edith and Opal I hoped they'd be getting a letter from Steve Inman addressed to me. They knew I'd tried before with Christmas letters to no avail. He probably didn't want to be troubled by a couple of relatives, so I held out little hope.

Sometimes when we went to the cemetery and saw the flags waving over veteran graves, I wondered if he had died in the military. I thought we were his only living relatives so no one would know about his death here in the small town on the prairie.

Chapter 48 - More Threats

At the end of the week, Julie and I walked home from Edith's talking about having a nice evening and maybe taking a bike ride, thinking Papa wouldn't return until the next day. My thoughts changed when I heard noises behind the house as we approached. In the backyard, we found Papa washing both cars.

Julie walked around the shiny blue car. "Does it run okay?"

Papa turned off the hose. "It's in fine shape. They did a good job on it." His face turned sour.

Julie looked closely at his face. "What's wrong? You look like you just sucked on a lemon. Are you mad, again?"

"Seeing the both of you makes me sick. It reminds me how much you cost me when I have all these accident bills to pay."

Julie stepped away from him. "It's not our fault you were drunk."

"Dammit, girl. Who told you that?"

To protect her, I answered. "I guess you don't remember. The cop who brought you home that morning said so."

"He needs to keep his mouth shut. The railroad would fire me if they knew."

"That would be terrible." I looked at the areas that had been damaged. "What do you think about the repairs?"

He wiped the windows with a dishtowel. "Perfect. Got rid of some scratches on the door that had bothered me." He threw down the towel. "Make yourself useful. Fix me some dinner."

I stiffened, hating his demand. "We were going to eat left-over stew. You can join us."

"I don't want that shit." He glared. "Too bad Tess never taught you how to cook. Make that beef stroganoff I like."

"I can't, we don't have any sour cream."

"Come on Julie. Get in the Chevy, we are going for a ride. You can run in the grocery store and get it. We'll be right back."

Julie did as she was told. Her eyes filled with fright. "I'll hurry Anna. We'll be right back, won't we Papa?"

He nodded, revved the engine and backed out. I watched them drive away. Julie's window down, she looked my way and grinned, her long blond curls blowing in the wind.

Fearing he wouldn't keep his word, I worried as I quickly fried the beef I had left over from the stew. I started water for noodles before changing into jeans and a blue long-sleeved shirt. By the time the meat was done, they still weren't back.

I turned off the burners and sat on the back step waiting. Minutes dragged by, then an hour passed. I fretted about what was taking so long and I thought about what Tess had told me about Dave taking her to the woods. I would die if that happened to my little girl. I went back in the house.

Another half hour passed before I heard the car engine. I finished setting the table. Two car doors slammed, and Julie skipped into the kitchen, smiling and carrying a large bag.

Papa strolled in behind her with a carton of sour cream. "We made a stop for some new clothes for Julie. They have a great kids' section at the Hot Shop."

"That's nice." I gave her a fake smile. "You'll have to show me in a few minutes, after I finish dinner." I turned to the stove, cooked mixed vegetables and finished the main dish with noodles, all the while fighting an ominous feeling, wondering what he had bought for her. Was he making plans?

I remembered when he brought me clothes and made me model them for him. New clothes and gifts were always payment for what followed, what he did to me.

My stomach flipped at the thought of eating at the same table as Papa.

Bad memories I'd been good at burying erupted, making me struggle with each breath. His eyes had that faraway look I'd seen many times.

Julie smiled, leaning toward him.

He smiled back and patted her arm.

Julie's smile made me sad and sick. I swirled my food around but ate little. Their interactions gave me an uneasy feeling. She was so vulnerable, wanting to please him.

Papa pushed himself away from the table, belched, left the house and drove off.

Julie sat at the table, her eyes downcast. "He didn't even say goodbye."

After cleaning up the kitchen and dishes, I found Julie in the bedroom trying on her new clothes. She modeled a darling shorts outfit in bright yellow with matching sandals.

"Daddy said I look great in yellow with my long blond curls."

She slipped out of the outfit and pulled her next gift from the bag, a pink lacey nightgown that made me cringe. She wore it to bed and was asleep in minutes, and I lay awake, still feeling the tension that had haunted me over a lifetime since Mama died.

Papa hadn't touched me in a couple months, not since he last hurt me so bad - when I decided I would never endure his abuse again.

I'd kill him if he touched Julie.

Chapter 49 - Caught

Papa was around for a few days and would unexpectedly walk in. He brought candy, something he seldom bought. One day we found a fresh pineapple on the counter. Since we had only eaten canned pineapple previously, I had to find a cookbook with instructions on how to cut and serve it.

Papa was paying more attention to Julie. That worried me.

After dinner as soon as Papa finished eating the pineapple, he went outside to tinker on his cars. Julie and I played a couple piano duets. He came in later and complimented us, saying how nice it was to hear our music outside where he was working. Kind words from him were so unusual, I had difficulty believing he meant them.

Julie said she loved piano lessons and reminded him he hadn't found a dance teacher for her, yet.

"I've been distracted, but I'll see what I can do if you promise to be a real good girl."

Julie spun around in a happy dance. "I'll be good."

"You can start by helping with my car. Could you come out with me?"

Julie rushed to his side. "I know how to use a screwdriver."

"Bring the hand-vac instead. The Chevy has some dirt on the floor from the repair shop that needs to be cleaned up."

She dug around in the hall closet and found the small vacuum. They went outside together, looking like a normal father and daughter. After the door closed, I peered out the back window and assumed the car was in the garage as I was unable to see them. I washed the dishes, practiced a few piano pieces, and then went outside to check on Julie.

When I opened the garage side door, I found them sitting in the back seat of the Chevy sharing a soda. Papa sat close, his arm around her shoulders. Through the window, I saw his belt was unfastened and zipper open.

I jerked the car door open. "What the hell are you doing?"

Julie looked at me in terror. Her face flushed. She jerked her hand away from his zipper as I pulled her from the car.

He was stunned, caught.

Julie broke away from my grip and ran from the garage crying.

"Damn you to hell! You're a pervert." I yelled, "You won't get away with it this time."

"Shut up, Anna. Nothing happened. Besides I'm her father. She belongs to me."

Papa got out of the car, closed the door and reassembled his clothing." He raised the garage door. "You won't see me for a while. I'm on my way out of town."

His crushing hands gripped my shoulders. "Don't do anything you'll be sorry for, Anna. Remember, you'll be missing, and Julie will be with me."

He backed out, laughing.

I stood in the yard, stunned, not sure what to do. First, I had to find Julie and see what he had done to her.

Chapter 50 - Julie in Danger

Julie didn't want to talk to me. She withdrew, stayed in bed the following day, and refused breakfast and lunch. Our fun weekend turned to chaos. I sat on Julie's bed and reassured her that whatever happened, was not her fault. "Papa is a bad man who is good at sweet-talking. Remember what he did to Penny and her mother? He sweet-talked them, too. Brought them treats and took advantage of them."

When I finally got Julie to tell me what happened, I did my best to explain what I thought we had to do to stop him and protect both of us. Tears streaked down Julie's flushed cheeks.

"Why does he pretend to be a good father when he is horrible? He is a good pretender. He made me do icky stuff after I told you I wouldn't let him hurt me. This time, he didn't hurt me." She dug in her little shorts pocket and pulled out a ten-dollar bill. "He told me it was a special kind of hug, worth a lot of money."

My heart broke.

He paid my baby for sex.

Julie said that Tess would want to know. I knew she was right. My dead mother was the only one we could tell. Otherwise, he'd do something terrible like kill me and keep Julie forever locked in his home like he had Tess and me.

Depression weighed us both down, too weary to walk to the cemetery. We thought bicycling with wind in our hair might make us feel better, so we set off with Julie in the lead.

We pedaled up the incline to Tess's grave following ruts in the dirt road. The flags from Memorial Day still waved on veterans' graves and scattered colorful flowers were teardrops of beauty left by mourners in the garden of the dead.

At Tess's tombstone, we laid our bikes in the grass and sat down. Julie softly ran her little fingers along my mother's name grooved into her headstone. "Tess you were too young to die. We really need you. Papa is scaring us, and we don't know what to do."

I swallowed sobs, listening to her soft voice, recalling my own words begging for my mother's help, telling her Papa was taking me to a place far away from her. "Tess, we're back and wish you could help us. Papa is worse. We have to get away from him."

A carload of visitors to a nearby grave interrupted us. To escape their eyes and possibly their questions, we bicycled to the bluff and sat in silence for a while. Julie said, "Is this our bluff, Ann? I think it must be. I feel better here, stronger, because here, Anna is gone, and my mother is with me. Papa is icky and mean. I hope he is gone for a long time."

We sat in silence for a while, then wandered along the river path for a distance admiring the expansive scenery, cattle off in the distance and a freight train rattling its way toward the eastern horizon. Julie took my hand. "Mother, I'm scared. I don't want him to come back because he is a liar. He makes me happy and sad at the same time. I like it when he's nice. When he gives me presents and money, I try to forget about him hitting me and hurting you."

"He won't change. He has been acting the same way for as long as I can remember and did it to Tess. She was a wonderful mother to me, but he kept us trapped in a horrible life with him. He is doing the same thing to us. We have to escape before he hurts you more."

Julie's eyes followed the disappearing freight. "Maybe he's driving that train and will never come back."

Seeing my little girl so troubled pained me, my stomach hurt, my knees wobbled. I bent down and hugged her. "Things will be better, soon. Let's go back to town and get something to eat."

Julie said she wasn't hungry but decided she could eat pizza. We bicycled to the Whistle Stop and bought a Hawaiian pizza to go. It was a little precarious riding home holding the pizza across my handlebars but made it to our picnic table without dropping it. We sat in the backyard talking to the Scarecrow and had a wonderful meal as the sky darkened.

That night, it took a long time to close my eyes and sleep with shadows racing across the ceiling and nighthawks screaming outside our windows. Julie was restless, kicking her covers off, uttering strange sounds, sometimes whimpering. When she finally slept, I drifted off.

In dawn's light, I saw her bed was empty. I listened and heard nothing. Did Papa come back and abduct her? My mind raced as I ran from the bedroom and into his room. He wasn't there.

I heard a noise from the bathroom and rushed to the door.

"Julie, are you okay?"

Silence.

I knocked, then tried to open the door.

Locked.

"Julie, you're scaring me. Are you okay?"

The door inched open. She stood there in her night-gown, scissors in hand, her curls cut off, strewn on the floor. Blood on her left wrist, oozed from cuts. Her face, plastic, no expression, her blue eyes, icy, blank. "I'm a bad girl. Papa won't like me if I'm a bad girl. He only likes good girls with long goldilocks hair."

My eyes went to her wrist. She looked into mine. "Cutting feels good. It makes me feel better, forget what he made me do. I thought I might go be with Tess where he can't hurt me."

Paralyzed by the pain in my child's eyes, I couldn't speak, couldn't stand. I sank to the floor and pulled her onto my lap.

Julie's bloody hands pressed against my cheeks. She made me look into her eyes. "Mother, will you help me?"

My arms circled her frail frame. "Yes. We both need help. I think we can get help at the clinic where I work." She relaxed and lay her head on my shoulder.

We sat on the floor for long minutes. My mind couldn't grasp the horror.

I put her in the bathtub, trimmed her hair to a curly pixie style and carefully washed her self-inflicted wounds. Two superficial cuts that carried great significance for the future, for her healing and for mine.

I dressed her in pale blue jeans to match her eyes and a white long-sleeved T-shirt to cover the Band-Aids on her wrist. She napped on her bed.

It was a challenge, but I cut my hair to match hers. When I finished, I liked the look and took a shower.

Three more hours until I had to work at noon. Papa was gone and we had some time to figure out what to do next. I dressed and sat down on Julie's bed.

She sat up, saw our images in the mirror beside her bed and laughed –a joyful sound I wasn't sure I'd ever hear again. "You cut your hair, too. We look like twins."

I smiled. "You look great in short hair, so I joined you. It's a statement to Papa. He's lost control of us."

Before we left the house, I showed her our escape bag with the car key, money and a few overnight things. We'd already left clothes at Edith's. I didn't tell Julie about the evidence of abuse on clothing I'd stashed in the bottom of the bag along with photographs of our injuries. We talked about moving in with Edith but planned to stay in Papa's house until my first paycheck from the clinic.

I didn't think Papa would be home for a week based on his typical schedule. Things had been strange recently with his train accident and car accident. I figured he'd be trying to work longer hours and make up for lost time.

Chapter 51 - The Escape

A shriek awakened me. I thought at first it was a dream or a night hawk. I listened. I heard it again and sat up. I turned on my bedside lamp.

Julie's bed was empty.

I tore out of the room into a dark living room and ran to Papa's bedroom.

Muffled noises inside shredded my heart.

I threw open the door. Papa was naked, on top of Julie, a hand over her mouth and nose.

Just like he'd done to me.

I screamed and seized one foot, pulling him sideways. He grabbed for me but lost his balance and fell hard onto the wooden floor. The room shook from the impact.

He struggled to his knees, yelling. "Get the hell out!" He huffed waves of alcohol breath.

I kicked him and dragged her from the bed. "Julie, run! Go to Edith's. Run!"

Papa's fingers circled my ankle, his other hand caught my wrist. I struck at him. He jerked me to the floor.

A hand went for my neck. I spun away and he punched my face below my left eye.

From the living room, I heard Julie's footfalls on the floor. Running. Good.

I rolled, jumped to my feet, knocking over a small table. I grabbed a metal lamp and swung it with all my might. I struck his head.

Stunned, he touched his scalp. His fingers dripped with blood. "Bitch! I'll kill you for that."

He blocked my escape

I swung the heavy lamp again. It hit his nose. Blood exploded from it.

He grabbed his face screaming.

I dodged past him and rushed out the door to our bedroom. Julie was gone. I snatched my bag of emergency things from the closet and ran for the kitchen. As I raced for the back door, Papa lunged at me. Naked, bloody and furious. He stumbled against the door casing.

I grabbed a broom and rammed it into his stomach.

He got ahold of it but tilted backwards. As we struggled, his foot caught a kitchen chair leg and he sprawled face down.

I backed toward the door while digging in my bag for the pepper spray. Finally, my trembling fingers closed around the canister and by that time he was on his knees trying to get up. I held by breath and sprayed. He coughed and collapsed, blinded.

I covered my face with my shirt and sprayed and sprayed him again and again.

He howled with pain and rage, clawing at his eyes.

Outside, I ran to the garage. The door stood open, the blue car gleaming in the streetlight.

I could have run the three blocks to Edith's as Julie had. But, no, I took his beloved car.

I scrambled in and locked the doors, still coughing from the spray.

My eyes watered so much from the irritant I could barely see.

I dug out my key and then sat on the bag as a booster. Afraid he'd show up pounding on the window, I quickly put the Chevy in gear and backed out. My legs trembled so much I was afraid I'd crash into something. I hit the brakes, changed gears and drove out of the alley onto the street toward Edith's.

Tears poured from my irritated eyes, blinding me as I turned the wheel, swerving this way and that.

A loud metallic crash!

I hit the brakes. Through my tears, I saw a galvanized trash can I'd hit roll to the side of the road. I sat shaking, gripping the wheel, then realized I'd been driving without lights. Thank God one of his cop friends didn't see me. I parked along the street in front of a dark house to gather my thoughts and calm down.

Lights behind me turned onto the dark neighborhood street where I'd stopped. I ducked my head and took my foot off the brake to avoid attracting attention to the lights, fearing someone would stop.

The car went on by. I sat a few minutes to clear my vision and opened the side window for some fresh air. My breathing calmed but in the rearview mirror my eyes caught the view of another vehicle. Headlights stabbed the dark, swerving. Papa's junker roared past me and turned west, heading out of town.

Drunk and bleeding, raving mad, blinded and wheezing from the pepper spray. Was he scared I'd turn him in? Since he didn't head to Edith's I thought he was trying to escape.

I waited a few minutes. My legs stopped shaking. With my headlights on, I carefully drove to Edith's.

A bright light in her living room window assured me Julie made it safely.

I parked behind the house in the alleyway to keep Papa's car out of view and ran to the back door.

It was locked. I pounded.

I heard running footsteps.

Julie opened the door, crying. Edith right behind her, screaming to come in.

Pounding on the front door. Papa?

Julie clung to me as I locked us inside and pulled her to the living room.

Edith opened the front door before I could stop her.

Opal and Jimmy rushed in.

Edith's safe refuge turned chaotic as we all cried and held each other. Julie stood shaking in her stained lacy nightgown. Edith sat on a chair and pulled the little girl into her lap.

I looked at my distraught friends and daughter, all of us safe.

A strange calm washed over me. I locked the front door then lowered myself to the couch. "Thank you for helping us."

Jimmy spoke first. "Edith called us for help and told us what happened. Where the hell is Dave? I want to get the police after him."

"Just headed out of town toward Falls City. He's crazy drunk and pepper-sprayed."

"Good for you. That son-of-a-bitch needs to be behind bars." Jimmy dialed Edith's phone. "There is a dark green old Ford headed west out of Riverside at a high rate of speed. Almost hit me. Drunk driver. He needs to be arrested. He just assaulted his kids."

I squeezed Julie's little hands. "Jimmy, we have to go to Falls City to the ER right away. Papa hurt Julie, bad."

"Sure honey," he said. "We'll go right away. You have blood all over you and your face is turning purple. You're hurt, too."

Words tumbled out of my mouth, a flood that couldn't be stopped. "Papa started raping me the day they put Mama in the ground. He said he'd kill me and throw me out like trash if I told anyone." I took a deep breath and hugged her. "Julie is my daughter."

Edith collapsed into her easy chair. "God almighty, how could I be so dumb not to see it?"

Opal gasped. "Why didn't I see it? I'm so sorry."

"I couldn't tell you. Papa said he'd kill me and keep Julie if I told anyone. Tonight, he attacked Julie. I want him dead." I told them what happened.

Opal scanned the room, fear in her eyes. "Does he know you're here?"

"Probably, but he is trying to get away, so he isn't arrested."

Julie and I dressed in pedal pusher outfits with T-shirts we had left in Edith's upstairs closet. I made sure Julie didn't wash and I explained a little about the examination that would be done. "I'm so sorry he hurt you. I won't leave you, so don't be afraid. He'll never hurt us again." I put her nightgown in my bag.

Edith sat with us in the back seat of the car. Jimmy drove too fast, swearing, using words I never imagined would come from his mouth.

Opal asked him to calm down.

At three a.m. Jimmy pulled into the ER entrance and dropped us off while he parked. I registered both Julie and me. My voice stayed steady as I told the clerk, "Julie's father sexually assaulted her and beat me." I'd expected her to show surprise, but she didn't, only her brow furrowed with concern.

Our waiting room looked like a living room. Edith, Opal, and Jimmy sat in soft chairs while Julie and I perched side by side on the couch, my arm around her. "This is the time we have been waiting for. It's our escape."

She nodded, her fingers laced on her lap, her chin quivering, trying not to cry.

A middle-aged nurse named Becky came in and greeted us. She discretely asked questions sorting out who was who. I explained Julie had been sexually assaulted by her father and mine, and that Julie was my daughter.

The nurse sat up straight, took a deep breath. "This is a complicated situation. I am so glad you got away. How old were you when Julie was born?"

"Twelve."

"How old are you now?"

"Julie is seven. I'm nineteen."

"Why weren't the police involved then?"

"He lied. He took me to another state, said I was older. They believed him. He said he'd kill me if I told the truth."

"Where is he now?"

"We don't know where he is. Driving, drunk and mad after I pepper sprayed him and escaped. I saw him swerving and headed out of Riverside toward the west."

I explained what our lives had been like for years, living under constant threat of death, too afraid to leave.

"I am so sorry," Becky said. "You have been through so much. Excuse me for a few minutes. We need him arrested and we need to call child protective services to get you the right help."

She opened the door to leave. "Everyone can wait here. I'll be back soon with a doctor."

After she left, our friends apologized over and over. Julie said, "It's okay. Now we're safe. You helped us get away."

Our friends sat crying.

Julie and I had no tears.

This was the day I'd been planning for.

Julie leaned against me. Her trembling finally stopped.

Chapter 52 - Missing

I was relieved when Nurse Becky returned with a young lady doctor. I had worried an old male doctor like one of the pompous church deacons or that ugly abortionist would come in to examine her. Our friends waited when the nurse and Doctor Lily escorted us to an adjacent exam room where everything was organized with swabs and trays. The doctor asked us many questions while Becky took careful notes on our two charts.

The questions were detailed. I began with the history my mother had told me and how abuse had begun with her rape, isolation, and domination. Then how Papa's pattern repeated itself, keeping me isolated, trapped and sexually abused over years following her death. "He bought me presents and pretty clothes for church, but like Mama, he raped me frequently and made me take birth control pills. I had no friends. No telephone. No money. No escape. And threat of death if I told anyone."

The doctor touched my hand. "Anna, I am so glad you are finally safe. I'll be sure you get the right help and counselling to get through this."

Julie stood beside me, then sat on my lap. "Papa is mean, but sometimes he brings us presents."

I agreed. "He's a railroad engineer and makes good money. He is gone for days. Those are our good days. Tonight, it was terrible." I broke into tears and hugged Julie. "He took my little girl from her bed. I woke up to her screams and found him on top of her, naked and smothering her."

The doctor carefully checked Julie and said it appeared I had stopped Papa before he penetrated her. There was some bruising. Her examination consisted of lots of swabs for the noisy humming air drier where she placed them. She explained to us that she swabbed body fluids for laboratory studies for the police.

I had Jimmy bring in my bag from the car. Becky put Julie's nightgown into a labeled paper bag. I gave her my stained gown for evidence, Papa's underwear, too. After the exam, a lab tech came in to draw our blood for tests.

A female police detective joined us after the exam and lab swabs to explain the legal side of things including the evidence collection she would secure. I handed her the photos I had taken of Julie's facial trauma from Papa a few weeks earlier. She commented, "You are very organized and calm. I'm surprised."

"For years, Papa told me that no one would believe me, so I researched information in the library. I wanted to be sure police would believe me when we finally had a chance to escape."

The officer photographed my black eye and swollen face. She placed the camera in a bag with her clipboard, ready to leave. "I think we have everything now. Is there anything else I should know?"

I hesitated, not sure how to say it. "We aren't the only ones."

The detective's eyes widened. She sat down, and pulled out her clipboard, pen in hand.

"He made a teenager named Penny Davidson pregnant and got her an abortion."

"How do I contact her?"

"Her mother's name is Charlene. She works at Mack's Shack in Riverside."

"Why wasn't he arrested?"

"Charlene went to the church deacons. They protected him."

She took notes including the name of the church and the pastor. "Thank you for telling me. This is even worse than I thought." She stood. "Let's go back in the other room with your friends. I spoke with them. They're very sad they didn't see what was happening and protect you."

"It's not their fault, it's mine. I couldn't tell them. He said he kill me. I think he would have killed me tonight if I hadn't escaped. I'm afraid to go home."

"I'll make some calls and see if they have him in custody, yet." The officer opened the door and signaled for Becky to join us. "Could you bring Julie something to wear home since I need the shorts she was wearing for evidence?"

Becky returned a few minutes later. "We have a little stash of new clothes for patients in need. I chose size six. Will that work?"

Julie nodded.

Becky said, "We have a shower. Would you like to bathe before you dress?"

Dressed in a patient gown that dragged the floor, Julie followed Becky into the bathroom. Soon, both emerged. Julie's hair wet, in tight curls, looking adorable in a little pink jogging outfit, wearing flipflops.

We joined Jimmy, Opal, and Edith in the waiting room for a few minutes before two male detectives in regular clothes came in with a woman from the state child protective services. They listened in the background as we finished talking to the doctor and listened to our friends' conversations.

"Oh, Jimmy, why didn't we recognize what was going on?" Opal patted my knee. "Tess left Riverside one summer after sixth grade. She moved back years later, married. She was so thin and sad but had her beautiful four-year-old little Anna to make her smile."

Jimmy said, "Working as the graveyard grounds keeper, I loved it when Tess and Anna would visit with me." He looked my way. "Anna was the cutest little grade schooler playing on the tomb stones while Tess sat and talked to Sally, her dead mother. Sometimes I'd stop to talk with Tess."

My friends all appeared upset and not sure what to say. "Julie and I still go to the cemetery where we could talk, where no one could hear our secrets. Sometimes we asked Mama for advice." I looked down at my hands. "I know it's magical thinking, talking to my dead mother, but saying things out loud, helped me sort through decisions I've had to make."

Julie stood with me. "My little girl helps me be happy. We take care of each other, but I'm really worried about her."

Julie rested her head on my shoulder. "Papa doesn't care about books or school. Tess wanted Anna to go to college. We tell Grandma Tess about our good grades." Julie looked at the others and then back to me. "It's nice out there. Flowers and no yelling."

Detectives and state workers waited, listening as we talked. Then they asked about Papa.

I answered, "He looks like a good father, churchman, and wage earner. We live in a good house. He has two cars. We look good on the outside, but he is an evil violent man."

Jimmy spoke louder than usual, hoping someone would get to the point. "We are all worried Dave will show up violent toward all of us. Did they arrest him?"

The detectives looked grim, one answered, "No. Riverside police went to his house. Lights on, door open, a mess inside, bloody. No cars. They're looking for him and put a warrant out for his arrest."

The other detectives suggested we go to a hotel at least for the night to be sure we'd be safe until they located him and locked him up.

Jimmy and Opal wouldn't hear of it. They wanted all of us, including Edith, with them.

Heavy rain and winds made the five-mile drive home from Falls City slow. Windshield wipers wacked back and forth at a high rate of speed. Jimmy pulled over and stopped for a while until the downpour subsided, making driving easier.

When we pulled up to their driveway, the sun was peeking through dark clouds. It was after nine when we sat down to a breakfast of scrambled eggs, toast, and fruit.

Julie and I slept together upstairs in one guest room, Edith in the other. I heard them both snoring long before I closed my eyes.

Chapter 53 - Freedom

The smell of coffee drew me out of bed in the early afternoon. I showered, dressed in yesterday evening's outfit and went downstairs. Julie slept on as I sneaked out and pulled the door closed. Edith was already up. I saw her bedroom door open and found her with Opal in the kitchen.

Opal announced, "Jimmy went to the police station to see if they had any information about Dave." She handed me a cup of coffee.

"Thanks. This is the happiest day of my life." I sat down with them. "Julie and I are free and he'll be in prison. It still seems like a dream come true. It is, but it's also the end of a nightmare."

Edith leaned back in her chair looking relaxed. "If he got caught speeding, maybe he's in a jail somewhere on the High Line. I don't know where he is, but I never want to see his face again."

"He was so drunk he shouldn't have been driving." The phone rang interrupting my thoughts.

Opal answered and nodded. Her eyes widened as she turned away from us, listened for a while and then hung up. She turned back. "Jimmy is leaving the police station and will be here soon."

I poured myself more coffee, adding cream and sugar. "I want to go clean up the house if you'll watch Julie. She needs to sleep besides I don't want her to see the mess."

Edith sipped her coffee. "Let's wait till Jimmy gets back and hear his news, then I will help you."

"That would be great. Opal, do you have rubber gloves I could borrow? I'm not sure how to wash pepper spray off stuff. My arm still burns where I got some on me."

She took a pair from beneath the kitchen sink and handed them to me, then went about serving breakfast cereal with strawberries. Julie joined us and we were nearly finished eating when Jimmy walked in looking upset.

He sat down beside me. "I have news about Dave. Troopers tried to pull him over. He made it to the Interstate and was swerving all over. He sped up when they hit the siren and lights." Jimmy hesitated, searching for words.

I sat silent, waiting for him to go on.

"Dave hit the shoulder, over-corrected and rolled the car. It was dark and rainy last night so the roads were slick. Medics took him to the hospital in Shelby, but they couldn't save him." Jimmy's face was hard to read, like a mixture of sadness and anger. "Dave is dead."

I gasped. Suddenly, I felt his death was my fault. So many times I'd wished he would never come home. Now my wish had come true.

Julie sat on my lap. Her shoulders slumped. "He isn't coming home anymore and can't hurt us. Why couldn't he be a good daddy like Jimmy?" She covered her face in sorrow, her shoulders shaking, tears flowing.

Jimmy reached over and hugged both of us. "Opal and Edith and I will be your family. We'll take care of you."

+

After some time to discuss the situation, Jimmy called the police station to tell them the name of the mortuary we wanted to use after the state lab released Papa's body following the autopsy. That would take about a week. They would contact us when that occurred.

I felt weak and empty, strange, as if I had no strength to do anything but remembered the condition of our house and thought it would be therapeutic to clean everything up. I explained, "The house is a mess. Overturned furniture, blood on the floor and pepper spray all over the kitchen. We probably have to open all the windows to get rid of the spray."

Jimmy suggested he take Julie to the hardware store with him, and he'd drop the rest of us off at the house. "I think we should change all the locks on your doors to be safe. We have no idea where Dave's keys are or who he might have given them to."

I said, "He was friends with the cops. I don't trust them, so that's a good idea." I looked to Julie for her response. She was happy to go on a shopping expedition to the hardware store with Jimmy.

I explained to her, "This is a memorable day for us for many reasons. A man who fathered us is dead, but he was a bad man, evil and mean. He harmed us but with help, we will be happy."

Edith suggested, "There is a very good counselor who has an office at the clinic. Would you like me to tell Sue what's happened, to give you some time off and find out about counselling?"

Julie and I agreed. She said, "That would be nice, but I want to go with Ann. Did you know that is her name now?"

Questioning eyes turned to her. "Anna was the girl Papa abused. Ann is my strong mother and we have happy plans. Right, Mother?"

"Right. No more secrets. A new life." I looked to all of them. "Let's get started with cleaning and get started on our new life."

+

Edith, Opal and I climbed out of Jimmy's backseat and went in the house with a bag of rags, gloves and Lysol. Opal scrubbed away the blood, purifying the living room and kitchen floors. I scrubbed Papa's bedroom, cleaned off the bloody lamp and up righted the table I'd knocked over. Edith vacuumed while I washed the linen from Papa's bed. Before we finished, Julie rushed in talking about eating popcorn and shopping for locks. She held a bag high with a big grin and then dumped a few things on the kitchen table. "Look at what Jimmy bought us!" She laid out new locks and dead bolts for the doors on the kitchen table. Then, pulled out a hummingbird feeder. She beamed, "It's for our porch."

Jimmy walked in carrying a small lawn chair. "These were on a special sale, and it fit her perfectly." He placed the chair in the middle of the kitchen.

Julie demonstrated how her feet touched the floor when she sat in it. "I'll bring it outside for another surprise. Come out to the picnic table."

Jimmy walked back out to the car and brought two pizzas to the table where we gathered. "I figured we could all use a little more food. You've been working hard. After I eat a couple pieces, I'll change the locks while you all rest."

Julie ate one piece and then walked toward the house with another. "I'm going to help Jimmy, then we'll hang the bird feeder." She skipped up the steps.

I watched my little girl. "Julie is looking joyful. It helps me to know she is finally safe. The doctor said Papa harmed her emotionally but not physically. The leftover feeling by being smothered by him last night to stop her from screaming might give her nightmares, but the real nightmare is over."

Opal took one box with a couple slices in it to the house. Edith and I placed the trash in the garbage can near the back door. When I opened the lid, I saw an empty whiskey bottle. "Isn't this interesting? He wasn't just drinking beer."

"I bet he was furious when he found his treasured car gone." Edith commented. "You said he loved that car."

"Yes. Unfortunately, more than us."

In the house, we watched Jimmy finish installing the back door locks with Julie standing by handing him screws. They tested the door closure with her on one side, him on the other, to be sure everything matched up. He smiled at us. "She may become an engineer or a mechanic. Julie is very good with tools."

While they finished and hung the bird feeder, the rest of us sat in the living room.

Edith telephoned her cousin, my boss Sue, that evening. She explained what had happened. Sue offered to give me the week off or longer if I wanted more time.

Julie and I stayed with Edith for the next week. I thought we could go home but our friends didn't want us alone until we had a little time to begin adjusting to all the changes in our lives. Jimmy had given the local police his phone number, acting as an adult guardian for us. I'm old enough but I appreciated his support. When we were still with Edith, he received a phone call from child protective services. They wanted to interview me and Julie and offer help. We made arrangements to meet with them in Falls City at their office. Jimmy drove us and Edith came along. She could confirm our stories and our support system with her, Opal and Jimmy.

After some time to unwind and rest at Edith's I decided to take a second week off, hoping Papa's body would be trans-ported to Riverside and I could complete all the arrange-ments, then return to work with a clear mind. When the call came to Jimmy from the local police, that the body was in the mortuary and ready for arrangements, we went to the po-lice department together to collect his belongings.

The disgusting cop friend who gave Papa the pepper spray walked out to meet us. His dark eyes scanned me from head to foot. A graying mustache trimmed his fat face. Buttons strained across his uniform shirt. He introduced himself. "I'm Dave's friend, Chief Bradberry. You're his daughter, right?"

"I'm Ann Stanton, here for his belongings."

The Chief left the room and returned with a large bag. He pulled out a wallet, keys and a checklist of items that included money he counted out, credit cards, a checkbook and keys. He returned the small items to an envelope. He handed everything to Jimmy, then offered his hand to me. "My condolences, Anna."

I stood and did not shake his hand. "Thank you, Chief. He was a horrible man you protected. He threatened us with your pepper spray. Luckily, I bought some of my own or we might be dead. Jimmy, let's go."

I turned to walk away but not before seeing the red-faced man standing, speechless.

Once in the car, I collapsed in sobs. "It's finally over. He can't hurt us anymore."

Jimmy waited until I settled down then asked, do you feel like going to the mortuary to finalize a burial?"

"Cremation. No funeral, just cremation. Yes, let's go tell them."

Jimmy said nothing and drove to the funeral home where I signed papers and asked them to mail me the bill. They said they'd would notify Jimmy by phone when the ashes were ready to pick up.

Chapter 54 - A New Beginning

In one day, our lives changed. After the violence, the telling, all the telling, told after so many years of silence. Experiencing the freedom of thought and body without his looming presence left me feeling lighter, as if I could fly.

Sue found another nursing student able to take my shifts for as long as I wanted. At first, I had no idea what to do with all the decisions, the freedom and the responsibilities. Without Papa's income, I had no idea how I'd be able to support us.

Two weeks after his death, we received a letter from the railroad. I expected it to be some sort of condolence. Julie and I read it and reread it. It was addressed to the daughters of David Stanton, deceased. "Survivor benefits calculated based on your father's duration of employment will provide a one-time payment of $1000 and a monthly survivor benefit for Julie until age eighteen. In addition, we recommend you contact the Social Security office in person for information regarding additional benefits.

We were shocked for two reasons, one the fact we would have money to live on and the other, that Papa had named Julie as his daughter.

Jimmy was good with math and a good saver. He agreed to accompany us to Papa's bank, the railroad administration office in Falls City and the Social Security office. It took time and patience to comply with all the information and forms. I found a key in Papa's desk and at the bank, found his safe deposit box contained Julie's and my birth certificates along with a life insurance policy for $10,000. We had to await a death certificate from the funeral home to finalize everything.

In the end, we received more money in savings than we ever dreamed of having and a livable monthly income. The house was paid off. We had a car and decided to have a phone installed. Plus, Papa had money in checking and savings accounts. With all that money, I wouldn't have to work, but I knew the experience would help me with nursing.

Child Protective Services made regular visits to be sure we were safe and recovering. They found a counselling clinic in Falls City where both of us could talk with professionals about our long-term psychological and physical abuse. Neither of us wanted to talk about it, but I realized I needed help because bad thoughts disrupted my sleep and my heart raced whenever I heard a train whistle. As a survivor of incest and isolation by a madman, I needed help.

We only had three real friends and were wary of people. After what the church did to protect Papa from the law, we never went back there. They were nice to me after Mama died, but Papa fooled them, too.

For a long time, Julie and I would tremble if a police car passed us or if someone knocked on the door. Little things jarred our senses. We had the premonition of Papa's anger re-entering the house. That's probably why we kept our home super clean and orderly the way he demanded it to be for so many years. We still felt his angry presence.

About a week after I'd returned to work, I left Julie at Edith's house and drove to the funeral home where I picked up a package labeled *David Stanton*. I stashed the box of his ashes in the trunk of his Chevy Malibu, his hearse.

I certainly didn't want them in the ground next to Mama. The only way she could escape his abuse was by dying. I wouldn't put him next to her for eternity. And I certainly wouldn't let him come in the house again.

We had a better plan.

One sunny day we rode our bikes out to visit Mama just like we used to do before we had a car. As usual it was a very windy day, one of those bright, big sky, no-cloud days with rolling tumble weeds and dust devils soaring.

We sat under the oak tree near Mama's headstone. I smiled at Julie. "Hey, Mama. We had Papa's ashes in the trunk of his favorite car until today. We wouldn't let him come in the house."

Julie pointed, "Look, the flowers we brought her are shaking as if she is laughing. Just wiggling a little bit."

"Mama, we're on our way to the bluff above the river where you and I used to sit. Where we watched dust devils swirl away and listened to beautiful meadowlark songs. You talked about flying away and making things better. We will follow your wishes." We left and waved, riding out to the bluff with his ashes in my bike basket.

At the bluff, I put the kickstand down and took the box.

Julie and I crawled between two strings of barbed wire. A strong wind blew from the west, pushing us along and stirring up dust as we walked. We left two long trails of our footprints across the expansive plowed field high above the river.

When we reached a spot nearly out of sight of the barbed wire fence, we opened the box. Each of us held a side and walked on, spilling the gray dust behind us with each step until the box was empty.

Seeing the last wisp of ash in the wind, we hugged each other for a very long time.

It was over. His evil hands would never touch us again.

We turned and walked beside our trail back to the rocky bluff and sat looking toward the eastern horizon. The wind blew through our hair and dried tears of relief.

A sudden gust blasted over the field crossing our path, picking up Papa's ashes. His remains swirled into a dust devil snaking along the ground, then spinning upward into a dense dark cloud. Rising higher, twisting like a tornado, traveling east, higher, and higher, scattering his ashes until he disappeared from our lives forever.

The End

Epilogue

J ulie and I are doing well. I am using the name Ann in our new life. I feel older and stronger. We moved to Falls City where we have both continued counseling to help us recover from abuse. Our new home is a rented duplex within walking distance of Julie's school and the college. Our adopted calico cat, named Callie, keeps us company. I will complete a four-year nursing degree at the time Julie enters middle school.

In the meantime, our lives have expanded to attending many movies to make up for lost time. I bought an electric keyboard, so we continue our music. We still love cooking together using Mama's recipes. We haven't forgotten that we said we'd share our cookie recipe with you.

We had hoped our uncle, Stephen Inman, could help us but he didn't receive our letters. His friend Buddy in Riverside put him in touch with us about a year ago. He is out of the military now and has been a great support. The three of us are close. He likes these cookies, too.

Love to all of you.

Ann and Julie

Montana Chocolate Chip or Raisin Cookies

Crisp on the edges, soft in the center

Bake at 350 degrees, 8-9 minutes till very light brown.

1 ½ cups butter

1 ½ cups white sugar

1 ½ cups brown sugar

1 Tablespoon vanilla

1 ½ Tablespoon molasses

3 Large eggs

4 ½ Cups flour

2 Tablespoons Malted milk powder

1 ½ teaspoon baking soda

1 ½ teaspoon salt

2 ½ Cups: semi-sweet chocolate chips or raisins

Combine butter and sugars. Beat until fluffy.

Add eggs one at a time.

Add vanilla and molasses. Mix.

Add flour, malted milk powder, salt, and baking soda.

Mix on low for 2 minutes. Add chocolate chips or raisins.

Cover dough and refrigerate overnight.

Form into walnut-sized balls and bake at 350 degrees for 8-9 minutes

Store them in plastic bags. They don't last very long because we eat them too fast. They freeze well.

References:

RAINN – Rape, Abuse & Incest National Network
https://www.rainn.org/

Sexual Assault Hotline: (800) 656-HOPE (4673)

Routes callers to the nearest sexual assault service provider

National Child Abuse Hotline Referrals to services.

Hotline: (800) 422-4453

Centralized call center. (140 languages)

Darkness to Light: Crisis intervention and referral services for child victims of sexual abuse Helpline: (866) FOR-LIGHT (367-5444)

Cyber Tipline – National Center for Missing and Exploited Children

Hotline: (800) THE-LOST (843.5678)

Questions and Topics for Discussion

Note: Incest is a difficult topic for many people to discuss because it generates emotion, guilt, shame and sometimes anger. Many victims refuse to reveal their pain, some have tried and were not believed. When a child is not believed, the emotional trauma is magnified.

In discussing the topic and the various components of this novel, your conversation must remain sensitive to those gathered. Incest is so common and unreported, friends and reading partners may be victims.

1. Recognizing possible behaviors displayed by a victimized child, silenced by the abuser, requires an astute observer. What are some of the behaviors you observed in both Anna and Julie?

2. How do you think Anna might have been rescued before she endured prolonged physical and emotional abuse? What were some of the missed opportunities?

3. How does this novel raise your awareness of this unspoken problem?

4. Knowing more about this form of hidden abuse, do you feel you could help a child in need? If yes, what are some actions you might take in your particular setting?

5. In the end, Anna and Julie survive with a path forward. The survivors who spoke to me about their abuse never reported it to authorities. Some who did seek private counseling found inadequate support. If you are aware of an abuse situation,

what are some of the things you should do before trying to rescue the child?

6. What authorities can help you without bringing more pain and risk to the child?

Note: If the perpetrator is a prominent community figure, disclosing the abuse is devastating to the entire family and their community standing. Both boys and girls may be incest victims over years. Even after rescue and skilled counseling, their lives are often complicated by Post Traumatic Stress Disorder, self-harm, drug and alcohol abuse, chronic illness and difficulty with interpersonal relationships. An intervention stopping the abuse, combined with proper counseling can result in a significant improvement in victim recovery.

Please write a review at your book retailer.

Please subscribe to: bettykuffel.com for new publications and updates.